THE DEEP WOODS

THE TWILIGHT WOODS

THE EDGELANDS

The Edge.

MIDNIGHT OVER
SANCTAPHRAX

Also available in The Edge Chronicles:

Book One: Beyond the Deepwoods
Book Two: Stormchaser

MIDNIGHT OVER
SANCTAPHRAX

BOOK 3 OF
THE EDGE CHRONICLES
Paul Stewart &
Chris Riddell

DOUBLEDAY
LONDON · NEW YORK · TORONTO · SYDNEY · AUCKLAND

TRANSWORLD PUBLISHERS
61–63 Uxbridge Road, London W5 5SA
A division of The Random House Group Ltd

RANDOM HOUSE AUSTRALIA (PTY) LTD,
20 Alfred Street, Milsons Point, Sydney,
New South Wales 2061, Australia

RANDOM HOUSE NEW ZEALAND LTD
18 Poland Road, Glenfield, Auckland 10, New Zealand

RANDOM HOUSE (PTY) LTD
Endulini, 5a Jubilee Road, Parktown 2193, South Africa

Published 2000 by Doubleday
a division of Transworld Publishers

1 3 5 7 9 10 8 6 4 2

Text and illustrations copyright © 2000
by Paul Stewart and Chris Riddell

The right of Paul Stewart and Chris Riddell to be identified as the Authors
of this work has been asserted in accordance with
the Copyright, Designs and Patents Act 1988

A catalogue record for this book is available
from the British Library

ISBN 0 385 600895

Printed in Great Britain
by Clays Ltd, St Ives plc

For Anna and Katy

· INTRODUCTION ·

Far far away, jutting out into the emptiness beyond, like the figurehead of a mighty stone ship, is the Edge. A great torrent once poured over this overhanging lip of rock. Now, however, the Edgewater River is shallow and sluggish. Its source, known in myths as Riverrise, is drying up, and the streams and tributaries which used to feed it are dwindling.

Straddling the river's broad and increasingly marshy estuary, is Undertown, a sprawling warren of ramshackle hovels and rundown slums. Its population is made up of strange peoples, creatures and tribes from the Edge, all crammed together into its narrow alleys.

Dirty, over-crowded and often violent, Undertown is also the centre of all economic activity — both above board and underhand. It buzzes, it bustles, it vibrates with energy. Everyone who lives there has a particular trade, with its attendant league and clearly defined

7

district. This leads to intrigue, plotting, bitter competition and perpetual disputes – district with district, league with rival league. Yet there is one matter which binds them all together: their *freedom*.

Everyone who dwells in Undertown is free. Born out of the second Great Migration, Undertown developed as a haven for those who had escaped a life of servitude and tyrannical bondage in the Deepwoods. Its founding fathers enshrined the principle of free status for all in the constitution. Today, that principle is still guarded fiercely. The punishment for anyone who attempts to enslave an Undertowner is death.

In the centre of Undertown is a great iron ring to which a long and heavy chain extends up into the sky. At its end is an immense floating rock.

Like all the other buoyant rocks of the Edge, it started out in the Stone Gardens – poking up out of the ground, growing, being pushed up further by new rocks growing beneath it, and becoming bigger still. The chain was attached when the rock became large and light enough to rise up into the sky. Upon it, the magnificent floating city of Sanctaphrax has been constructed.

With its elegant schools and colleges, Sanctaphrax is a seat of learning, home to academics, alchemists and their apprentices. The subjects studied there are as obscure as they are jealously guarded and, despite the apparent air of fusty, bookish benevolence, the city is a seething cauldron of rivalries and rancorous faction-fighting. For all that, however, the citizens of Sanctaphrax have a common aim: to understand the weather.

To this end the academics – from mist sifters and fog-probers, to windtouchers and cloudwatchers – observe and examine, calibrate and catalogue every minute feature of the ever-changing climatic conditions which roll in from open sky, far beyond the Edge.

It is out there – in that vast, uncharted void where few have ventured and none returned – that the weather is brewed up by the Mother Storm herself. White storms and mind storms, she concocts: rains which bring sadness, winds which cause madness, and dense, sulphurous fogs which steal the senses and play tricks with the mind.

Long ago, the ancient scholar, Archemax, wrote in his introduction to the *Thousand Luminescent Aphorisms* that 'To know the weather is to know the Edge.' The current academics of Sanctaphrax would do well to heed his words for, cut off in their floating city, they are in danger of forgetting the link between the two.

The Deepwoods, the Stone Gardens, the Edgewater River. Undertown and Sanctaphrax. Names on a map.

Yet behind each name lie a thousand tales – tales that have been recorded in ancient scrolls, tales that have been passed down the generations by word of mouth – tales which even now are being told.

What follows is but one of those tales.

·CHAPTER ONE·

OPEN SKY

Out in the vast cloudscape, a lone sky ship in full sail cut through the thin air. Ahead, at the end of a rope-tether, a gigantic bird flapped its mighty black and white wings as it led the ship ever further into that place of terror for all the creatures from the Edge – open sky.

'Weather vortex straight ahead,' the small oakelf shouted from the caternest at the top of the main-mast. His voice was shrill with fear. 'And it's a monster!'

Down at the helm of the *Edgedancer*, a young sky pirate captain in a hammelhornskin waistcoat raised his telescope to his eye with shaking hands. As he focused in on the dark, swirling air, his heart missed a beat. The approaching vortex was indeed monstrous. It was as if the great milky clouds were curdling and falling in on themselves, swirling into a great blood-red throat at the centre of which was an inky blackness that threatened to swallow the tiny sky ship whole.

'I see it, Spooler,'
the young captain
called to the oakelf.
'It's coming in at a rate of
about a hundred strides
per second, Captain Twig,
sir,' Spooler shouted, panic
plain in his voice.
'We've precious little
time till impact.'

Twig nodded grimly.
Already the currents of air
around them were beginning to
spin unpredictably. They were passing in
and out of great banks of cloud; plummeting as they
went in, soaring up again as they emerged on the other
side. With the binding tether taut, the caterbird continued its steady, relentless flight.

'Surely this is madness!' complained the wiry weasel-
faced quartermaster in the gaudy brocaded coat. He
pulled the large tricorn hat from his head and wiped his
sweaty brow. 'It's heading straight for the vortex.'

'We must follow where the caterbird leads, Sleet,'
Twig shouted back.

'B . . . but . . .' stuttered Wingnut Sleet, his voice a thin
whine.

'Sleet!' Twig called back. 'We are all in this together.
Just make sure those tolley-ropes are securely cleated.'

Muttering under his breath, the quartermaster went to
do the young captain's bidding. On the lower deck, he
found a heavy flat-head goblin clinging to the rigging, its
eyes white with fear.

'Nothing to worry about, Bogwitt,' Sleet said through gritted teeth. 'If our young captain really does believe that that great scraggy bird can lead us to his long-lost father rather than to certain death in the heart of the vortex, then who are we to argue?'

'Who indeed!' shouted a stocky figure with the tell-tale flame-red skin and hair of a Deepwoods slaughterer. 'You signed on with Captain Twig, just like the rest of us. And I reckon, just like the rest of us, you saw something special in him – like he saw something special in each of us. We're the chosen few, we are, and we'll see this through to the end.'

'Yes, well,' replied Sleet uncertainly. 'The end seems rather closer than I'd expected.'

'Vortex, a hundred thousand strides and closing,' came the nerve-racked voice of Spooler from the caternest.

'It's all right to be afraid, Sleet,' murmured a soft, hissing voice from the shadows behind them.

Sleet dropped the tolley-rope and turned. 'Reading my thoughts again, were you, Woodfish?' he said.

Woodfish recoiled. He was a slight, reptilian individual with webbed hands and feet and enormous fanned ears which were constantly aquiver.

'I can't help it,' he apologized. 'It's what we water-waifs do. And I can tell you this, too. The young captain knows this caterbird well. He was there at its hatching, and for that the creature is bound to watch over him as long as they both shall live. It was the caterbird who discovered Twig's father marooned in a wreck of a ship in open sky. It enlisted Captain Twig's help, and he enlisted ours. We are behind him all the way. Besides,' he added, 'the caterbird knows what it's doing – even though its thoughts *are* a bit tricky to read.'

'Oh, well, that makes me feel *much* better,' Wingnut Sleet replied sarcastically.

'I know,' said Woodfish quietly. 'I can read *your* thoughts quite clearly.'

Sleet's smile froze, and his sallow cheeks reddened.

'The tolley-ropes, Sleet!' shouted Twig.

The young captain stared ahead into the great open void. The *Stormchaser*, his father's sky pirate ship was out there somewhere, deeper in open sky than any sky ship had ever sailed before, and he would find it, whatever it took.

They had already travelled for twenty days and twenty nights, with the caterbird out ahead, leading them on unfalteringly into the treacherous void. Now, as the pink light from the rising sun spread out across the sky on that twenty-first morning, the seemingly tireless creature was taking them still further. And all the while, the winds were becoming more and more unpredictable as the dominant south-westerlies collided with the tunnel of air coming in from the east.

'Take the helm, Goom,' Twig said to the great shaggy mountain of hair and tusks standing behind him. Every sky pirate captain needed a faithful lieutenant, and Goom the banderbear was Twig's. 'Hold a steady course. We've got to keep on after the caterbird.'

Goom grunted, his feathery ears fluttering.

Twig turned his attention to the two rows of bone-handled levers that controlled the sky ship. With dextrous expertise, his hands played over them – raising the stern-weight and lowering the prow-weight; lowering the starboard hull-weights, small, medium and large, as far as they would go, while raising their counterparts on the port side completely.

The sky ship dipped and listed sharply to starboard as Twig attempted to follow the caterbird's erratic path. Cries

of alarm went up from the lower decks. Twig gritted his teeth and concentrated. Flying a sky ship was a difficult skill at the best of times, but with a vortex looming in from open sky, Twig was being tested to the limit.

With one hand, he positioned the neben- and klute-hull-weights. With the other, he adjusted the angles of the sails – tilting the staysail, slackening off the mainsail, bringing the jib gently round . . . Easy does it . . .

'Angle, speed and balance,' Twig muttered to himself.

They were the three fundamentals of skysailing. Yet as the wind became more turbulent with every passing minute, it was difficult to maintain any of them.

'Harder to starboard, Goom!' Twig bellowed, as he realigned the hull-weights. 'We've got to maintain the angle of . . .'

All at once a fearsome juddering went through the sky ship. The hull creaked, the masts trembled. Abruptly it flipped up and listed to the other side.

'Tether down!' Twig bellowed at his crew. At any moment, the *Edgedancer* could turn turvey – and, with no land below them, anyone who fell would fall for ever.

Spooler, the oakelf, disappeared into the caternest. Wingnut Sleet grabbed a tolley-rope and lashed himself to the fore-mast. Tarp Hammelherd the slaughterer and Woodfish the waterwaif clung to the bowsprit, while Bogwitt the flat-head goblin simply threw back his head and howled.

At the centre of the ship, on a platform above the flight-rock, a figure in a great pointed hood and coat stood, calm and still and silent. This was the last member of Twig's crew – the Stone Pilot.

The wind buffeted the sky ship violently: now on the port bow, now on the starboard. Twig raised the prow-weight completely and held his breath.

For a moment, the *Edgedancer* juddered more violently than ever. But it remained upright. Heartened by this, Twig made fine adjustments to the mainsail and jib. The sky ship listed slightly to port and leapt forwards. The tether slackened off. In the distance, the caterbird flapped towards the great gaping chasm of the vortex.

'Seventy-five thousand strides and closing,' Spooler shouted out.

'Stay tethered!' Twig cautioned his crew loudly. 'I don't want to lose anybody overboard.'

'Anybody?' Sleet mumbled. 'More like *everybody*! We're all doomed if we pursue this foolish course.'

Tarp Hammelherd glared round at him. 'Sleet!' he warned.

Sleet stared back at him defiantly. 'Someone's got to tell him,' he said. 'He's going to get us all killed.'

'The captain knows what he's doing,' said Tarp.

'Besides, we've come too far to turn back now.'

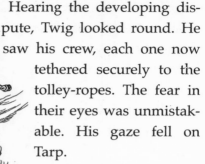

Hearing the developing dispute, Twig looked round. He saw his crew, each one now tethered securely to the tolley-ropes. The fear in their eyes was unmistakable. His gaze fell on Tarp.

'What's going on down there?' he said.

'Nothing, cap'n,' said Tarp, with a shake of his shaggy red head. 'Just Sleet here got a touch of the jitters.'

Wingnut Sleet turned and looked up. 'So far as I'm aware,' he said, 'no captain has ever steered his sky ship into a weather vortex and lived to tell the tale.'

The others listened but remained silent. They were all too loyal – and grateful – to the captain to question his commands, yet their fear of the approaching weather storm kept them from leaping to his defence. Twig looked at them sadly.

How different the scene before him was now compared with the night the *Edgedancer* had set off on its long journey. Then, under a bright full moon, the entire crew had sat down together on the lower deck to a hearty supper of roast snowbird, wood pumpkin and blackbread. Their spirits were high, the woodale loosened their tongues, and they regaled one another with stories of their lives before Twig had signed them up to sail with him.

For the crew of the *Edgedancer*, this was their first voyage together. There was Spooler the oakelf – small, wary, but with vision so sharp he could spot a white raven in the mire at a thousand strides.

Goom, the young banderbear, was already a giant, his tusks newly grown; a single blow from one of his massive paws could kill a hammelhorn. And then Woodfish, the reptilian creature from the black depths of the Deepwoods whose fan-like ears heard everything, spoken or unspoken. Twig had rescued all three from the clutches of Flabsweat, an unsavoury retailer in exotic pets, and earned their lifelong gratitude in the process.

Tarp Hammelherd, the slaughterer, was a Deepwoods dweller who had been lost to the taverns of Undertown.

Bogwitt, a flat-head goblin and fierce warrior, had once been a Sanctaphrax guard. Both had been treated harshly by capricious fate; both had been offered succour and a second chance on board the *Edgedancer*.
Neither would ever forget the young captain's kindness.

 And then there was Wingnut Sleet – who owed nothing to him – a clever, yet sly, quarter-master on whom Twig had taken a chance. Only the silent Stone Pilot had been known to Twig – and had sailed with him before.

'To our first adventure together!' Tarp had said, and raised his glass. 'And may the caterbird guide us quickly to the cap'n's father, and bring us all safely back to the Edge.'

A ripple of assent had greeted his words.

'To our first adventure,' the sky pirates had cried.

Now, three weeks later, that adventure was reaching its climax.

'Vortex, fifty thousand strides,' Spooler shouted above the roar of the approaching vortex.

'Listen up, all of you,' Twig called loudly. He turned to the banderbear at the helm, still holding a steady course despite the treacherous battering from the wind. 'You too, Goom,' he said. 'Can you all hear me?'

'Yes,' came the chorus of voices and the crew, as one, turned to look up at their captain.

All round them, the clouds writhed and squirmed, yellow and grey, with flashes of electric blue. The wind gusted treacherously as the weather vortex – with the gaping opening to the spinning tunnel face-on – drew closer. Twig looked up nervously, his hammelhornskin waistcoat bristling. The caterbird was still heading straight for it.

'I did not force any of you to come,' said Twig. 'Yet come, you did. And I am grateful for that – more grateful than you could imagine.'

Woodfish nodded his head knowingly.

'I thought I had lost my father for ever. Now I have been given a chance to find him. I shall never forget that it is you who have made this possible.'

'I would follow you to the end of open sky, cap'n!' Tarp Hammelherd shouted back.

'Wuh-wuh!' Goom agreed.

Wingnut Sleet lowered his head and shuffled around awkwardly.

'We have already come a long way together,' Twig continued. 'Now we are about to be tested to the limit. Sky willing, we will find Cloud Wolf and return to the Edge,' he said. 'But if . . .' He paused. 'If we fail, then I swear that so long as you are members of my crew, come what may, I will never abandon you. Never! As captain of the *Edgedancer*, I give you my word.'

Tarp Hammelherd looked up. 'I can't speak for the others,' he said, 'but I'm with you, cap'n, all the way.'

'Me, too,' said Woodfish.

A rumble of agreement echoed round the deck. Even Wingnut Sleet nodded.

'Though I still don't see why we have to make things so difficult for ourselves by sailing straight into the mouth of a weather vortex,' he grumbled.

'Have faith in the caterbird,' Twig replied. 'It knows what it's doing . . .'

'Vortex at twenty-five thousand strides,' cried Spooler. 'Approximately four minutes to impact.'

The *Edgedancer* flew into a bank of grey, sticky cloud. The gale-force gusts of wind tipped it this way, that way. While Goom gripped the helm, Twig ran his fingers over the bone-handled levers in a frantic effort to keep the sky ship steady. All round them, blue lightning forked and flashed. The cloud was so dense that the sky pirates could barely see their hands before their faces.

'Angle, speed and balance,' Twig muttered. For once the words offered no comfort. With the thick air in his eyes, his nose, his mouth, he felt his nerve beginning to go.

At that moment, the *Edgedancer* burst through the bank of cloud. To a crew-member, the sky pirates started back in horror. Twig gasped. Even the caterbird seemed surprised by the sight which confronted them. The swirling entrance to the vortex was suddenly there, directly in front of them. Its great blood-red mouth gaped so vast, it took up most of the sky.

'V . . . v . . . vortex, ten thousand strides and c . . . closing,' Spooler stammered.

'A little higher, Twig,' the caterbird's voice floated back to them as it soared upwards, pulling the tether taut once again. 'We must enter the vortex at the still point in the very centre of the spinning tunnel of air.'

Without giving the command a second thought, Twig's hands danced over the levers once more, raising the prow-weight, lowering the stern-weight and realigning the stud and staysails.

'That's it,' the caterbird shouted back. 'Now hold this course. So long as we remain at the centre of the weather vortex, we stand a chance.'

An icy shiver of unease ran the length of Twig's spine. The swirling vortex roared closer.

'Five thousand strides,' Spooler cried.

Hurricane-force winds battered the *Edgedancer* with immense power, threatening at any moment to send the sky ship into a fatal spin. The charged air smelt of sulphur and toasted almonds; it made the hair of the sky pirates stand on end.

'A thousand strides!'

The ship trembled and creaked. The crew grabbed onto anything they could. They held on desperately.

All at once, the frayed edge of the spinning vortex was swirling round the sky ship. It was like staring down a monstrous throat. There was no turning back now.

'Five hundred strides!' cried the oakelf. 'Four. Three. Two. One . . .'

'Brace yourselves!' Twig cried. 'We are entering the weather vortex . . . *now!*'

·CHAPTER TWO·

THE WEATHER VORTEX

It was a world of red they were plunged into. There was a blast of furnace-hot air, and a terrible screaming which filled Twig's ears. His stomach knotted, his breath came in gasps and, when he managed to half-open an eye, the wind caused scalding tears to course down his cheeks.

'Sky above!' he exclaimed.

They were inside the raging red gullet of the monstrous weather vortex. All round them, the swirling currents wailed and screeched. Yet here, at the central still point, there was a clammy, eerie calm.

'Heavy on the mainsail, Tarp,' Twig bellowed above the roaring air. 'And double-check that the tolley-ropes are secure.'

'Aye aye, cap'n,' he shouted back.

The weather vortex was vast beyond imagination. It was as if the sky itself had turned into a great voracious beast. And the *Edgedancer* was inside it: swallowed up, consumed.

'Hold fast!' Twig roared. 'Goom, chain yourself to the helm and keep us steady.'

The banderbear leapt to obey. Twig concentrated on the sail and hull-weight levers. With the wind spinning faster and faster – an angry red wall that surrounded them, constantly threatening to draw the sky ship off course and into its terrible turmoil – it was vital to maintain balance as they were sucked in deeper and deeper.

'What now?' Twig called out to the caterbird.

'There is no going back,' the bird boomed. 'We are entering the turbulent heart of the Mother Storm, the birthplace of tempests and tornadoes – a place of terrible madness. Yet at its very centre, there is ultimate calm and . . .'

'And?' Twig called back. The air had turned icy blue, and tiny vicious hailstones stung his face.

'And,' boomed the caterbird, half lost in a bank of swirling fog far ahead, 'it is there we shall find your father – if any of us survive.'

All of a sudden, Twig was gripped by a feeling of intense sadness. He fell to his knees, great sobs racking his body. Woodfish screamed with high, piercing sorrow. Sleet lay curled in a ball at the feet of a weeping Bogwitt. The tiny hailstones beat out a terrible rhythm on the decks.

What was happening? Twig wondered. What was this all-consuming sorrow? He hauled himself to his feet. It was almost too much to bear.

Tarp Hammelherd knelt on the ground, his head hung low, and bellowed like a wounded tilder. 'Why?' he howled, and his body convulsed with grief. 'Why did you have to die?'

Spooler swung down the mast and crouched down beside him. 'Tarp, my friend!' he implored.

But Tarp couldn't hear him. And when he looked up, his unseeing eyes stared past the oakelf.

'Oh, Tendon. My brother!' he cried. 'My poor, poor brother . . .' He collapsed on the deck, shielding his head from the hailstones.

Twig gripped the helm. Behind him, Goom the banderbear's loud howls drowned out all other sounds. Then the swirling green fog broke silently over the bow. Thick and evil, it coiled round the deck, cloaking the crew from sight. With the abrupt change in the weather, the sobs of the crew turned to howls of fear.

Twig shuddered as the green fog hit him. It pierced his skin, chilling him to the very marrow in his bones. Blind panic gripped him.

'We're doomed!' he screamed. 'We'll never escape. We're all going to die here in this terrible place. We . . .'

'After sorrow, fear,' the voice of the caterbird floated back. 'This too will pass. Be brave, Captain Twig.'

Twig shook his head. The fog thinned and the terror began to release its hold. A light drizzle was now falling, the raindrops glittering and shimmering like tiny jewels. Wingnut Sleet threw back his head and roared with laughter. Twig drank in the rain. His head swam. It was all so wonderful, so beautiful, so unutterably . . .

'*Aaaaargh!*' screamed Sleet.

Below him, Twig could see the quartermaster staggering back from the balustrade, clawing desperately at his face. Encasing his head and shoulders was a ball of lightning, with worm-like tendrils of light squirming over his terrified features. Woodfish screamed and dived for cover as more sparking twists of lightning crackled across the deck.

'Get down!' yelled Twig, all feelings of elation abruptly gone.

Wingnut Sleet, seemingly lifeless, was slumped on the deck next to the body of Tarp Hammelherd.

'Save us! Save us!' screamed Woodfish, his voice high and sibilant.

'We must go on!' Twig shouted back.

And then the red mist descended.

Thick, penetrating and acrid with the stench of wood-smoke, the mist blurred Twig's vision. He found himself consumed with rage. His eyes blazed. His nostrils flared. His teeth ground together.

'No going back!' he raged, pounding at the helm.

The *Edgedancer* bucked and juddered alarmingly. Twig hit out at the bone-handled levers, scattering them this way and that. The sky ship seemed to gasp as its weights and levers pulled in opposite directions. Beside him, even Goom was unable to resist the effects of the red mist.

'Wuh!' he bellowed as, gripped by a frenzy of rage, he tore at the balustrades and punched holes in the sides of the sky ship. 'WUUUUH!'

Twig's inner fury intensified. It was all the caterbird's fault, this turmoil, this madness: the fact that they had set off into open sky in the first place.

'Curse you!' he bellowed. 'May you rot in open sky!'

Behind him, the banderbear roared fiercely as he ripped at the doorways and battened-down hatches and tossed each wrenched-off piece of splintered wood over the side. Creaking and cracking, the *Edgedancer* was now out of control. At any minute the swirling vortex would tear it to pieces.

Twig raced down to the main deck and over to the bowsprit. The red mist filled his mouth, stained his eyes and filled his muscles with a wild and unfamiliar strength. The madness grew; his senses closed in. He became blind to what his eyes were trying to show him, deaf to what his ears could hear. With his sword in his hand, he was cutting, hacking, stabbing and all the while, the terrible roars of the banderbear screamed in his head.

Then everything went black.

Twig opened his eyes to find a milky whiteness all around him. The *Edgedancer* hung in space at a crazy angle, perfectly still.

'We made it,' he said quietly to himself. He looked about in astonishment. Everything suddenly seemed clearer and sharper than ever before.

Tarp Hammelherd lay in a heap, still softly sobbing. Wingnut Sleet, hands clasped to his face, didn't move. Bogwitt was unconscious, a section of mast pinning his right leg to the deck. Beside him, and utterly exhausted, the banderbear's great hairy form lay in the wreckage of mast and rigging, heavy rasping breaths showing that he lived still. One great paw rested against Spooler the oakelf. His whimpers revealed that he, too, was clinging to life. Woodfish sat in the bows, shaking his head from side to side.

'I can't hear a thing,' he repeated monotonously.

The Stone Pilot appeared at the top of the bridge staircase.

Twig smiled weakly. 'Look,' he said. 'I'm fine. Are *you* all right?'

From deep inside the hood came a muffled voice. 'Oh, captain,' it said softly.

'What?' said Twig. 'I . . .' He followed the line of the Stone Pilot's pointing finger. It led to his own hands. He looked down, to see a piece of limp rope in one hand, his sword in the other. 'What have I done?' he murmured.

Slowly, fearfully, he pulled the rope-tether towards him. It offered no resistance. All at once, the end flicked over the balustrade and landed on the deck at his feet. It had been severed neatly.

'Caterbird!' Twig screamed. 'Caterbird, where are you?'

There was no reply. The caterbird – his guide and protector – was gone. Horrified, Twig turned to the Stone Pilot.

'What has happened?' he whispered.

'I . . . I tried to stop you,' the Stone Pilot said. 'But you were too strong for me. Swearing and cursing, you were. You seized the rope and tugged it towards you. The caterbird cried out as its wings clipped the bowsprit. Then you raised your sword and thrust forwards . . .'

Twig gasped. 'Did I kill it?' he asked.

'I don't know,' the Stone Pilot replied. 'The last thing I remember is Goom knocking me to the floor.'

'My crew, my crew,' said Twig, shaking his head. 'What is to become of them now?'

The great heavy hood of the Stone Pilot turned from side to side. Out of the corner of his eye, Twig saw something black and white sliding across the sloping deck. He looked round, just in time to see one of the caterbird's tail feathers sliding under the balustrade and slipping over the jutting ledge. As it fluttered away into the glistening void, Twig shuddered at the enormity of what he had done. The great caterbird, who had watched over him since its hatching, was gone, perhaps dead – and by his own hand. Twig was on his own now.

'What do I do?' he said miserably. He pulled out his telescope and looked all round him. The milky whiteness now glittered with all the colours of the rainbow: intoxicating, mesmerizing – red and orange and yellow and . . .

The Stone Pilot seized him by the elbow and cried out urgently. 'Look there!'

Twig pulled the telescope from his eye and squinted into the white light. 'What? I . . .' And then he saw it. There, looming from the mist, was a shadowy shape suspended in mid-air. It was almost upended; its mast was broken, the sails hanging limply like broken wood-fly wings. Twig's skin tingled; his heart thumped.

'Oh, caterbird,' he murmured. 'You did not fail me, after all. You led me to the *Stormchaser*.'

With his heart in his mouth, Twig leaned over the balustrade. He cupped his hands to his mouth.

'Father!' he bellowed. 'Father, if you're there, answer me!'

But no sound came from the floating shipwreck save the creaking of its cracked hull and the *tap-tap-tap* of a loose tolley-rope knocking against the broken mast. The *Edgedancer* drifted closer to the wreck of the once-proud *Stormchaser*. Twig peered at the sky ship. It shimmered with a brilliance that hurt his eyes.

'I must know if my father is on board,' he said.

He seized one of the fore-
deck grappling-hooks, swung
the rope round his head and
launched the heavy hook
down through the air at the
other sky ship. It seemed almost
to pass through the *Stormchaser*
until, with a shudder and the sound
of splintering wood, it struck something solid – and held. The Stone
Pilot secured the end of the rope
to the bowsprit. Twig climbed
up, placed a length of broken wood over the rope,
and clutched it with both
hands.

'Wish me good fortune,'
said Twig, and with that he
was gone – sliding off down
the rope before the Stone
Pilot could answer.

The descent was steep
and fast, and Twig's arms
felt as if they were being
wrenched out of their sockets. Below him the gaping
void blurred past as he gathered speed and – *crash* –
thumped down onto the deck
of the *Stormchaser*.

For a moment Twig remained still, scarcely believing he had made it in one piece. He looked about. The sky ship was battered almost beyond recognition. The wood and rigging seemed drained of colour. With a jolt, Twig realized that they were almost transparent, and he could see down deep inside the ship. Then he heard a voice. ·

'Twig? Twig is that really you?'

Twig swung round. A gaunt, pale figure sat beside the shattered helm. 'Father!' he cried.

Cloud Wolf looked older. His fine clothes hung in rags, his hair was white and his eyes were bluer than Twig remembered – unnaturally blue. Across his right shoulder were the raw scars from a recent wound. Twig ran towards him, his heart clamouring inside his chest, and fell at his side. 'Oh, Father,' he said tearfully. 'I have found you.'

'I have waited so long, my boy,' Cloud Wolf whispered wearily. He pulled Twig closer to him. 'You have come far to reach this place,' he said. 'The caterbird who found me said you would. He was right. No father has ever been prouder of his son than I am of you.'

Twig lowered his head modestly. Tears splashed onto his leather breastplate.

'So much emotion,' said Cloud Wolf gently. 'I know, I know.' His voice grew harder. 'Twig,' he said urgently. 'You must listen closely, for I shall say this but once. This is a dangerous place I have drawn you to.' He sighed. 'If I had known beforehand, I would never have asked the caterbird to enlist your help.'

'But, Father, I *wanted* to . . .'

'Don't interrupt, Twig,' said Cloud Wolf. His body glistened from head to toe. 'I don't have much time left. The perilous vortex has brought me – us – here to the very heart of the Mother Storm. It is a place of calmness, of enlightenment – yet there is a terrible price to pay for the knowledge she imparts.'

'Price to pay?' said Twig anxiously.

'Those who arrive here slowly become one with the Mother Storm, Twig,' his father continued gently. 'She enters through the eyes, the ears, the pores of the skin. She fills you with knowledge of the weather itself – knowledge which the academics of Sanctaphrax have, for centuries, been striving to attain – but she claims you for herself in the process.'

Twig gasped. 'You mean . . . ?'

'I have been becalmed here too long, my boy. I can't hold on to my thoughts for much longer . . .' Cloud Wolf waved a pale, almost translucent hand in front of Twig's face.

'Oh, Father,' Twig murmured. 'What is . . .?'

'I am disappearing, Twig – becoming one with the Mother Storm. My greatest sorrow is leaving you when we have only just been reunited. But before I do, there is something I must tell you – something I have learnt here. The Mother Storm will soon return.'

'To the Edge?' Twig gasped.

'Aye, Twig,' said Cloud Wolf. 'This mighty storm which first seeded the land with life is coming back, as she has done every several thousand years since the beginning of time itself. She will sweep in from open sky, pass over the Mire, the Twilight Woods and on to the highest point of the Deepwoods. Riverrise.'

'Riverrise?' said Twig. 'But surely the place is only a myth . . .'

'Riverrise exists,' said Cloud Wolf firmly. 'When she reaches it, the Mother Storm will rejuvenate its waters, the Edgewater River will flow vigorous and strong once more, and her energy will spread out all across the Edge, bringing new life, new hope – a fresh beginning.' He paused, and Twig looked down to see the pain in his father's eyes. 'At least,' he murmured, 'that is what *should* happen. But all is not well.'

Twig frowned. 'I don't understand,' he said.

Cloud Wolf nodded patiently. 'That last time the Mother Storm visited the Edge her journey to Riverrise was clear,' he explained. 'Now, there is something which stands in her way . . .'

Twig gasped. 'Sanctaphrax!' he said.

'Sanctaphrax,' whispered Cloud Wolf, his eyes misting over. 'Our floating city, with its shining spires and venerable institutions – once, long ago, when it was truly great, my home . . .' He cleared his throat. 'It lies directly in the path of the storm. It will be destroyed by the energy of the Mother Storm when they meet.'

'But . . .' Twig began.

'Hush,' said Cloud Wolf wearily, 'for there is worse to come. If the Mother Storm is blocked by Sanctaphrax, then she will never reach Riverrise to seed it with new life. The waters of the Edgewater River will dry up completely. And with their going, the darkness at the black heart of the Deepwoods will spread out like a vast fungus, until it has engulfed every inch of the Edge.' He looked up at his son. 'Twig,' he said. 'Sanctaphrax must not block the path of the Mother Storm.'

'But what can I do?' said Twig, searching his father's ghostly face for some clue.

'The Anchor Chain . . . it holds the floating city in place . . . it must be . . . severed,' Cloud Wolf told him, every word an effort.

'Cut the Anchor Chain?' said Twig, astonished. 'But . . . but . . .'

'Sanctaphrax will soar away and the Mother Storm will sweep on unhindered to Riverrise. The Edge will be saved, but . . .' His voice grew fainter. '. . . Sanctaphrax will be lost.'

As he spoke, his entire body began to glisten and sparkle.

Twig gasped, and started back. 'Wh . . . what's happening?' he stammered.

Cloud Wolf held up his hands and looked, bemused, as they shimmered like countless million dancing atoms. 'Finally, she has come for me,' he sighed.

'What do you mean?' said Twig. 'What's going on?'

'I told you, Twig. I have been here for too long,' his father whispered barely audibly. 'The Mother Storm has filled me with herself. That is how I know what is soon to take place. But with that knowledge, I have lost myself, Twig. The brighter I glisten, the fainter I get.' As he spoke, the glittering grew more intense, and the form of Cloud Wolf the sky pirate captain became more difficult to make out. 'She has claimed me for herself. I must leave you, Twig.'

'No!' said Twig. 'I shan't let you go!' He shifted round onto his knees and tried to sweep his father up in his arms. But it was like cradling light. 'Father!' he cried out.

'Be still, Twig,' said his father. 'You must know one last thing . . . *when* the Mother Storm will strike . . .'

'When, Father?' said Twig. 'When?'

Cloud Wolf's glittering mouth moved, but not a sound left his lips.

'Father?' Twig shouted desperately. 'When?'

Tethered together the two sky pirate ships circled each other slowly. Twig left the fading *Stormchaser* and swung back across the yawning void to the *Edgedancer* – brought lower in the sky by the Stone Pilot. He landed with a heavy thud on the deck. Behind him, the rope went limp. The *Stormchaser* had finally disappeared completely.

The Stone Pilot stared into Twig's ashen face. 'What happened?'

Twig struggled to clear his head. 'It ... it was so strange,' he whispered. 'Unearthly ...'

'Captain Twig,' said the Stone Pilot, shaking him by the shoulders. 'Snap out of it! Tell me what happened on the *Stormchaser*. Cloud Wolf, your father? Did you find him?'

Twig looked up as though hearing the words for the first time. Tears welled in his eyes. He nodded. 'Yes, but ... Oh, I don't know what to think...'

Without saying a word, the Stone Pilot reached up and unfastened the internal bolts which secured the glass eye-panelled hood to the shoulders of the greatcoat. The catches opened and the Stone Pilot removed the hood to reveal the slight figure within. Her red hair fell down over her pale cheeks and slender neck.

'Twig, it's me, Maugin,' she said gently. 'Remember? You once saved my life.' She paused. 'Now calm yourself and tell me what happened over there.' She rolled the heavy Stone Pilot suit down off her shoulders and took him by the hand.

Twig shook his head. 'I did see my father,' he said, 'but he is gone now. For ever.' He sniffed and tried in vain to swallow the painful lump in his throat. 'Before he disappeared, he told me what I have to do. Sanctaphrax must be destroyed.'

'Sanctaphrax destroyed?' Maugin gasped. 'Why?'

Twig silenced her with his hand. 'We must return to Sanctaphrax so that I can warn the Most High Academe.'

'But, Twig,' said Maugin. 'We are becalmed in the middle of open sky.'

Twig clutched his head in his hands and rocked from side to side.

'Twig, you must tell me what you know,' Maugin persisted. 'Sky willing, at least one of us will survive to pass on your father's message.'

'Yes,' said Twig, pulling himself together. 'You are right.'

Maugin's eyes grew wider and wider as Twig began telling her what Cloud Wolf had told him.

'The Mother Storm,' she murmured. 'Riverrise . . . I had always thought such matters were merely the subject of legends.'

'I, too,' said Twig. 'I . . .' His jaw dropped. 'Sky above!' he exclaimed. 'What's happening now?'

The pair of them looked round. The glistening air seemed to be coalescing, and rushing in towards them.

'Quickly Twig,' said Maugin urgently. 'Tell me everything. Before it is too late.'

As the whiteness closed in, the air pressure increased. The pain in Twig's ears became intolerable.

'He told me . . . He said . . .'

All round him, the light intensified. His ears whistled. His head throbbed. Despite the intensity of his memories, the words of explanation wouldn't come.

'When, Twig?' said Maugin. 'When will the Mother Storm strike? Did he tell you or not?'

Twig clutched his head. The air grew denser, heavier. 'I . . . he . . .' he murmured. His eyes filled with bewilderment. 'When the water stops flowing . . .'

He fell silent and winced with pain as he struggled to

remember his father's last fateful words. His eyes throbbed. His head felt as though it had been clamped in a vice.

'When ... when the very last drop falls, she will arrive. Dawn over Riverrise,' he whispered faintly. 'Midnight over Sanctaphrax ...'

But Twig could not know whether Maugin had heard him or not, for a wind whisked his words away, whiteness filled his vision and a high-pitched whine whistled in his ears.

'Put ... your hood on,' he shouted to Maugin, and stepped forwards to help her back into the heavy suit.

The air grew even whiter. Bright white. Dazzling white. It filled his eyes, shutting out everything else till he was utterly blind. The sky ship trembled. He fell away from Maugin and stumbled backwards – slowly, impossibly slowly – through the viscous air.

'Maugin!' he cried out – or rather, *tried* to cry out – for his voice could no longer escape his mouth.

He landed on the deck. Muffled noises echoed round him: splintering, cracking, crashing. The whiteness intensified. The high-pitched whine grew to a scream. Twig screwed his eyes shut, clamped his hands over his ears and rolled himself up into a tight ball.

But it was no use. He couldn't keep it out. The terrifying whiteness was inside him, as blinding and deafening within as without. It blunted his senses. It gnawed at his memory.

'Maugin,' Twig mouthed. 'My crew ...'

Whooooopff!

Unable to withhold the mounting pressure a moment longer, the white storm imploded in on itself. For an instant there was stillness. Then, with a cataclysmic thunderclap, the dazzling sphere – with the *Edgedancer* at its centre – exploded outwards with such force that the very sky juddered.

·CHAPTER THREE·

THE LOFTUS OBSERVATORY

Far away, the floating city of Sanctaphrax keeled and bucked in a fearsome storm. The Anchor Chain which moored it to solid ground was being tested to the limit. Inside the sumptuous buildings, its citizens – the academics and apprentices, the servants and guards – huddled together in silent groups of their own kind, terrified at the thought that the chain could snap.

Only the Professor of Darkness remained alone. As Most High Academe of Sanctaphrax, it was his duty to continue working while the others sought refuge. When the violent storm had first broken, he had hurried up the winding staircase to the top of the Loftus Observatory as fast as his frail, old legs would take him. The various pieces of measuring equipment which represented every academic discipline in Sanctaphrax awaited his inspection. He arrived to find them all going wild.

'Sky above!' he exclaimed as he entered the airy room.

He scratched his bushy beard and pushed his steel-rimmed spectacles up his nose as he took a closer look at the instruments. 'But such readings are unheard of.' He glanced out of the window of the high tower. 'And little wonder.'

The storm that night was greater than any he had ever witnessed before. Hurricane-force winds and driving rain were sweeping in from beyond the Edge, battering the jutting spur of land with unprecedented violence.

'Come on, now,' the professor muttered to himself. 'Readings must be taken. Calculations calibrated. Facts and figures logged.' He gripped his staff tightly as he crossed stiffly from one side of the swaying observatory to the other. 'But where should I begin?'

The brass anemometer was spinning furiously, registering wind speeds far in excess of any previously recorded. The rain-gauge was overflowing and bleeping loud the concentrated presence of anti-magnetic sour-mist particles.

The professor shook his head. 'Unbelievable,' he muttered. 'Quite un . . .' He paused. 'But never mind the anemometer or the rain-gauge!' he cried. 'What in Sky's name is the sense-sifter doing?'

The object of the professor's sudden feverish interest was a small, silver box which stood, at an angle, on a tripod. Each of its six sides was inlaid with a small square panel made of a soft, glimmering material derived from the wings of woodmoths. Like the creatures themselves, the material was sensitive to emotions, changing its colour according to the mood surrounding it. Anger would cause it to turn red; sadness, blue; fear, yellow, and so forth.

There were two sense-sifters in Sanctaphrax: one, here, in the Loftus Tower, the other in the rundown Department of Psycho-Climatic studies. Normally, the weather-sensitive apparatus glowed a neutral white. A particularly depressing downpour might tinge it with pale blue; a long stretch of balmy breezes and sunny skies might turn it a delicate shade of pink. But always pastels. Nothing extreme was ever registered. Certainly no more than would cause a slight sense of disappointment or an increased tendency to smile. For though the weather undoubtedly affected all the creatures of the Edge, its effects were always mild.

Until now!

As the professor stared at the sense-sifter, his jaw dropped and his heart pounded. The apparatus was pulsing with multi-coloured intensity. Flashing, sparking, fizzing. Now dazzling red, now ultramarine, now gleaming emerald green. And purple – deep, dark, crazy purple.

'A *mind* storm,' he gasped. He had read of such phenomena in the dusty tomes of *The Elemental Treatise*. 'No wonder my own mind has been in such turmoil.'

At that moment a bolt of lightning zigzagged down out of the swirling sky to the north. For a moment, night became day. The needle on the light-meter shot off the scale and jammed, while the sound-recorder shattered completely in the thunderclap that followed immediately after.

The professor stared at the broken instruments. 'What frauds we are, pretending to *understand* the weather,' he murmured, then checked furtively over his shoulders, in case someone was listening. There were many in Sanctaphrax, twisted with ambition, who would leap at the chance to exploit the Most High Academe's deepest misgivings. Thankfully, no-one was there to hear his blasphemous words.

With a sigh, the Professor of Darkness hitched up his black gown and climbed the ladder which led into the glass-domed attic. He pressed his eye to the viewfinder of the great telescope in the centre of the floor.

As he adjusted the focus, the professor found himself staring deeper and deeper into the dark void beyond the Edge. If he could just see that little bit further . . .

'What mysteries lie out there?' he wondered out loud. 'Wh . . . what in Sky's name is *that*?' A small dark fuzz had crossed his field of vision.

With trembling fingers, he readjusted the focus. The blurred object became solid. It looked like a sky ship. But what was a sky ship doing out there, untethered and so far away from land? Scarcely able to believe what he was witnessing, the professor pulled away, removed his pocket handkerchief and wiped his eyes.

'No doubt about it,' he muttered feverishly. 'It *was* a sky ship. I know it was. Unless . . .'

He glanced round at the sense-sifter. It was pulsing a deep shade of purple.

'No,' he shuddered. 'I can't have imagined it. I'm not mad.'

He spun back, grasped the telescope and peered back down the sight anxiously. There was nothing there in the swirling depths. With trembling fingers he played with the focus. Still nothing. And then . . . The professor gasped. From the point where the sky ship had been – at least, where he *thought* it had been – several bright balls of light were spinning off into the dark sky.

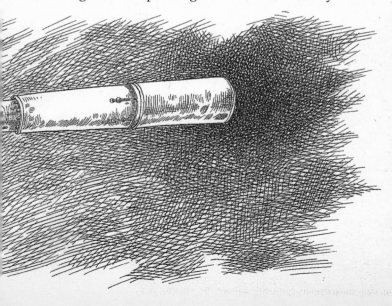

Perplexed, he let go of the telescope and hurried to the window.

'Shooting stars!' he cried.

One after the other, the dots of light flew up and hurtled across the night sky towards the Edge in wide flaring arcs. Seven in all there were, the professor noted. No, eight; two were flying close together. Apart from this pair, each of them was heading in its own direction, at its own speed and describing its own unique parabola.

The professor sighed. The characteristics of light were outside his field of expertise, yet he would like to have one of the shooting stars for himself to examine its make-up; to prove, once and for all, that it was darkness that lay at the heart of all light. The trouble would be in finding one where it landed.

Already the shooting stars were falling; some, quite near. Others continued over the Mire and on to the Deepwoods beyond. While one – shining more brightly than the rest – went on further than the professor could even see.

'Curious,' he whispered. The wind howled and the tower creaked. 'Very curious.'

Far below the battered floating city, the streets of Undertown had turned to a quagmire. Its hapless inhabitants squelched about the sucking mud, trying desperately to salvage something from the trail of destruction the maelstrom was causing.

'Sky above, what is to become of us all,' the frightened voice of a mobgnome cried out as a bright flash lit up the

sky. 'Why were we not told about the arrival of so fearsome a storm?'

The wind screeched. The roof rattled. A shooting star
hissed across the night sky above her head. Glancing up
too late to see it clearly, she wiped the hair from her eyes
and peered through the sheets of driving rain at the
floating city. Her face twisted with rage.

'Why didn't the academics warn us?' she demanded.

'Academics? Don't make me laugh, Glim,' her companion shouted down angrily as he struggled to rope
their flapping roof into place. 'Barkslugs, the lot of them!
Slow, slimy and full of stinking . . .'

CRASH!

'TOG?' Glim shouted in alarm. 'Are you all right?'

There was no reply. Heart pumping with anticipation,
Glim gathered up her skirt and climbed the ladder. The
roof was empty. There was a gaping, jagged hole in the
corrugated ironwood panels.

'TOG!' she cried again.

'I'm down here,' came a muffled voice.

Clutching tightly with trembling fingers, Glim pulled
herself forwards across the roof and peered down into
the hole. The sight which greeted her made no sense. A
huge piece of wood lay in the middle of the floor.
Beneath it lay Tog.

'Help me,' he whispered. 'Can't move. C . . . can't
breathe.'

'Just hang on,' Glim shouted back. 'I'll be right with
you.'

Shakily, she eased herself back down the roof and felt

for the top rung of the ladder with her feet. The wind tugged at her fingers. The rain lashed at her face. Slowly, carefully, she descended the ladder and ran inside.

'Oh, good gracious!' she exclaimed, and her fingers flew to the lucky amulets around her neck.

Close to, the piece of wood looked even bigger. It was curved and varnished, and along its side, gold letters gleamed in the lamplight. EDGEDA . . . The word ended abruptly in a jagged mass of splinters.

'It looks like a bit of a sky ship,' said Glim. 'Though why anyone would want to go skysailing in *this* weather . . .'

'Never mind all that,' Tog wheezed. 'Just get it off me!'

Glim started back guiltily. 'Yes, Tog. Sorry, Tog,' she said.

Brow taut with concentration, she tugged at the wood with all her might. It was heavy – much heavier than it looked. Despite all her efforts, it hardly moved. Yet move it did. And just enough for Tog to release his trapped legs and scramble backwards.

'Yes!' he cried.

'*Unnkh!*' Glim gasped, and the wood fell to the floor with a bang. 'Oh, Tog,' she said. 'Are you all right?'

The mobgnome inspected his body carefully, up and

down. 'I think so,' he said finally. 'Leastways, no bones broken.' He nodded towards the section of broken sky ship. 'Which is more than can be said for the crew of this thing, I dare say.'

'Do you think they were leaguesmen or sky pirates?' said Glim.

Tog ran his fingers over the fine wood and gold lettering. 'Hard to say, really,' he replied at last. 'But I'll tell you this for nothing. This sky ship must have been a real beauty when she was all in one piece.'

Glim shuddered. 'Oh, Tog,' she said. 'Can you imagine what it must be like being up in the sky when so terrible a storm strikes? Nowhere to run. Nowhere to hide . . .' She looked up at the hole in the roof. 'Puts our problems into perspective, don't it?' she said.

'Certainly does,' said Tog thoughtfully. 'I'd best get it repaired before the whole place floods.'

It wasn't only the mobgnomes who suffered damage. There were others, in various parts of Undertown, who lost their homes, their property, even their lives, to the falling debris.

In the main commercial centre, a broad section of hull flattened one side of the aviary run by Flabsweat the pet shop owner, killing half the captive birds outright and leaving the rest dazed but free to escape. The bowsprit flew down through the air like a spear, skewering an unsuspecting hammelhorn – penned up and ready for the following morning's sale – as it landed. The heavy main mast crushed a row of market stalls where it fell.

The west side of the town fared no better. A volley of falling hull-weights brought considerable damage to the opulent dwellings of several prominent leaguesmen. And the rudder-wheel – a great circular slab of rock which keeps a sky ship on an even keel – smashed through the roof of the Leagues' Chamber itself. It broke the ceremonial ring-shaped table in two, and killed three leaguesmen in the process.

The three unfortunates were later identified as Simenon Xintax, the current Leaguesmaster, Farquhar Armwright, a slight, nervous individual who represented the League of Gluesloppers and Ropeteasers, and Ulbus Pentephraxis – a bull of a leaguesman known more for his ferocity in battle with the sky pirates than for any business acumen: none of them had stood a chance.

Even Sanctaphrax itself suffered damage from the

wreck of the sky ship. First, a large section of poop-deck completely destroyed all the intricate apparatus on the high balcony of the Cloudwatchers' College. A moment later, a heavy fore-harpoon speared the side of the dilapidated – and thankfully abandoned – Raintasters' Tower and remained there, swaying precariously, half-way up the crumbling wall.

The noise from the blow was tremendous. It echoed round the entire city and juddered through the floating rock itself.

'That's it,' the Professor of Windtouchers groaned. 'We're all doomed now.' He turned to the Professor of Cloudwatchers who was crouched beside him beneath his desk. 'It has been an honour and a pleasure knowing you, my friend,' he said.

'The pleasure has been all mine,' the Professor of Cloudwatchers replied, beaming brightly.

The Professor of Windtouchers frowned. '*All* yours,' he said. 'If it was *all* yours, I wouldn't have derived *any* pleasure from our acquaintance. And I did.'

The Professor of Cloudwatchers nodded sagely. 'But I derived *more* pleasure.'

'Why, you obstinate, hog-headed . . .'

'Who are you calling hog-headed?'

A second, and louder, noise filled the air and, as the city rocked, the contents of every shelf and cupboard in the study tumbled down to the floor with a crash.

'That's it,' the Professor of Windtouchers groaned. 'We're certainly all doomed now.'

The third loud noise was the loudest of all. It boomed and thundered with such force that the two professors fell down flat on the floor. All over Sanctaphrax, academics and apprentices, servants and guards, did the same.

Only the Professor of Darkness, the Most High Academe of Sanctaphrax, knew what had happened. At the sound of the first crash, he had looked from the window of the Loftus Observatory to see a nearby tower swaying precariously, to and fro.

'The Raintasters' Tower,' he murmured, and swallowed nervously. 'Thank Sky I was not in it.'

Up until only a few days earlier, his own study had been situated at the top of the tower. But what had caused it to rock so? He looked down. And there, half-way up, he saw a gleaming spike of metal and wood buried deep in the shattered stonework.

The professor scratched his head. 'It looks like a sky ship harpoon, but . . . *whooah!*'

He stared in horror as the great harpoon juddered, slipped and, in a flurry of rocks and mortar, tumbled down through the air, landing with a loud crash on the roof of the covered cloisters far below. The first stone pillar crumpled; the rest toppled, one against the other like a line of dominoes, until all of them were down.

Then, just as the air was clearing, the weakened wall of the tower finally gave up the struggle to remain standing, and the whole lot came tumbling down to the ground in an explosion of rocks, rubble and dust.

The professor's jaw dropped. Deep furrows crisscrossed his brow. He was recalling the sky ship which had disappeared so mysteriously. The curious falling debris. The shooting stars . . .

The sound of insistent tapping interrupted his musings. He spun round and there, perched on the broad sill beyond the window, was a white bird with yellow eyes and a vicious-looking beak which it was hammering at the glass.

'Kraan!' said the Professor of Darkness.

Years earlier, he had found the bird as a bedraggled fledgling, half-dead in a snowstorm. He'd taken it back to his warm study where he'd both nursed it back to health and taught it the rudiments of speech. Now Kraan was fully-grown and powerful, and despite – or perhaps because of – its unpromising start in life, it had gone on to become leader of the flock of white ravens which roosted in the Stone Gardens, right at the tip of the Edge.

The professor hurried to the window and pushed it open. The gale-force wind burst in, ruffling his beard and setting his black robes flapping. 'Kraan, my loyal friend,' he said. 'How good to see you – but what has brought you here in such terrible weather?'

The white raven cocked its head to one side and stared at him with one unblinking yellow eye. 'Strange lights in sky,' it said, its voice raucous and rasping as it shouted above the noise of the storm.

'Shooting stars,' the professor nodded. 'I saw them too. I . . .'

'Shooting stars,' the white raven repeated. It turned its head and fixed him with the other eye. 'One in Stone Gardens.'

The professor started with surprise. 'You mean . . . You're saying . . .' A broad grin spread over his face. 'One of the shooting stars has come down in the Stone Gardens, yes?'

'Stone Gardens,' Kraan repeated.

'But this is wonderful news you bring,' the professor said.

'Stone Gardens,' Kraan called for a third time. It flapped its heavy wings, launched itself off from the sill and swooped away into the night.

'Quite so,' said the professor, as he hurried across to the top of the stairs. 'I must go and investigate for myself at once.'

·CHAPTER FOUR·

THE STONE GARDENS

The Stone Gardens lay at the very tip of the jutting Edge promontory. There were no plants there. No shrubs or trees. No flowers. Nothing grew in this ghostly place but the rocks themselves.

Seeded long long ago, they had been growing in the Stone Gardens for as far back as anyone knew. *The Elemental Treatise* itself made several mentions of '*The wondrous spheres of rock which do grow and, in their immensity, float skywards.*' The great floating rock upon which Sanctaphrax had been built had its origins there.

New rocks appeared beneath the old ones, pushing those above them higher as they grew. Over time, stacks had formed with the rocks standing one on top of the other, and each one larger than the one below. Strange eerie groans and deep sonorous rumblings accompanied the rocks' growth – noises which, combined with the towering silhouettes of the rock stacks, made the Stone Gardens a place of fear to Undertowners.

If left untended, the uppermost rocks would become

so large, so buoyant, that they would break free with a crumbling sigh and sail upwards into open sky. But the Stone Gardens *were* tended. The colony of great white ravens over which Kraan ruled – sleek descendants of their smaller, scraggier cousins in the Mire – had been roosting in the stone stacks for centuries. It was they who monitored the growth of the rocks.

Their sensitive talons could detect the shifts of a ripe flight-rock. Their acute ears could pick up the whisper of a rock about to float free. Once, occasionally twice, a season, the great flock would take to the sky and circle round the Raintasters' Tower. Then, like a great drift of snow, they would alight on the sloping roof of the Loftus Observatory, signalling to the academics of Sanctaphrax that the rock harvest should begin.

Under the watchful eye of the Most High Academe,

the ceremonially blessed and ritually purified academics would descend from Sanctaphrax and go to work. With stone-nets and rock callipers, they secured the flight-rocks one by one as, with ghastly howls, they broke free.

Superstitious at the sight of the great white flock – like a visitation of ghostly spirits from beyond the Edge – the Undertowners quaked with fear. The howling of the Rocks and the shrieking of the ravens – known by most as *the chorus of the dead* – was almost too much to bear. It panicked the animals, it sent youngsters scurrying indoors with their ears stopped and struck terror into even the bravest of hearts. The Undertowners would clutch their best-favoured talisman or charm and whisper urgent prayers that death might spare *them* a while longer.

Yet, for all their fears and superstitions, the Undertowners would have been still more alarmed if the noise ever failed to come. For, terrifying as it was, the ghoulish clamour heralded the delivery of the flight-rocks upon which each and every one of them depended. If the supply of flight-rocks ever dried up, no ship would ever again be able to take to the sky.

Richly rewarded by Undertown for the flight-rocks,

the academics were only too aware of the importance of this material side to their duties. It brought them both great influence and enormous wealth, allowed them their elevated existence in the magnificent floating city, and enabled them to continue their own lofty studies.

Despite the importance of the rocks, the academics felt no need to guard the Stone Gardens. That task could be safely left to the white ravens. The moment the academics finally completed their work and departed, the great white birds would swoop down noisily from the Loftus Observatory to gorge on the hammelhorn and tilder carcasses left out for them – or, when death had visited Sanctaphrax, on the ceremonially laid-out bodies of the deceased academics themselves.

It was into this place of death, and growth – the Stone Gardens – that the shooting star had fallen. Above the sound of the wind which whistled in and out of the stone stacks, a faint hissing had been heard and the white ravens had looked up to see a tiny ball of light flying in from beyond the Edge.

As it came nearer the sizzling, spitting sound had grown louder; the light, bigger, brighter. Abruptly, a bank of dark cloud had blotted out the moon, but the Stone Gardens had become lighter, not darker, as the glowing ball of light had hurtled towards them. It had turned the water in the dips and hollows to black mirrors, and the stacks of spherical rocks to orbs of burnished silver.

The white ravens had flapped their ragged wings and screeched with terror. It was a shooting star, and it was heading straight for their rocky home.

Down, down, down and ... CRASH! The object had landed with a loud muddy splash beside the highest stack of rocks. And there it had remained. Dazzling, yet motionless.

Hopping forwards inquisitively, the white ravens had formed a circle around the shiny object. Was it danger-ous? Was it edible? They had screeched and flapped and stabbed at it nervously before Kraan had stopped them with an angry shriek.

'Waaaark!'

Any unusual intrusions into the Stone Gardens had to be reported to the Professor of Darkness without delay. And, as leader of the flock of white ravens, it had been Kraan's duty to do so.

'Waaaaark!' it had screeched a second time, as it flapped away.

The white ravens were to guard the shining object until his return.

*

'Faster, you addle-brain!' shouted the Professor of Darkness. 'Good grief, you must be the slowest barrow-driver in all of Undertown!' He leaned back and struck the lugtroll on the shoulder with his wooden staff. 'Faster,' he bellowed. '*Faster!*'

Instead of speeding up, the lugtroll stopped completely and lowered the wooden shafts to the ground. The professor slumped backwards, braced himself against the side rail and turned on the lugtroll furiously.

'What is the meaning of this?' he bellowed.

'This is as far as I go,' came the reply.

The professor looked round and was surprised to see that they were at the edge of the Stone Gardens. 'And not before time,' he said gruffly. 'But I'm not done with you yet. I need you to take me into the Gardens themselves.'

The lugtroll shook his head.

'Did you hear me?' the professor demanded.

Scuffing his bare feet in the dust, the lugtroll looked away. 'I'm not going another step,' he said firmly. 'I've already brought you further than I like coming.' He shuddered. 'I hate this place. Gives me the creeps, it does.'

'I see,' said the professor curtly. He climbed down from the barrow and straightened his robes. 'You will wait for me here,' he said.

'Oh, but . . .' the lugtroll whined.

'It will be the worse for you if you do not,' the professor warned him. 'If you are not here when I return, I shall see to it that you never push another barrow so long as you live.'

The lugtroll looked over his shoulders anxiously. 'All right,' he said at last. 'But ... try not to be too long.'

The professor surveyed the grim, rocky landscape and shivered with foreboding. 'Believe me,' he muttered. 'I shall be as quick as I possibly can.'

Wrapping his gown tightly around him and raising his hood, the professor set off. His feet stumbled and squelched; his wooden staff tapped at his side. He felt weary and increasingly ill at ease. The Stone Gardens, groaning and creaking all round him, suddenly seemed uncomfortably immense – and the prospects of finding the fallen shooting star pitifully small.

Where should he try first? What should he look out for?

Looking round, as the low moon brightened and dimmed with the passing clouds, the professor caught a flash of flapping wings far ahead. His heart missed a beat. The savage birds that roosted in the Stone Gardens were both unpredictable and dangerous and, hearing their raucous cawing fill the air, he was about to head off in the opposite direction when a horrible thought struck him.

'Since it was Kraan who told me about the shooting star,' he said to himself, 'there is every likelihood that it is the shooting star they are all flapping around now. Ah me,' he sighed. 'Be brave now. Show no fear, or they will be upon you at once.'

As the moon sank down beneath the horizon, the temperature fell sharply. Mist, coiling up from the ground, swirled around the professor's shuffling feet and tapping staff.

'Sky protect me,' he murmured in a quavering voice as the screeching of the white ravens grew louder.

Guided only by the incessant noise of the raucous birds, he stumbled on over the uneven ground, half-blinded by the thick mist.

All at once, a tall stack of rocks loomed out of the misty shadows before him. He paused. Half a dozen of the great white ravens were perched on the boulder at the top, squabbling for position. Others clung to the sides. A dozen more – massive specimens, each of them – were down on the ground, wings outstretched, loping round in their strange, weightless dance. They were guarding something, that much was clear.

The professor took a step closer. His heart thudded – not only with fear, but also with excitement. Whatever the white ravens were clustered around, it was still glowing. He took another step. And another . . .

'*Waaaaark!*' the white ravens cawed furiously as their attention was grabbed by the intruder.

Those on the stack flapped their wings and rose up screeching into the air. Those on the ground loped for-wards and thrust at him with gaping beaks and savage talons. They were angry – and hungry.

'D . . . do you not know me?' the professor cried. He held out the heavy gold seal of high office which hung from the chain around his neck. 'It is I, as Most High Academe who sees to it that you are fed, who . . .'

He fell still. The birds were paying no heed to his words.

They were all around him now in a wildly flapping circle, and beginning to test his strength. To keep them at bay was a hopeless task. Even while the professor was lashing away at those in front of him with his heavy wooden staff, others were snapping viciously at his back.

'Kraan!' he bellowed. Surely his old friend wouldn't let any harm come to him. 'KRAAN!'

From above his head came a flurry of wings as the largest and most powerful white raven of all spiralled down out of the sky. Its talons glinted. Its beak gleamed. It was Kraan. Staggering backwards, the professor watched it land on the back of an attacker and sink its beak in its neck. A loud shriek echoed round the Stone Gardens. Blood trickled down over white feathers.

'WAAAARK!' Kraan screeched menacingly.

The other white ravens fell back.

'Dangerous here,' Kraan croaked, spinning round to snap viciously at a bird that had ventured too close.

'The shooting star . . . ?' the professor stammered.

'Shooting star,' Kraan confirmed raucously, turning and cutting a swathe through the gathering of dis-gruntled white ravens. The professor followed him, nervous still. If the colony banded together they could overpower their leader in an instant.

As they approached the glowing object, the professor squinted down into the dense mist. He trembled, hardly daring to believe what he was seeing. It must be his imagination. Or a trick of the light and shade. He moved closer still, crouched down and reached out. His fingers confirmed what his eyes had already told him. This was no fallen star. No fireball. No blazing rock.

It was the body of a sky pirate, lying on its front, face turned away – and glowing from head to toe more brightly than a flaming torch.

'I knew I hadn't imagined seeing the sky ship,' he muttered. 'It must have exploded. And the shooting stars I saw, those eight balls of light . . .' He looked back at the glowing sky pirate. 'Could they have been the crew?'

The cawing of the white ravens grew louder than ever. Now the professor understood why they had been guarding their find so jealously, and why his arrival had aroused such fury. To them, the sky pirate who had dropped into their midst was a free meal – a free meal Kraan and this gowned intruder were preventing them from enjoying.

He reached forwards and seized the sky pirate by the shoulder. As he did so, his fingers brushed against something as sharp as needles. He pulled back and looked more closely.

'Hammelhornskin fleece,' he said thoughtfully. He noted the sky pirate's build, his youth – and the thick, matted hair. This time when he took hold of his shoulders he did so more carefully. He rolled him over and stared down at the face.

'You!' he gasped. The body pulsed with the eerie luminous glow. 'Oh, Twig, what has happened to you? What have you done?'

All around them, the white ravens screeched and squawked, the bravest of them hopping forwards to stab at Twig's legs with their cruel beaks.

'Twig!' the professor called desperately. The intrepid young sky pirate captain was alive still, but fading fast. 'Twig, wake up. I'll take you back to Sanctaphrax. *Twig!* You wouldn't listen to me. Oh no! "I'm a sky pirate captain," you told me. "Like my father, and his father before him," you said. "It's in the blood." And look where it's got you! Why, if your father, Quintinius Verginix, could see you now . . .'

At the sound of his father's name, Twig stirred. The professor smiled. The white ravens hopped back, squawling with fury.

Twig's eyelids fluttered. The professor observed the movement with excitement.

'Or, perhaps I should call him by his other name. The name of the most feared and respected sky pirate captain ever to sail the skies. Cloud Wolf . . .'

Twig's eyes snapped open. 'Father,' he said.

'No, Twig,' said the professor gently, 'not your father. It is I, the Professor of Darkness.'

But there was no sign of recognition in the eyes as they stared round, wild, unseeing. Nor did Twig speak another word. The professor shivered with apprehension. Apart from the strange glow it gave off, the young sky pirate's body appeared unscathed, yet his mind had clearly suffered.

The ravens moved closer once again. Kraan stabbed at the most inquisitive of the birds and turned to the professor. 'Go,' it said. 'Take shooting star, now!'

From the urgency in its raucous voice, the professor knew that Kraan would not be able to keep the other white ravens at bay for much longer. Trying hard to ignore the disconcerting confusion in those blindly staring eyes, the professor supported Twig under his arm and heaved him up.

'Now, walk,' he muttered. 'Come on. You can do it.'

The sky lightened to the east as the professor hobbled back through the Stone Gardens, one hand round Twig's shoulder and the other holding his staff.

'That's it, Twig,' he said encouragingly. 'Just a little further.'

·CHAPTER FIVE·

COWLQUAPE

'A shooting star!' The solitary figure of a junior sub-acolyte, a tousle-haired youth in ill-fitting robes, peered out into the night. 'How curious,' he murmured.

The storm had passed, and the academics were stirring from their numerous hiding places.

'What have we here?' came a sneering voice from behind the youth. 'A little runt of a leaguesman's son. Why aren't you in the library with your nose stuck in a scroll, Cowlquape?'

The voice belonged to a tall apprentice in the fur-lined robes worn by all those in the College of Cloud. Several others stood behind him, dusting off their clothes and sniggering.

'I thought . . .' mumbled the youth. 'I thought I saw something, Vox.'

'Leave sky-watching to those of us who are qualified,' Vox said nastily. 'Don't you have a latrine or something to slop out?'

'I . . . I was just going,' said Cowlquape, all fingers and thumbs as he gathered up his bundle of scrolls. He hurried off down the rubble-strewn walkway.

'Undertown scum!' Vox's voice floated after him.

Barely fifteen years old, Cowlquape was small for his age. He was lowest in the pecking order of Sanctaphrax – slopping out the latrines was just one of his tasks. He was at the beck and call of any who had a menial task that needed per-forming: running errands for the various sub-professors, mistsifting and windgrading, helping to maintain the spotless and gleaming appearance of the floating city.

Cowlquape, however, dreamt of better things. Whenever he could, he would seek refuge in the Great Library of Sanctaphrax – now sadly neglected – and immerse himself in the countless dusty old barkscrolls that were housed there.

The library wasn't fashionable. It had neither the glamour of the College of Cloud or the Academy of Wind, nor the power and influence of the School of Light and Darkness – but then Cowlquape himself wasn't fashionable. His father, a burly, overbearing bully of a leaguesman by the name of Ulbus Pentephraxis, had bought him into Sanctaphrax.

'You'll never make it in the leagues, you frightened little barkworm,' he had said. 'Perhaps those pompous weather-watchers up there can make something of you. It's certainly beyond my capabilities!'

And so he had secured sub-acolyte tenure for his son. At first, Cowlquape had been overjoyed. He was soon to discover though that the floating city could be as harsh a place to live as the streets of Undertown. For although they were undeniably wealthy, the leaguesmen were universally despised by the academics of Sanctaphrax, and those acolytes and apprentices who gained entrance to the floating city with their money were despised all the more.

As he hurried through the deserted avenues of the majestic floating city, Cowlquape paused to take in every detail of the splendour which surrounded him: the magnificent towers, with their minarets, domes and spires, gleaming pink in the glow of the rising sun, the ornately carved pillars, the statues and fountains, the sweeping staircases and arched walkways. He knew that he could never, ever take it for granted. It was all so elegant. So opulent. So grand.

Cowlquape sighed. It made him feel even smaller than usual to gaze up at it all. Vox's taunt came back to him. 'Undertown scum!'

Would he ever be accepted in this magnificent city, he wondered, or would he never be anything more than a frightened little barkworm?

One thing was for certain. He could never go back to Undertown. The noise, the filth, the blows and kicks

from his father – and the look of disappointment in his mother's eyes before she'd died. His life in Undertown had all but crushed him completely. No, come what may, Sanctaphrax was his home now. His father paid good money to the College of Cloud to keep him here. And he, Cowlquape, would earn the respect of those snooty professors!

'Be brave,' he whispered to himself. 'Be confident.'

He was rounding the corner of the Institute of Ice and Snow when he heard a voice from the landing-stage ahead of him.

'Crushed to death by objects falling out of the sky,' it was saying.

Cowlquape started, then shrank back into the shadows. A thickset gnokgoblin was talking to a fellow basket-puller on the jutting platform.

'Whatever next?' said the gnokgoblin's companion.

'I know,' said the gnokgoblin. 'I just come up here from Undertown a minute ago. Lucky to escape with my life, I can tell you. I was in the Bloodoak tavern when Mother Horsefeather – the old bird who owns the place – comes bustling in all of a quiver with news that a sky ship had been struck by the full fury of the storm. Smashed to smithereens, it was, with lethal bits of debris dropping down all over Undertown. 'Parently the giant rudder-wheel came smashing through the ceiling of the Leagues' Chamber – and flattened three bigwig leaguesmen.'

'No!' said his companion, wide-eyed with gory interest.

'On my mother's life,' said the gnokgoblin. He raised his hands and counted off the victims one by one. 'First, the Leaguesmaster,' he said. 'Simon or Simeon something or other. Then whassisname Armwright, the Rope and Glue character. And then . . .' He frowned thoughtfully. 'Ah, yes. Captain of one of them league patrol boats. Pentephraxis. Ulbus Pentephraxis.'

Cowlquape felt as if he had been hit by the full weight of the rudder-wheel himself. His father, dead! He could never mourn the loss of so unpleasant a father, yet his breath came in short, anxious gasps as the terrible implications of the news sank in.

When a leaguesman died, the League took everything. Even now his father's erstwhile colleagues could be stripping the family mansion of everything they could lay their hands on, like ravenous white ravens. And who was to stop them? Certainly not his weedy only son up in Sanctaphrax.

'Sanctaphrax!' Cowlquape groaned, his head in his hands. Who would pay his fees? The College of Cloud would throw him back on to the streets of Undertown as soon as the money dried up. He was finished, ruined – fit only to be fed to the ravens.

The journey from the Stone Gardens had taken longer than it should have and the sun was up long before the lugtroll finally made it back to Undertown. For a start, although no bones were actually broken, Twig's experiences in the storm had left him weak and slow. He'd had to stop for several rests as the professor steered him on towards the barrow. And when they arrived there, the lugtroll had insisted that the terms of their deal be re-negotiated since there were now *two* persons returning from the Stone Gardens, rather than the *one* he had taken there.

'Weigh more, pay more!' the lugtroll had insisted, and refused to budge until the professor gave way.

Then, when the amount had at last been settled and they set off, it was soon clear that the lugtroll had taken on a bit more than he could chew. On the flat he had puffed and panted as he crept along at a snail's pace, while on the hills he had wheezed so badly that the professor had wondered at times whether they were ever going to make it at all.

Twig, for his part, hadn't registered a single thing that was going on. Apart from that one word, he had not spoken. Withdrawn and passive, he had allowed the Professor of Darkness to bundle him into the barrow. And as the trip had got underway, the luminous glow which had drawn the professor to Twig in the first place had faded away.

'Soon be back,' the Professor of Darkness said encouragingly.

Twig gave no indication that he had heard.

'Do you remember how we first met?' the professor said, trying to stir Twig's memory. 'When you came to my old study at the top of the old Raintasters' Tower . . .' He chuckled. 'By Sky, Twig,' he added. 'You helped Sanctaphrax in her hour of need then. Now Sanctaphrax will help you. I swear this shall be so.'

He stared into Twig's troubled face and trembled with helpless sympathy.

'Oh, Twig,' he continued. 'What in Sky's name made you venture, untethered, into open sky in the first place? Did you not realize the perils you would have to face?' He gripped him by the shoulders. 'What happened out there?'

But Twig made no reply. The young sky pirate captain's head was clearly in turmoil. If he didn't receive attention soon, there was surely a danger that he could lose his mind completely. The professor looked round him and was gratified to find that they were just reaching the outskirts of Undertown. Five minutes later, the lugtroll lowered the shafts of the barrow to the ground.

'We're here,' he wheezed, and bent over double, gasping for breath.

As he climbed out of the barrow, the professor glanced up at the floating city hovering over them. One of the hanging baskets was directly above his head. He raised his arms and cupped his hands to his mouth.

'Anyone up there?' he shouted.

Still standing in the blustery shadows, Cowlquape stared up the broad paved avenue, his heart heavy, his eyes misting up. His gaze darted from building to magnificent building, each one designed to suit the school or college it housed.

'And I shall never see any of this again,' Cowlquape muttered, tears in his eyes. 'Soon I'll be a beggar on the streets of Undertown.'

Just then there was a commotion at the end of the platform. The Professor of Darkness stepped out of a basket as it came to rest on the landing-stage. He had someone with him – someone barefoot, bony, with matted hair and tattered clothes. Cowlquape forgot his troubles for an instant. Who was he? he wondered. And wasn't that the Professor of Darkness with him?

As the gnokgoblin lowered his basket again and disappeared from view, leaving the professor and the stranger on their own, Cowlquape stepped out of the shadows.

'You there, lad!'

'Who me, sir?' Cowlquape stammered, dropping his bundle of scrolls.

The Professor of Darkness looked him up and down. 'Yes, you,' he said. 'Help me to get Tw . . . er, my friend to the School of Light and Darkness and, er . . .'

'Of course, sir. At once, sir,' said Cowlquape, hauling the youth up onto his back.

'I take it that you can keep your mouth shut,' said the professor, leading the way. 'I don't want a lot of gossiping academics disturbing my friend.'

'Y . . . yes,' said Cowlquape softly.

The professor looked at him warily. 'What's your name, lad?' he asked.

'Cowlquape, if it pleases you,' came the reply. 'Junior sub-acolyte of Sanctaphrax.'

'Junior sub-acolyte of Sanctaphrax,' the professor repeated, his eyes narrowing. 'An Undertowner, by the look of you. Rich father in the leagues, I'll be bound.'

They had almost reached the entrance to the school.

Cowlquape nodded. 'Yes, sir. My father is . . .' He checked himself. '*Was* a leaguesman, sir.'

'Very good, very good,' said the professor absent-mindedly.

They arrived at the studded door of the School of Light and Darkness – for Cowlquape, all too soon.

'Thank you, my lad,' the professor said, as he bustled the stumbling figure inside the school. The great studded door slammed shut.

Cowlquape stood alone in the avenue, feeling lost. What now? He turned and wandered back the way they'd come. How long did he have? A day? A week? Probably no more than that, and then he'd be out, his few possessions in a bundle under his arm as he stepped into the basket to return to Undertown for ever.

'Well, Cowlquape,' he said to himself. 'Until then I'll find the darkest, dustiest corner of the Great Library and, who knows?' He smiled bravely. 'Just like all those barkscrolls, they may forget all about me!'

·CHAPTER SIX·

INSIDE AND OUT

The huge dinner gong clanged mechanically from the Refectory Tower. As one, the doors of the schools and colleges of Sanctaphrax burst open and a great throng of chattering professors, apprentices and acolytes streamed hungrily towards it. Head down and heart pounding, Cowlquape joined them. He slunk into the bustling refectory, took a brass bowl and platter from the racks and mingled with the seething crowd of those waiting for lunch.

Ten days had passed since the Professor of Darkness had asked for his help. In that time, Cowlquape had spent his time hiding, curled up in a dusty corner of the Great Library with his beloved barkscrolls, lost in the fantastic tales and legends they held. Nobody had disturbed him, and he had ventured out only to forage for food – a latrine cleaner's pie, an apprentice's tilder sausage dropped absentmindedly.

But it had been at least a day since he'd last eaten anything. When he had heard the dinner gong, his hunger
had got the better of him. He was so ravenous that he was
prepared to risk being caught by those in the College of
Cloud and expelled from Sanctaphrax for ever for the
sake of a hot bowl of delicious, spicy tilder stew.

At the long high tables, the senior professors were
being waited upon. In the galleries lining the walls, academics and senior apprentices jostled noisily over large
communal stew-pots. Whilst in the 'pit' below, a great
clamour of acolytes jostled and shouted round the stew-
pipes that snaked down from a huge central cauldron.
As he made his way through the clamouring throng
Cowlquape couldn't help but catch snatches of conversation.

'The Department of Psycho-Climatic Studies confirmed that it definitely was a mind storm the other
night,' an apprentice was saying. 'And we're still feeling
its after-effects.'

His colleague nodded. 'I know,' he said. 'I'm beginning to wonder if the skies will ever clear again.'

In the continuing gloom that had followed that fateful
night, more treacherous weather had been blown in from
beyond the Edge. Rain – registering deepest indigo on
the sense-sifters both up in the Loftus Tower and in the
garret of the Department of Psycho-Climatic Studies –
had prompted an outpouring of communal grief across
the region. A thick and oily mist had rendered the
residents of some northern districts of Undertown
temporarily deaf and dumb. While, the previous night, a

heavy downpour led to outbreaks of terrible violence amongst the cloddertrogs in the boom-docks.

The abrupt change in the character of the weather was bringing the hitherto insignificant Department of Psycho-Climatic Studies into the limelight. Its dean, a rotund pen-pusher by the name of Lud Squeamix, now sat self-importantly at the highest of the long tables, slurping stew up through his teeth, pausing only to belch loudly.

'I'm thinking of going for a place in the Department,' a third apprentice was saying. 'That's where the action is these days.' He looked round furtively. 'I hear that the windtouchers and cloudwatchers are forming an alliance.'

'*Pfff!* Fat lot of good it'll do them,' snorted his companion. 'Has-beens, the lot of them.'

All around the refectory the feverish conversations were the same. Plots and counterplots had become rife. And as if this wasn't enough, there were other rumours going round that even the most level-headed of academics could not ignore.

Up in the College of Rain gallery, a senior apprentice turned to his neighbour. 'And *I've* heard he's up to something,' he said. 'Something suspicious!'

Cowlquape's ears pricked up.

'Something suspicious?' said his companion. 'What, the Most High Academe?'

'That's the one,' the first senior apprentice replied. ''Cording to my sources in the School of Light and Darkness, he's got someone locked up in there. They say he was found in the Stone Gardens, and I can well believe it. He looks like a vagrant, and never speaks – though he can freeze your blood with one icy stare.'

'Absolute madman, by the sound of him,' an apprentice cloudwatcher in an upper gallery called down. 'He howls!'

'Howls?' said the apprentice raintasters as one.

'Like a woodwolf,' the cloudwatcher continued. 'Every night. 'Course, you wouldn't hear it from your faculty, but it echoes all round the College of Cloud. Spooky, it is.'

Cowlquape frowned. He, too, had heard the curious night-time howling from his hiding place in the library, but hadn't made the connection between that and the staring-eyed character he had encountered with the Professor of Darkness that blustery morning.

As he inched his way forwards to the stew-pipes, his thoughts stayed with the stranger.

Gossip had it that the mysterious individual was none other than Twig, the young sky pirate captain who had returned to a hero's welcome in Sanctaphrax only weeks earlier. It was said that he had done what no-one had ever done before – set out into open sky, untethered. Something must have happened to him out there, the stories maintained. Something unearthly, inexplicable; something that had left him both dumb and distracted. It was curious then that, according to the rumours, the Most High Academe had conferred upon him the title of Sub-Professor of Light.

The crowd shuffled towards the pipes. Behind

Cowlquape, two sub-apprentice windtouchers were bemoaning their lot.

'Windgrading, windgrading and more windgrading,' one of them complained. 'And the professor's such a tyrant!'

'The worst type,' came the reply.

Cowlquape sighed. At least your futures are secure, he thought bitterly. Unlike my own. He shuddered, and the brass platter slipped from his grip and clattered to the stone floor.

The raintasters and cloudwatchers around him looked at the thin, tousle-haired boy with amusement.

'Then again, at least we're not sub-acolytes,' one of the windtouchers commented sniffily.

'Undertowner!' said the other scornfully.

'Sky above!' a voice bellowed from the highest of the long tables, and all heads turned. It was Lud Squeamix and he was almost choking on his stew. 'Who'd have thought it?' he spluttered.

A flagon was dropped in surprise.

'Upon my word,' someone else exclaimed, 'it *is* him.'

Every eye looked towards the highest long table. There, where the most prominent academics were eating, the Professor of Darkness was to be seen ushering the mysterious, wild-eyed individual to an empty seat.

The apprentices forgot all about the junior sub-acolyte in their midst.

'I can't believe that's Twig,' Cowlquape heard one of them say. 'I mean, look at him!'

'Like a crazy one,' another agreed.

'And he's meant to be the new Sub-Professor of Light!' said a third. 'I wouldn't fancy being *his* apprentice.'

'Yeah,' laughed the first apprentice raintaster. 'Definitely a couple of raindrops short of a shower.' And they all burst out laughing.

All, that is, except for Cowlquape. While the apprentices were too empty-headed to see anything beyond his outward appearance, Cowlquape looked again. There was something about the young sub-professor – a fierce intelligence ablaze in those bright, staring eyes. Perhaps Twig hadn't lost his mind at all, Cowlquape thought with a sudden jolt. Perhaps he had simply turned his gaze inwards.

Beneath the stew-pipe at last, he pulled the lever, taking care that none of the steaming tilder stew missed his bowl. He grabbed a hunk of oak-bread from the basket beneath the pipes, soggy from stew others had let fall, and pushed his way towards the mass of low stools that sprouted like mushrooms beneath the galleries. Looking up, he could see Twig clearly.

The newly appointed sub-professor was staring into mid-air, oblivious to his surroundings. Occasionally, prompted by the nudging elbow of the Professor of Darkness, he would start picking at his food like a bird. But only for a brief moment – and never long enough actually to eat anything.

As Cowlquape continued to watch the twitchy young individual – only a few years older than himself – he asked himself what horrors Twig must have endured when the *Edgedancer* received the full brunt of the mind storm. After all, if a passing rain cloud could lead to the cloddertrogs attacking each other, then what must it have done to the sky pirate captain who had seen his ship destroyed?

Just then, a blanket of blackest cloud swept in across the sky and plunged the refectory into darkness. The Professor of Darkness – for whom the sudden gloom was of particular interest – pulled a light-meter from the folds of his gown. Concentrating intently, he failed to notice his young sub-professor get up from his seat and make his way down the wooden steps.

'Curious,' muttered Cowlquape.

A heavy hand landed on his shoulder almost knocking him off his stool. 'Well, well, well,' came a familiar mocking voice. 'If it isn't our favourite little Undertowner!'

'Vox!' gasped Cowlquape, looking up into the arrogant face of the tall cloudwatcher apprentice.

'I hear somebody hasn't been paying his fees,' he said. '*Tut, tut.* That won't do at all.'

Cowlquape trembled. 'Please!' he begged. 'It's just that my father, he . . .'

'Save it for the Professor of Cloudwatching, bark-worm!' Vox's voice was hard, his grip vice-like on Cowlquape's shoulder.

Outside, a dismal angry drizzle began to fall. Rage at the unfairness of it all flared in Cowlquape's eyes. It wasn't his fault that his father had been killed!

'Professor of Cloudwatching?' he said. 'Professor of Cloudwatching?' His voice rose to a shout. Vox stared in amazement. 'You can give this to your Professor of Cloudwatching in place of payment!' And with that Cowlquape hurled the bowl of steam-ing stew into the tall apprentice's face.

'*Aaaargh!*' Vox shrieked, falling into a gaggle of mistsifters and sending bowls and stew flying everywhere.

Cowlquape took to his heels, ducking and dodging as he made for the door, and bowling a couple of indignant latecomers off their feet as he dashed from the refectory.

It was even darker outside than it had been inside and, away from the noise of the refectory, far more for-bidding. Purple-edged black clouds twisted and swirled overhead like bubbling wood-tar. The wind was sul-phurous. And even though he could not know how the sense-sifters were glowing orange, Cowlquape felt an unfamiliar tumult of emotions within him: anger, exulta-tion, and a nerve-tingling fear as chaotic and swirling as the weather around him.

Chicker-chacker-cheeeesh. Crimson lightning darted this way and that across the sky, and the thunder which followed crashed all round the floating city, shaking it to its very core.

Head spinning, Cowlquape set off for the refuge of the Great Library. He kept to the shadows as he hurried silently across the greasy tiles. Around a corner, he halted. He looked back and forth. The coast was clear. From the guard turret to his right to the landing-stage far away on his left, the place was deserted.

As he set off again the sky lit up for a second time, and Cowlquape caught a sign of movement out of the corner of his eye. He spun round and squinted into the dim light. There was the young sub-professor. He was standing atop the stone balustrade of the landing-stage, legs apart, head up, arms outstretched and palms raised. All round him, the lightning cracked and splintered.

'Twig!' Cowlquape bellowed. He didn't know whether it was his own inner confusion or simply the madness of the weather that made him call out the professor's name. Could he really be going to jump? 'Stop! Stop!'

His urgent cries were drowned out by a second rumble of thunder. Twig tottered on the edge of the balustrade, flapping his arms.

'NO!' Cowlquape yelled. He raced forwards, heart in his mouth, and seized the hem of Twig's waistcoat. '*Ouch!*' he cried, as the hammelhorn fur turned instantly to sharp needles which pierced his skin. Droplets of blood welled up on his fingertips.

The lightning flashed again. The thunder rolled. And, as the wind grew stronger, a light sparkling rain began to shower down. All over Sanctaphrax, the mood changed to elation. Cheers echoed from the refectory. Cowlquape, gripped by a sudden feeling of intoxicating strength, grasped Twig's arm and pulled him off the balustrade. Twig fell to the ground.

'Forgive me, Professor,' Cowlquape whispered. 'I thought you were going to jump.'

Twig stumbled to his feet. 'You spoke?' he said.

Cowlquape's jaw dropped. '*You* spoke!' he said. 'They said you were dumb . . .'

Twig frowned and touched his lips with his fingers. 'I did,' he whispered thoughtfully. He looked round, as if seeing for the first time where he was. 'But . . . what am I doing here?' he said. 'And who are you?'

'Cowlquape, Professor,' came the reply. 'Junior sub-acolyte, if it pleases you.'

'Oh, it pleases me well enough,' said Twig, amused by the young lad's formality. Then he frowned. 'Did you say . . . *Professor*?'

'I did,' said Cowlquape, 'although Sub-Professor would have been more accurate. You are the new Sub-Professor of Light − at least, if the rumours are to be believed.'

A look of bemusement passed over Twig's face. 'This must be the Professor of Darkness's doing,' he said.

'He was the one who brought you to Sanctaphrax,' said Cowlquape. 'From the Stone Gardens, they say. He . . .'

'The Stone Gardens,' said Twig softly. 'So I didn't imagine it.' Looking lost and bewildered, he turned to Cowlquape. 'And yet . . .' He frowned with concentration. 'Oh, why can't I remember . . . ?' He scratched his head slowly. 'It's as if I've been in a dream. I remember my crew, the voyage, entering the weather vortex and then . . . Nothing!' He paused. 'Until just now, when you obviously stopped me from throwing myself to my destruction.' He smiled. 'Thank you. What did you say your name was?'

'Cowlquape,' said Cowlquape, 'and I don't know what came over me. I shouldn't have saved you at all.' He stared down at the ground disconsolately. 'I should have joined you. I have nothing to live for!'

'Come, come,' said the young professor gently. He lay his hand on Cowlquape's shoulder. 'You can't mean that.'

'I do,' said Cowlquape, hanging his head. 'I'm an Undertowner. My father is dead and I have no fees to pay for my apprenticeship. When they find me, they'll throw me out of Sanctaphrax. What have I got to live for?'

Twig looked at the bookish young acolyte. 'You saved me,' he said simply. 'I think I ought to repay the debt. You say I'm a Sub-Professor of Light.'

Cowlquape nodded.

'In that case, I hereby appoint you as my apprentice, Cowlquip.'

'Cowl*quape*,' said Cowlquape excitedly. 'Do you really mean it?'

'Of course,' said Twig, smiling. 'I'll need a smart young apprentice to look out for me now that I've finally woken up. I've got a lot to do.'

'I'll look out for you, professor,' said Cowlquape. 'You see if I don't.'

CHAPTER SEVEN

THE SHOOTING STAR CHART

Cowlquape strode out of the Great Library, brushing the dust from his fine new robes. The costly black material showed up every speck, and the fur trim seemed somewhat extravagant – but the clothes fitted splendidly. He clutched the ancient barkscrolls to his chest and hurried towards the School of Light and Darkness.

Turning into a narrow alley next to the Windtouchers' Tower, he stopped. There, blocking his way, stood Vox, the cloudwatcher, his face pasty with woodsalve.

'Alone at last,' the tall apprentice snarled.

Two more cloudwatcher apprentices appeared behind Cowlquape. He was trapped.

'I believe you and I have some unfinished business, barkworm,' said Vox, producing a mean-looking cudgel from the folds of his gown. He swung it through the air, catching Cowlquape a glancing blow to the side of the head, and sending him sprawling.

'Vox!' he gasped. 'You great big bully . . . *Unnkhh!*'

'Where's your so-called professor now, Undertowner, eh?' Vox sneered. 'Where's brave Captain Twig, saviour of Sanctaphrax?'

'Right here,' said Twig, seizing Vox's upraised arm and twisting it neatly up behind his back.

'*Aaargh!*' yelled the apprentice, dropping the cudgel.

Twig shoved him away. 'I believe my valued apprentice, Cowlquape, needs a hand,' he said.

'Y . . . yes, sir,' stammered Vox, cowering before the young professor.

'And dust off his robes while you're about it.'

Vox clumsily helped Cowlquape to his feet and brushed him down.

'Now be on your way,' said Twig. 'And don't ever let me catch you bothering him again or you'll find yourself on a one-way basket trip to Undertown. Do I make myself understood?'

Vox nodded sullenly and sloped off. His friends had long since fled.

'Thank you, Professor,' gasped Cowlquape.

Twig smiled. 'How many times do I have to tell you?' he said. 'Call me Twig.'

'Yes, Prof . . . Twig,' said Cowlquape.

'And Cowlquape.'

'Yes, Twig?'

'You dropped this.' The young professor handed the crumpled barkscrolls to his apprentice. 'And don't get bark dust all over your nice new robes.'

'No, Twig,' said Cowlquape happily; and followed the Professor towards the School of Light and Darkness.

Twig's study was situated at the top of the west tower in the School of Light and Darkness. It was a small room, yet with its soft hanging armchairs and blazing stove, a comfortable and cosy place. The wall was lined with shelves brimming over with rows of leather-bound books, stacks of papers tied up with ribbons, and intricate light-orientated scientific apparatus. A furry layer of dust covered it all.

Twig watched Cowlquape as his young apprentice sat with his nose in a barkscroll, reading avidly in front of the open-doored stove that glowed with purple flames. It must be lufwood he's burning, Twig thought, and was once again taken back to his childhood with the woodtrolls, when he would sit on the tilder rug before the fire listening to Spelda – his adoptive mother – as she recounted her tales of the dark Deepwoods.

The lufwood logs gave off a lot of heat but, being buoyant when burned, they had a tendency to fly out when the door to the stove was open. Every so often, Cowlquape would look up and nudge back into the stove a blazing log which threatened to escape.

'What's that you're reading?' Twig didn't hide the boredom in his voice. It was plain to his young apprentice that Sanctaphrax, and the stuffy confines of the School of Light and Darkness in particular, stifled the young sky pirate captain.

'An old barkscroll, Professor,' said Cowlquape. 'I found it in the Great Library – it's fascinating . . .'

'Call me Twig,' he said impatiently. Then, in a gentler voice, 'I envy you, Cowlquape.'

'Me, Twig? But why?'

'You can pick up a barkscroll and be transported off to goodness knows where. I've watched you sit there for hours, poring over some scrap of bark, half eaten by woodmoths and barkworms, as if in a trance. You're a born academic, Cowlquape. Whilst I . . .' He paused. 'I'm a sky pirate!'

Twig climbed to his feet, crossed the stuffy study and flung open the window. Icy rain splashed down on his upturned face and trickled down the back of his neck. 'That is where I should be,' he said, pointing beyond Sanctaphrax. 'Out there. Sailing the skies as captain of a sky pirate ship. Like my father and his father before him. It's in the blood, Cowlquape – and I miss it so.'

Cowlquape put down the barkscroll and caught an escaping lufwood log with the fire tongs.

'Oh, Cowlquape,' Twig continued, his gaze still fixed on the endless expanse of sky outside. 'You have never heard the wind singing in the rigging, or seen the world laid out below you like a map, or felt the rushing air in your hair as you sail across the sky. If you had, you would know what misery it is to be stuck in this poky study. I feel like a bird whose wings have been clipped.'

'I love Sanctaphrax,' said Cowlquape. 'I love its towers, its walkways; the Great Library – *and* this poky study. But I wouldn't be here if it wasn't for you.' He looked down, suddenly embarrassed. 'And I'd follow you anywhere, even . . .' He gestured to the open window. 'Even out there, into open sky.'

Twig flinched. 'There were others who followed me there,' he replied quietly.

'Your crew?' said Cowlquape.

'My crew,' Twig whispered sadly. He could see them all now, the diverse yet loyal bunch he had assembled: the flat-head goblin, the slaughterer, the oakelf, the waterwaif, the Stone Pilot, the banderbear and the bespectacled quartermaster. They had believed in him, followed him into open sky – and had perished there. 'I don't know how, but I killed them all, Cowlquape. You see how dangerous it can be putting your trust in me.'

'Are you sure they're dead?' said Cowlquape.

'Of course they're dead,' said Twig irritably. 'How could they possibly have survived?'

'*You* did,' said Cowlquape. Twig fell still. 'I mean, did you actually see what happened to them?'

'See?' Twig repeated. 'I can't remember!'

'Can you remember *anything* of that fateful voyage into open sky?' he prompted.

Twig hung his head. 'No,' he admitted glumly.

'Then how do you know they're dead?' Cowlquape persisted. 'How many were on board the *Edgedancer* when you set sail?'

'Eight, including myself,' said Twig. 'But . . .'

'The Professor of Darkness said eight shooting stars were seen flying through the sky,' Cowlquape blurted out.

Twig frowned. 'Cowlquape, what are you saying?'

'I've said too much.' Cowlquape stumbled over the words. 'The professor told me not to talk to you about your former life. He said that it would only upset you . . .'

'Upset me? Of course it upsets me!' Twig stormed. 'If I thought for an instant that any of them were still alive, I'd leave this place right now and find them, whatever it took.'

Cowlquape nodded. 'I think that's what the professor is afraid of,' said Cowlquape. 'Forget I spoke, Twig.'

'Forget!' Twig turned on him. 'I can't forget! Eight shooting stars, you say. One for each member of the *Edgedancer*. Cowlquape, think now, did the professor say where these shooting stars landed?'

'Well, I . . . I mean, I think . . .'

'I can answer that,' came a voice. The Professor of Darkness stood in the study doorway. 'I should have known I couldn't make a professor out of you, Twig, my boy,' he said sadly. 'You're just like your father, a born adventurer – and like him, you're probably destined to be lost for ever in open sky.'

Twig seized the professor's hand. 'My father?' he said. 'You know what happened to my father?'

The professor shook his head. 'Only that he was swept away in the Great Storm many weeks ago, and hasn't been seen since.' He looked deep into Twig's troubled eyes. 'Did you . . . ? Out there . . . ?'

'I don't know,' Twig said unhappily. 'I can't remember.' He grasped the professor's hand in his own and squeezed it tightly. 'Professor, you must help me find my crew. As their captain, I made a promise never to abandon them, come what may. If there is even the *slightest* chance that any of them are alive, then it is a promise I must keep.'

'But Twig,' said the professor. 'Even if . . .'

'And maybe,' said Twig, cutting through the professor's objections, 'just maybe, my crew might help me retrieve my memory.' He pulled away from the professor and looked into his eyes. 'For who knows what I might have forgotten – out there, in open sky. Something useful perhaps? To you, Professor. To Sanctaphrax.'

The professor nodded uneasily. Twig had a point.

Having sailed so far into open sky he had experienced what no-one before had ever experienced; what the aged academic himself had only dreamed of doing – namely, entering the source of the weather itself. What was more, Twig had survived and returned to tell the tale. For the moment, of course, his mind was shut tight, but if it could be unlocked . . .

'Very well,' said the professor. 'I can see your mind is made up. Go in search of your missing crew, Twig, and with my blessing.' He pulled a leather pouch full of gold pieces from the folds of his robes and placed it into Twig's hand. 'For your journey,' he said. 'Use it wisely. Now follow me to my study and I shall show you the chart I made the night you fell to earth. It shows the approximate position of the other shooting stars – if my calculations are to be trusted. A few fell not far, some-where in Undertown. A couple fell farther off in the Deepwoods, Sky help them. And one – the final one – fell so far away that I couldn't track it with any certainty.'

'Show me, Professor!' said Twig excitedly. He turned to his apprentice. 'We're going to find my crew, Cowlquape. To be reunited . . .' He paused. 'Perhaps they will even be able to tell me about my father . . .'

'Twig,' said the professor sternly. 'Go charging off on this shooting star hunt if you must. And indeed, I see that you must. But for Sky's sake leave the lad here, safe in Sanctaphrax where he belongs.'

Cowlquape stepped forwards, grasped Twig's arm and faced the professor. 'I'm sorry, Professor,' he said. 'But I too have made a promise!'

·CHAPTER EIGHT·

THE LULLABEE INN

'Cowlquape,' said Twig gently. 'The basket will soon be here.' Cowlquape looked up from the old barkscroll he was examining. 'Trust you,' Twig smiled. 'We're just about to set off on an arduous, not to say possibly futile, quest and you've got your nose stuck in a scroll.'

'Sorry, Twig,' said Cowlquape. 'But this particular scroll really is fascinating.'

Twig smiled. 'You're dying to tell me about it, so go on then.'

'It's *The Myth of Riverrise*, Prof . . . I mean, Twig,' said Cowlquape excitedly.

'What, that old tale?' said Twig. 'Spelda, my mother – or rather the woodtroll who raised me as her own – used to tell it to me when I was a young'un.' A smile played on his lips as his eyes glazed over. '*Once upon a velvet blackness came a spark . . .*' Twig murmured. 'Oh, how my heart thrilled when she spoke those words. Of all the many tales she told, *The Myth of Riverrise* was always my favourite.'

'*The spark turned. And the wind breathed. And the rain cried . . .*' Cowlquape read.

Twig nodded. '*And the sun smiled. And the first minute of all minutes came to pass,*' they said together.

'You know it off by heart!' said Cowlquape, delighted.

'*The Myth of Riverrise* is told in every corner of the Edge,' said Twig. 'I heard it in the caverns of the termagant trogs, I heard it on board the *Stormchaser* – different versions, but essentially the same. What you've got there is the classic.'

'It makes sense of things,' said Cowlquape.

Twig tugged at the ends of the scarf around his neck. 'Sometimes there is truth buried in the old tales,' he said seriously.

'Do you think, then,' said Cowlquape, 'that somewhere out there is the place where it all began?'

'That *the Mother Storm did strike the highest point of that barren, jutting rockland and seed it with life*?' said Twig. 'Why not? I've seen many strange things out there in the Deepwoods, in the Twilight Woods . . .' He fell silent.

'What is it, Twig?' asked Cowlquape, concerned.

Twig was staring into the empty sky beyond the Edge. 'There *is* something,' he whispered. 'I'm sure of it. Something I can't remember.' His voice grew more urgent. 'Something I *must* remember . . .'

'Twig,' said Cowlquape, and nodded behind him. 'The basket-puller's arrived.'

Without another word, Twig and Cowlquape climbed into the basket. Cowlquape trembled giddily. The basket-puller, a gnokgoblin, unhitched the rope and began winching them slowly down from the floating city. 'A lot of weather we've been having recently,' he said, and looked at them askance. 'But then I'm sure I don't have to tell you two that.'

They were being pumped for information. Like all Undertowners, the gnokgoblin was desperate for any explanation of the treacherous weather that, of late, kept blowing in from beyond the Edge. Twig said nothing, and Cowlquape followed his example.

As the basket was lowered, Twig and Cowlquape removed their gowns and rolled them up, so that they could travel incognito. The smells of Undertown grew stronger, the lower they got. Pungent smells. Familiar smells. Roasting pinecoffee beans, burnt tilder oil, and, the sickly sweet scent that so many used to mask the stench of untreated sewage.

And noises. The clatter of ironwood wheels on cobble-stones, the banter and badinage, the endless bustle of feverish activity.

The gnokgoblin brought the basket down in the artisans' quarter – a sprawling hotchpotch of iron-mongers, leatherworkers and glassblowers.

Stepping out of the basket, Twig pointed down a winding alleyway to his left.

'This way, Cowlquape,' he said. 'We need to be methodical, so let's start by visiting all the taverns in the east of Undertown.'

'But I'm not thirsty,' said Cowlquape nervously.

'Nor am I, Cowlquape. But there's plenty that are – traders, slavers, merchants and skysailors. And when they drink, Cowlquape, they talk. And when they talk, we'll listen. And maybe, just maybe we'll hear some-thing. Stay close,' Twig told him, 'and keep your eyes and ears open.'

'I'm a good listener,' Cowlquape smiled as he fol-lowed him into the crowd.

Cowlquape soon lost count of the inns, taverns and drinking dens they visited – the Running Tilder, the Rusty Anchor, the Hook and Eye – the names merged into one another. By the end of that first day, however, they had heard nothing! Weary and footsore, Cowlquape followed Twig out of the Redoak. Night had fallen long ago and the oil street lamps had all been lit. Cowlquape looked round, bleary-eyed. 'Which one should we . . .' He stifled a yawn. '. . . we try next?'

Twig smiled. 'No more for this evening,' he said. 'We'll take lodgings for the night and resume our search tomorrow.'

Cowlquape looked round uncertainly. 'You want to spend the night here in Undertown?' he said.

'We're on a quest to find my missing crew, Cowlquape,' Twig reminded him. 'We can't go scurrying back to Sanctaphrax every time we get cold or wet or tired, can we?'

Cowlquape shook his head. 'No,' he said a little sorrowfully. 'I suppose we can't.'

They secured lodgings that night in a small, dark room above the Redoak. It was simple, yet adequate. There were two straw mattresses against the walls, and a large pitcher of fresh water in the corner enabled them to swill out their mouths and wash away the smell of stale smoke.

'Goodnight, Cowlquape,' said Twig.

'*Look for your roots, captain,*' whispered a voice.

'What did you say? Cowlquape?' said Twig. But there was no reply. Cowlquape had fallen into a deep, dreamless sleep.

They woke late the following morning and, after a hearty breakfast, set off once more. And so it continued. For three days – from noon to midnight – they trudged round the eastern quarter of Undertown, resting up for the night in the tavern they had ended up in when the clock struck twelve. On the fourth day, they found themselves outside a tavern – the Lullabee Inn – in a particularly rough part of Undertown down by the boom-docks.

'*The lullabee tree shares your roots,*' said a soft, sibilant voice by Twig's ear.

Twig turned to Cowlquape. 'What do you know of lullabee trees?'

'Me?' said Cowlquape, puzzled. 'Nothing, Twig.'

Twig frowned. 'Well, we might as well try here,' he said.

Cowlquape looked up at the tavern sign of a Deepwoods tree with a broad knobbly trunk and fan-like upper branches. The artist had even painted a suspended caterbird cocoon hanging from its branches.

'Come on, look lively,' said Twig, stepping forwards. 'We . . .'

CRASH!

A heavy log bench came bursting through the window to the right of the door. Twig and Cowlquape ducked down. Just in time, for the next moment, a heavy barrel came hurtling through the glass in the door itself. It missed their heads by a fraction, struck the ground with a resounding *crack* and spilled its contents.

'Like I say, Motley, accidents can happen,' an angry voice shouted from inside.

'Yeah,' said a second voice menacingly. 'Troughs can get damaged. Barrels can get broke.' The statements were accompanied by the sounds of splintering wood.

'And faces can be rearranged,' hissed a third. 'If you get my drift.'

'Yes, yes,' came a fourth voice – a small and anxious voice.

Twig and Cowlquape pulled themselves up and peered cautiously through the broken door. Three hefty hammerhead goblins were standing round the hapless landlord, a slight character with tufted hair and mottled skin. His body was trembling from head to toe. 'Times are hard,' he stammered. 'Takings are down. I just d . . . don't have the money.'

Twig looked at Cowlquape, his eyes burning with indignation. 'How I hate to see the strong picking on the weak,' he said.

Cowlquape placed a hand on his arm. 'There are too many of them,' he whispered. 'You'll get hurt . . .'

But Twig brushed Cowlquape's hand aside. 'Perhaps I should also have left you to be beaten up by that apprentice cloudwatcher,' he said.

Cowlquape reddened with shame.

'It's OK, Cowlquape. You stay here if you want to,' said Twig. 'But I'm going in.' He climbed to his feet and pushed the broken door open.

The hinges creaked. The hammerheads spun round.

'Evening,' said Twig calmly. 'Evening, Motley. A goblet of your finest sapwine if you'd be so good.' He glanced round and a smile flickered over his lips; Cowlquape had followed him in after all. 'And one for my friend here, as well.'

'I . . . we're just about to close,' said Motley.

Twig glanced up at the cluster of customers skulking in the shadows at the back of the tavern, too cowardly or too inebriated to come to Motley's aid. None of them looked as if they were about to leave.

'No wonder business is bad,' the hammerhead said gruffly. 'Turning away your customers like that!' He looked Twig and Cowlquape up and down, and smirked. The dark-grey ironwood of his false teeth gleamed in the turquoise glow of the lullabee flames. 'Take a seat,' he said, pointing with a knife towards one of the benches that was still upright.

Cowlquape moved to obey the goblin. Twig laid a reassuring hand on the youth's shoulder.

'Sit down!' roared the hammerhead.

'Just do as they say,' said Motley weakly. 'I'll be with you directly.'

Twig and Cowlquape remained where they were.

'Did I not make myself clear?' the hammerhead growled between clenched teeth. The other two turned and made towards them, fists clenched and eyes blazing.

'Riverrise clear!' Twig replied steadily, and drew his sword with its great curved blade: the sword his father had thrust into his hands just before being swept away in the Great Storm. It flashed in the turquoise light.

For a moment, the surly goblins were stunned to silence. Then they turned, looked at one another and laughed with disbelief.

'You little pipsqueal!' the nearest one bellowed at the

young captain and drew his own weapon; an evil-looking sickle. 'Come on then,' he growled, sneering, beckoning, shifting his weight from foot to foot.

'Go on, Tabor,' the hammerhead with the knife grunted encouragingly. Motley seized the opportunity to slip away. 'That's it!' Stepping back smartly from the shadows, Motley swung his club. '*UNNKH!*'

The blow struck the hammerhead on the side of his head, felling him like a tree and sending his knife skittering across the floorboards. It came to rest at Cowlquape's feet. Cowlquape hesitated, then bent to pick it up.

The heavy knife felt strange in his grasp. Despite his father's best attempts to teach him, Cowlquape had never mastered the art of self-defence. He turned on the second hammerhead nervously. 'You'd better just watch it,' he said, as threateningly as he could. 'Don't make me have to use it.' His voice was thin and unconvincing.

Behind him, the sickle of the third hammerhead sliced through the air. Twig leapt to his young apprentice's side, sword raised. The sickle struck it with a ferocious blow that jarred the length of his arm. He held his ground.

'The uglier they are, the prettier the victory,' Twig muttered. He lunged forwards ferociously, once, twice, at the two hammerhead goblins.

The sickle hissed through the air again, low and from the side this time. Twig jumped back. The cruel tip to the blade missed his stomach, but snagged on the fastener of his hammelhornskin waistcoat. Cowlquape spun round and stabbed furiously at Twig's attacker.

'*Aaiii!*' the cloddertrog squealed, as the sharp blade cut into the thumb of his fighting hand.

'Attaboy,' Twig shouted out encouragingly. He raised his arm and thrust the sword forwards. It found its mark and the hammerhead's sickle clattered to the ground.

Cowlquape kicked it over to the side wall. Twig pressed his sword against the hammerhead's neck.

'Leave now,' he said coldly, 'or so help me, I shall finish the job off.'

The two hammerheads exchanged glances. 'Let's get out of here!' one of them bellowed, and they both spun round and beat a hasty retreat. Neither of them once looked back at their fallen comrade.

'Sky above,' Cowlquape muttered. He held out the hammerhead's knife to Twig.

Twig smiled. 'Keep it,' he said. 'You earned it. That was excellent, Cowlquape,' he said. 'I didn't know you had it in you.'

117

Cowlquape lowered his head bashfully, and slid the knife down behind his belt. Neither did he.

'Not exactly known for their loyalty to one another, hammerhead goblins,' Motley chuckled, as he hung the club back on the wall. He turned to Twig and Cowlquape. 'Yet dangerous for all that,' he said. 'Thank you for coming to my aid, gentlemen.' He righted one of the upturned benches. 'Take a seat. You shall drink of my finest barrel – and on the house, of course.'

Twig and Cowlquape sat down. Cowlquape was drenched in sweat, his hands shaking. He looked around the tavern for the first time.

The other drinkers, sipping and slurping in the shadowy corners, seemed unaware of the recent disturbance. Some sat beneath the rows of hexagonal barrels set into the far wall like woodbee honeycomb; some hunkered on low logs by the drinking troughs. In the corner, the covered brazier glowed turquoise and echoed with the melancholy singing of the burning logs.

'It sounds like lullabee wood,' Cowlquape remarked unsteadily. He still felt shaken.

'We *are* in the Lullabee Inn,' said Twig, and smiled. 'Takes me back to the Deepwoods when I was a boy. Spelda – the woodtroll mother I told you about – would put a lullabee log on the fire at bedtime. The mournful songs used to lull me to sleep.'

'They sound eerie to me,' Cowlquape shuddered.

Motley returned with three goblets brimming with golden liquid. He sat down between them.

'To your very good health,' he said, and they all raised

the sparkling sapwine to their lips. *'Aaaah!'* Motley sighed appreciatively. 'Pure nectar.'

'It's very good,' said Twig. 'Eh, Cowlquape?'

Cowlquape winced as the pungent liquor burnt his throat and sent stinging vapours up his nose. He placed the goblet down and wiped his eyes. 'Very nice,' he rasped. He frowned and turned to Motley. 'But aren't you afraid the racketeers will be back?' he said.

Motley chuckled. 'Hammerheads are cowards at heart,' he said. *'Once bitten* and all that. Once word gets round that the Lullabee Inn's no pushover they'll leave me alone – for the time being at least. And it's all thanks to you two!'

'Oi, Motley!' came a gruff voice from the far corner. 'More woodgrog, now!'

'Coming up!' Motley shouted back. He climbed to his feet and wiped his hands on his apron. 'No peace for the wicked,' he said. 'Give me a shout when you need a refill.'

Motley scuttled away. Twig turned to Cowlquape who was trying a second sip of the sapwine. 'Take your time,' he said. 'I may as well have a look round while we're here. Chat to some of the locals. See if anyone knows anything.'

Cowlquape placed the glass down for the last time, nodded eagerly and jumped to his feet. 'Good idea,' he said. 'I'll come with you.' He didn't fancy being left on his own in this rough, shadow-filled place with its strange mournful music.

There were a dozen or so individuals in the tavern all

told. Trogs, trolls and goblins: heavy drinkers with lined, leathery faces and blank staring eyes.

'Greetings, friend. Can I get you a drink?' said Twig, tapping the shoulder of a small figure hunched over the drinking trough. 'Interesting weather we've been having.'

The creature turned, revealing itself as a lugtroll. He focused in on Twig's face. 'What d'ya want?' he snarled.

Twig raised his hands. 'Just a drink,' he said. 'And a little conversation. Motley! Fill my friend's trough here. He looks thirsty.'

Several pairs of eyes looked round and stared at him blankly.

'Thank you, sir,' said the lugtroll. Twig had got his attention.

'Like I said, interesting weather – strange rains, hailstones as big as a goblin's fist, all sorts of things falling out of the sky. Why, I even heard tell of shooting stars falling to earth right here in Undertown.'

The lugtroll shrugged. 'I ain't seen nothing,' he said. 'Just got off a sky ship from the Great Shryke Market. Carrying slaves we were.' He grunted. 'Never again! The noise was horrible – screaming and moaning they was, all the way. Can't get it out of my head. I came straight here to forget.' He buried his face in the brimming trough and Twig moved on.

'Cap'n?' came a gruff, questioning voice to his right.

Twig spun round. Cowlquape peered into the shadows, trying to see who had spoken.

'Cap'n, is that you?' A heavy seat scraped back on the wooden floor and a stocky individual scrambled to his feet, rubbing his eyes as if he had just woken from a sleep. Twig stared as the figure approached. It was a Deepwoods slaughterer: hair wild and blood-red skin, deep purple in the shadowy darkness. His morose features twisted round into a grin. 'Cap'n Twig, it is you, isn't it?' he said. 'Tell me it is?'

'Tarp?' said Twig. 'Is that you, Tarp? Tarp Hammelherd? From the crew of the *Edgedancer*?' Twig cried out. 'Yes, it's me! It's me, your captain!'

The two of them fell into one another's arms.

'Oh, cap'n,' Tarp said, tears welling in his eyes. 'I feared I would never live to see this day.'

Twig broke away from Tarp's stifling embrace and gripped the slaughterer's arms. 'But you *did* live, Tarp! You're alive! You're really alive!' he said, his voice quivering with excitement. 'And now I have found you!' He turned to Cowlquape. 'Look, Cowlquape,' he said. 'We've found one of my . . .'

He fell silent. His young apprentice looked as if he had seen a ghost. He was standing stock-still, mouth open and eyes almost popping out of his head. At his side, Motley looked equally dumbstruck.

'Cowlquape, what in Sky's name is the matter?' said Twig.

'Y . . . you're b . . . both glowing,' came the stammered reply.

'Like a pair of tilder-oil lanterns,' said Motley, staring in awe.

Twig looked at Tarp. It was true. A luminous light was glowing brightly from the top of the slaughterer's blood-red hair to the tips of his tooled leather boots. He looked down at his own body. Chest, legs, arms, hands, wiggling fingers – they were all aglow.

All round them, the regulars were muttering to one another. They wagged their fingers, they shook their heads. The lugtroll next to Cowlquape fingered the amulets around his neck. 'Spirits,' he hissed. 'Spirits in the boom-docks. And now spirits here. It ain't natural, I tell you.'

A couple of mobgnomes climbed to their feet. 'I'm not staying here,' said one nervously, and scuttled to the door.

'Me neither,' said his companion. He turned to Motley as he hurried past. 'Things in Undertown are weird enough these days without spirits turning up at the Lullabee Inn!'

'Yeah,' muttered the lugtroll, hurrying after them. 'Spirits is where I draw the line.'

'But ... but they were just leaving,' said Motley. 'Weren't you?' he added, as he ushered all three of them hurriedly to the door. 'Nothing personal,' he muttered to Twig. 'But you're upsetting the customers. And trade is trade you understand.' He pushed them gently but firmly outside.

As the door slammed behind them, Twig turned to the others. 'There's gratitude for you!' he chuckled. 'But who cares? You're *alive*, Tarp! That's what matters.'

'It's good to see you too, cap'n, but ...' Tarp frowned. 'We did look a bit odd, glowing 'n all. It's enough to put the frighteners up anyone.' He frowned. 'I was glowing when I first landed back in Undertown,' he said, 'but it soon faded. Until just then,' he added uncertainly, 'when we met again.'

'It was the same with me,' said Twig. 'Yet there we were, reunited and glowing once more. Something must have happened out there,' he said, his voice low and breathy. 'Something which even now binds us together.' He seized Tarp by the arm. 'Do *you* remember what happened? To the rest of my crew? To my ship? And, my father! Do you know if we found Cloud Wolf ...?'

But the slaughterer was shaking his great, shaggy red head sorrowfully. 'If only I *could* remember, cap'n,' he said. 'But I can't recall a darned thing after we entered that weather vortex.'

Twig smiled and squeezed his arm warmly. 'No matter,' he said. 'I have found you, Tarp, and that is a start. An excellent start! Now all we have to do is find the others.' His face clouded over. 'But where?'

'Spirits,' said Cowlquape softly.

'What was that, Cowlquape?' said Twig. 'Speak up.'

Cowlquape turned to him. 'I overheard that lugtroll saying that you must be a spirit.' He paused. 'Just like the ones in the boom-docks!'

'The boom-docks?' said Twig. 'Spirits in the boom-docks? Just like us?'

Cowlquape nodded. 'That's what I heard him say.'

'Oh, well done, Cowlquape!' Twig exclaimed with delight, and clapped him on the shoulder. 'That is where we shall go. To the boom-docks!'

Cowlquape lowered his head. 'I said I was a good listener,' he muttered happily.

·CHAPTER NINE·

THE CLODDERTROGS

The moment they had stepped outside, Twig and Tarp
Hammelherd had stopped glowing. The sun, though
low and golden in the late afternoon sky, was neverthe-
less bright enough to obscure their curious luminous
glow.

And thank Sky for that! Cowlquape thought, as they
set off.

They headed eastwards, through streets that they
were getting to know well, and on down towards the
swampy boom-docks beside the sluggish Edgewater
River. Twig was in reflective mood.

'We've done well, Cowlquape, finding Tarp alive,' he
said, 'but as for the others . . .' He fell silent. 'Do we
really dare hope that these ghosts, these spirits, could
possibly be . . . Who? Goom? Spooler? Wingnut Sleet
perhaps, or Woodfish?'

'Well, the lugtroll did say *spirits* not *spirit*,' said

Cowlquape, 'so there must be at least two of them there.'

Twig pulled from his bag the scroll of paper the Professor of Darkness had given him, and opened it out. It revealed a map of the Edge annotated with lines and crosses which charted the trajectories and approximate landing places of the eight shooting stars. The cross drawn over the Stone Gardens had been circled. That was where Twig himself had landed. He took a charcoal-stick and circled one of the four crosses dotted around Undertown.

'One down,' he said, turning to Cowlquape. 'And three still to find.' He smiled hopefully. 'Maybe they're *all* down in the boom-docks.'

'Maybe,' said Tarp Hammelherd. 'Though, to be honest, cap'n, I'm not sure how much I give for their chances if they *have* ended up there. It's cloddertrog territory, and they don't take kindly to outsiders at the best of times.'

'And what with all those stories of fighting we've been hearing,' Cowlquape added, with a shudder.

'Courage, Cowlquape,' said Twig. 'Stories is probably all they are. If we stick together, we'll be fine. Trust me.'

Cowlquape smiled bravely. Since they had first arrived in Undertown he had been overwhelmed by Twig's determination. Although they might well have been on a fool's errand, not once had the young captain contemplated giving up. And now, with Tarp Hammel-herd found, the young captain's determination had paid off. But what lay in front of them – bloodthirsty cloddertrogs – would test that determination to the limit.

Cowlquape shuddered again.

All round them, the cosmopolitan atmosphere of the thronging eastern quarter was coming to an end as they entered the hinterland of the boom-docks. The rows of shops and houses gave way to a maze of narrow alleys lined with ramshackle huts and shacks, each one over-run with huge families of cloddertrogs.

'Just watch your step,' Tarp Hammelherd cautioned, looking round furtively over his shoulder. 'Keep to the centre of the alleyways – cloddertrogs are suspicious of anyone going too near their property. And avoid eye-contact at all costs.'

Initially, Cowlquape complied with Tarp's instruc-tions, yet as they continued through the noisy, bustling streets, he began to relax. The overspilling taverns were raucous but relaxed. The markets buzzed with friendly banter, while the cramped houses resounded with snatches of song, young'un-play, infant-wail and gales of infectious laughter. It was a poor area, certainly, but there was nothing about its atmosphere which struck him as threatening.

'I can't see what I was fretting about,' Cowlquape said, as he punted a stray bladderball back to a rowdy group of youngsters.

'Yeah, well,' said Tarp Hammelherd grimly. 'First impressions can sometimes be deceptive. Things can turn nasty in a moment . . .'

'*Wurrgh!*' Cowlquape cried out.

'What is it?' Twig asked.

Cowlquape turned away and pointed back into a dark

and empty doorway. Twig peered into the shadows. The sudden pungent smell of decay snatched his breath away.

'Bones,' Twig muttered.

Cowlquape gagged.

'See what I mean!' said Tarp Hammelherd darkly. 'Now be on your guard.'

Cowlquape looked round, suddenly seeing the lumpen trogs in a different light. He noticed how large their yellow teeth were, how bloodshot their eyes, and he saw the heavy, studded clubs they carried over their shoulders and the knives on their belts.

Sticking closer together than ever, he, Tarp and Twig headed off down a dark, rubbish-strewn alley which led to the river's edge. Here, the homely smells of stale woodale and boiling mire-cabbage were overwhelmed by the odour of rotting fish. Above them, the early evening sky darkened as thick, billowing clouds swept in.

At its end, the alley opened out into the sprawling filth of the boom-docks themselves. The dwindling Edgewater River lapped half-heartedly at the recently exposed mud-banks. A light, greasy drizzle began to fall. Even though the light was fading – oil lamps had been lit and shone dimly from the rotting clapboard warehouses which lined the banks – they could still see the bones scattered over the mud. Lots of them, large and small. Each one had been picked clean by scavenging white ravens and the piebald rats which splashed and squealed as they fought over the waste that the encrusted sewage-pipes discharged into the sluggish water.

'I don't like this one little bit,' said Cowlquape uneasily.

'Neither do I,' said Twig, shaking his head. 'It's a pity that lugtroll wasn't more specific about where the spirits had been seen.'

Cowlquape nodded. 'I . . .' He gulped. 'You're beginning to glow again,' he said. 'Both of you.'

Twig examined his outstretched arm and saw for himself the faint, yet discernible, light it was giving off. 'It must be because it's getting dark,' he said.

'Then we . . . we'd better split up,' said Tarp nervously.

'Split up?' said Twig.

'The closer we are, the brighter we glow. I noticed that back inside the Lullabee Inn . . .'

'No, Tarp,' said Twig. 'I told you, we stick together. Besides, as I noticed *outside* the Lullabee, if it's bright enough we don't glow at all.'

'But Twig . . .' Cowlquape began.

'Cowlquape!' said Twig sharply. 'We'll go on a little further. Together!'

They continued in silence, picking their way past stacks of boxes and piles of empty barrels, through towering mounds of rusting chains and rotting fish, and on underneath the raised jetties which creaked as the tolley-ropes of the cumbersome tug ships pulled at the tether-rings.

The drizzle stung as a wind got up. Cowlquape winced as, with every step, his boots sank deep into the slimy mud. 'This is hopeless. We're never going to find them here,' he said. 'And you're glowing even brighter.'

'We'll try this way,' said Twig evenly.

They turned away from the river and went back up through the narrow alleys. Beneath the street lamps, the curious luminosity was barely visible. Yet, as they went on, Cowlquape thought he noticed a difference in the re-action of the cloddertrogs they passed. Before, they had simply been ignored. Now – unless it was his imagin-ation – they were being studiously avoided; eyes were averted and those approaching stepped to one side or disappeared into doorways until they had passed.

'I think they've noticed,' Cowlquape hissed.

'Come on,' said Tarp Hammelherd. 'Let's get out of here. We don't want to draw attention to ourselves.'

'It's a bit late to worry about that now,' Twig said out of the corner of his mouth. 'Look.'

They were standing at the edge of what seemed to be a junction, like the hub of a great spoked wheel, where dozens of the narrow alleyways met. At its centre stood an immense wooden vat, around which a seething mob of carousing cloddertrogs jostled together. The rowdy scene was bathed in the bright purple light of lufwood torches which cast grotesque shadows on the leering cloddertrog faces – and masked Tarp and Twig's luminous glow completely.

Shoved forwards by those just arriving, Twig, Cowlquape and Tarp Hammelherd found themselves being impelled deeper into the crowd and towards the great vat. The atmosphere of the place struck all three of them in the face like a blast of bad breath: hot, humid and foul. Cowlquape struggled hard not to heave.

'Fish,' said Twig. 'Rotten fish and . . .' His nose wrinkled up. 'Tripweed.'

From his childhood, Twig had always loathed the smell of the pickled tripweed on the woodtrolls' breath. Here, the stench was overwhelming. Pungent. Acrid. Fermenting. It seemed to be coming from the frothing vat.

'Tripweed beer,' he groaned.

'Three jugs, is that?' came a voice from beside the wooden vat. A squat cloddertrog with a filthy cloth draped over his arm motioned them to approach. They picked their way past the heaving bodies of drunken cloddertrogs asleep in the mud.

'I . . . errm . . . You haven't got any woodgrog, have you?' said Twig.

'Nah!' the cloddertrog scowled. 'This is a drinking pit. We don't cater for the hoity-toity here.'

Twig nodded. 'Then three jugs of tripweed beer it is,' he said amiably.

The cloddertrog climbed a wooden ladder and thrust three filthy jugs into the vat.

'Best to keep him happy,' Twig said to Cowlquape. 'Though I wouldn't drink it if I were you. It's fermented from rotted tripweed and the entrails of oozefish.'

Cowlquape shivered with disgust. The cloddertrog returned.

'There you go,' he said, thrusting the overflowing wooden jugs into their hands.

'Thanks,' said Twig, slipping a coin into the cloddertrog's outstretched paw of a hand. 'And tell me . . .'

But he had already turned his attention to a scrum of thirsty cloddertrogs who were standing to one side, cursing and swearing, demanding to be served. Twig nudged Cowlquape and nodded towards the jugs. 'Let's see if these can buy us some information.'

Taking care not to knock into anyone – '*spilled beer and spilled blood oft flow together*' as the cautionary saying went – they picked their way through the heaving mob.

The stench from the tripweed beer grew stronger. It steamed from the jugs, it hung in the air, it oozed from the pores of the cloddertrogs all round them.

One of them – a colossal individual – turned and peered at the outsiders with glassy-eyed interest. His gaze rested on the jugs in their hands.

'Are they for me?' he exclaimed, his voice booming and slurred. 'You're too kind!' He seized the jugs, swallowed long and deep and beamed back at them. 'Nectar of the clods,' he boomed, and roared with laughter. He threw the two empty jugs aside and started on the third. Behind him, a group of ruddy-faced indi-viduals burst into song. A roar of laughter went up from the drinking pit.

'So what line of work are you in?' said Twig.

'Same as most round here,' the cloddertrog replied. 'Dock work. Loading. Unloading . . .' He grinned. 'Wouldn't swop it for the world.'

The cloddertrog beside him turned and punched him good-naturedly on his fleshy arm. 'That's coz your soft in the head, Grom,' he said. He turned to Twig. 'I'll tell you what, I for one wouldn't mind swapping places with one of them academical types up in Sanctaphrax. Living in the lap of luxury, they are.'

'*Pfff*,' said the first, and spat on the ground. 'I'd sooner be down here, Tugger, as you very well know – with a jug in my hand and surrounded by mates.'

'See?' said Tugger, turning to Twig and Cowlquape, and screwing a thick finger into his temple. 'Soft in the head. Finest sapwine they drink up there in the floating city, out of cut-glass goblets. Or so I've heard.'

'They certainly do,' said Twig. 'We were up there only the other day – on business,' he added. It seemed unwise to let the cloddertrogs know of their true connection with Sanctaphrax. 'You wouldn't believe the wealth.'

'Oh, I would,' said Tugger.

'Mind you, none of them seemed as happy as anyone here,' said Twig, looking round.

'Told you!' said Grom triumphantly. He drained his jug and folded his arms.

'In fact,' Twig went on, 'they all seemed rather distracted. Apparently reports have been coming in that spirits have been sighted in Undertown. In particular in the boom-docks . . . Mind you, it's probably all a load of nonsense,' he said. 'You know what they're like with their lofty ideas – it's what comes of living with their heads in the clouds the whole time . . .'

The two cloddertrogs exchanged glances. 'Yet maybe there is some truth in the stories this time.'

Twig's eyes narrowed. 'You don't mean . . .'

'I've seen them myself,' said Grom.

'Me, too,' said Tugger, nodding earnestly. 'Two of them.' He leant forwards conspiratorially. 'They glow!'

Cowlquape's heart began to thump. He looked Twig and Tarp Hammelherd up and down for any trace of their own tell-tale luminous light. Thankfully, the lufwood torches were blazing so brightly that there was none.

'Glow?' he heard Twig saying. 'How peculiar. But tell me, where exactly did you see them?'

'Once down by the river, glowing in the darkness,' came the reply. 'Once up in the market-place, late at night when all the lamps had been put out.'

Grom nodded. 'And once, at midnight, I seen them floating along an alley. There one minute, they were, then gone again.' He shrugged. 'Sky alone knows where they came from or where they go to – but they give me the heebie-jeebies, so they do.'

Tugger laughed heartily and slapped Twig on the back. 'Enough of this talk of spirits,' he said. 'I got a mighty thirst on this evening. Another jug?'

Twig smiled. 'I'm afraid not,' he said. He turned to the others. 'Come on Tarp, Cowlquape. If we're going to complete our business this side of midnight, we'd best be going.'

'Please yourself.' The cloddertrog turned away. 'Too good to drink with the likes of us,' said Grom, nudging Tugger.

Twig, Tarp and Cowlquape retreated. The light drizzle turned to great heavy drops of rain. Twig felt a surge of irrational anger welling up inside him. He fought against the feeling. Beside him, Tarp's and Cowlquape's faces were drawn and tense.

'*Waaargh!* You stupid oaf!' bellowed an angry voice.

'Me, stupid?' a second voice roared. 'You ridiculous dunderhead!' There was the sound of a clenched fist slamming into a jaw.

'It's . . . it's the weather doing this,' Twig muttered through gritted teeth, and grabbed Cowlquape by the arm.

The next instant, the whole place exploded into violence as each and every cloggertrog turned on one another. Fists flew. Teeth were bared. Clubs were drawn. Curses filled the air.

'Quickly, Cowlquape,' Twig said, steering him forwards. 'Let's get out of here.'

But there were cloddertrogs everywhere, gripped by rain-rage, blocking their way, lashing out blindly at any who came too near. Punching. Kicking. Snarling and biting.

The great vat was splintered and leaking. A scrum of half a dozen of the furious creatures fell screaming to the ground, where they squirmed and writhed in a flood of tripweed beer, still scratching and scraping and scuffling with each other.

'I'll rip off your head.' 'I'll tear you limb from limb!' 'I'll yank out your liver and swallow it whole!'

And all the while, the terrible rain grew heavier. It hammered down torrentially, flooding the narrow streets and dousing the blazing lufwood torches, one by one.

'Come on, Tarp,' Twig called as he and Cowlquape attempted to squeeze through the crush of thrashing bodies. 'I . . . *wurrrgh!*' he grunted as a particularly large cloddertrog seized him from behind and clamped a fleshy hand over his mouth. Another cloddertrog had hold of Cowlquape. A third pinned Tarp against a wall.

Half a dozen more torches sputtered and died. Then, all at once, the last of the blazing lufwood torches went out, and the whole area was plunged into darkness.

'WAAAAH!' the cloddertrog screamed in Twig's ear and shoved him roughly away. He careered into Tarp. Their luminous glow became brighter than ever.

'Spirits!' the cloddertrogs howled and fell back – enraged still, yet too terrified to attack.

'Quick,' Twig whispered to the others. 'Let's get out of here before they realize we might not be spirits after all.'

He grabbed hold of Cowlquape's arm, and the three of them made a dash for it. The cloddertrogs bellowed after them, but did not follow. Yet there were others out there on the streets – everywhere they looked – all driven to bloodthirsty violence by the madness of the weather.

'What do we do?' said Tarp, running first in one direction, then back again. 'We're done for! We're doomed!'

'*This way*,' hissed a voice in Twig's ear.

'Very well, this way!' he shouted and ran up the narrow alley, the others hot on his heels. 'Stick together!' he bellowed. 'And pray to Sky that . . .'

'*Aaaaargh!*' they all cried out in horror as the ground beneath them seemed to give way.

Falling. Down, down, down. Tumbling through the dark, fetid air, arms and legs flailing wildly. Above their heads there was a loud bang as a trapdoor slammed shut.

· C H A P T E R   T E N ·

THE CISTERN

'Goodness!' Cowlquape gasped as the rapid descent came to an abrupt halt. Something soft, silken and oddly springy had broken his fall. With a cry of surprise he bounced back, and grunted with pain as Tarp Hammelherd crashed heavily into him. The two of them fell back down onto the bouncy mesh of fibres. Twig landed on top of them both.

All at once, there was a click. Then a thud. Then, with a hissing swish, a rope drawstring tightened up. The mesh-like material gathered around them, gripping them tightly and thrusting the three hapless individuals close together.

The first thing that hit Cowlquape was the incredible stench, so powerful it felt like the fingers of an invisible hand reaching down his throat and making him gag. Encased in the thick netting, the glow from Twig and Tarp was muted, but by the faint light that *did* penetrate outside, Cowlquape slowly began to make out his surroundings.

They were suspended high above a great, steaming underground canal. All around them, pipes protruded from the walls of the immense tunnel through which the canal flowed. A constant stream of filthy water poured from the pipes and into the foaming torrent below.

'The sewers,' Cowlquape groaned. 'I . . . *Ouch!* That hurts!' he yelped as Twig's bony elbow pressed sharply into his back. 'What are you doing?'

'Trying to draw my knife,' Twig grunted. 'Though I can't . . . seem to . . . move . . .'

'*OWWW!*' Cowlquape howled, still louder.

Twig gave up the struggle. 'It's hopeless,' he muttered. 'I just can't reach it.'

'Wouldn't do you much good if you could,' came Tarp Hammelherd's muffled voice from below them. His face was pressed into the bottom of the net. 'It's made of woodspider silk.'

Twig groaned. Woodspider silk was the material used in the manufacture of sky pirate ship sails – light as gossamer, yet tough enough to withstand the battering of the gales which swept in from beyond the Edge. His knife would be as good as useless against the thick spun fibres from which the net had been constructed.

'This is terrible, cap'n,' Tarp Hammelherd complained. 'I'd have sooner chanced my luck with those crazy cloddertrogs than ended up strung up like a great tilder sausage.' He winced miserably as the steaming vapours of the passing filth swirled up into his nostrils. Piebald rats sniffed the air and squeaked up with frustration at the glowing bundle dangling above them. 'Somebody, or something, set this trap,' he said, 'and we've fallen into it.'

'What do you mean, *something*?' said Cowlquape, alarmed.

'I've heard that muglumps live in the sewers,' came Tarp's hushed and muffled voice. 'Fearsome beasts they are. All claws and teeth. But clever, devious – perhaps one of them might have . . .'

'*Shhh!*' Twig hissed.

From far in the distance came a harsh, clanking sound.

'What's *that*?' Cowlquape whispered, dread setting the hairs at the back of his neck tingling.

'I don't know,' Twig whispered back.

The clanking grew louder. It was getting closer. Twig, pinned against Cowlquape, couldn't turn his head. Tarp, beneath them, couldn't see a thing. Only Cowlquape, whose head was fixed so that he could gaze back along the tunnel, faced the direction of the sound. He gulped.

'Can you see anything, Cowlquape?' said Twig uneasily. He knew that it wasn't only piebald rats and muglumps that lived in the sewers. There were trogs and trolls who had left their underground caverns in the Deepwoods for the promise of a better life in

Undertown, only to find that the frantic bustle above ground was too much to take. Some starved. Others had taken up residence in the sewerage system underground, where they scavenged a brutal existence.

The clanking was closer than ever now, harsh and clear above the gushing pipes. *Clang!* Metal scraped on metal. *Clang!* The pipes seemed to shudder.

And then Cowlquape saw it: a great metal hook which swung through the air, clanged against a pipe jutting out from the tunnel wall and took hold. The hook was fastened to a gnarled wooden pole around which two bony hands tightened their grip and pulled.

A shadowy figure standing awkwardly in a bizarre craft of lashed-together driftwood emerged from the gloom. He swung the hook again. *Clang!* It gripped the next pipe, and he pulled his barge against the current of the foaming canal, closer and closer.

Cowlquape gasped. 'I can see something,' he whispered.

CLANG!

The boat was almost beneath them now. A huge flathead leered up at him.

'Twig,' Cowlquape squeaked, 'it's . . .'

The hook sliced through the air in an arc, then ripped back, releasing the net. Like a hot flight-rock – with the three hapless individuals still bound up inside – it fell with a heavy thud into the bottom of the goblin's barge, just as the current took it underneath.

They hurtled along the stinking canal, buffeted by waves of filth, the driftwood craft dipping and rocking in the swell. The goblin, balanced expertly on the stern, loomed over them. In his bony hands was the long hook, now acting as a rudder and guiding the makeshift boat on its way. Faster and faster, and . . .

CLANG!

The boat jolted to an abrupt halt as the goblin's hook latched fast to a jutting pipe overhead. Twig, Cowlquape and Tarp struggled inside the net.

'What have we caught today, Bogwitt?' came a voice from above.

'Bogwitt?' breathed Twig.

Dagger in hand, the goblin reached down and pulled the slip-knot that held the top of the net. The net fell away. Twig leapt to his feet, glowing brightly. Mouth agape, the astonished flat-head goblin dropped his dagger.

'Sleet!' he yelled. 'He's glowing! He's glowing like us!'

'Don't you recognize me, Bogwitt?' said Twig, trying to sound calm as the barge rocked dangerously beneath his feet. 'It's me, Twig.'

'*I* recognize you, *Captain* Twig,' came the voice from above. 'Though I never thought to see you alive again, least of all in the sewers of Undertown.'

Twig looked up. There in the entrance of a wide, gaping pipe stood a gaunt figure dressed in the heavy longcoat and tricorn hat of a sky pirate. He, too, was bathed in the same luminous glow.

'Sleet!' cried Twig, almost losing his balance. 'Wingnut Sleet!'

But the former quartermaster of the *Edgedancer* had already turned away and disappeared into the pipe.

'Don't you mind him, captain,' said Bogwitt, clambering awkwardly from the boat, his right leg dragging behind him. 'I'm sure he's more pleased to see you than he's letting on. And as for me, I couldn't be happier.'

'Nor I, to see you,' said Twig. 'I can scarcely believe what's happening.'

He followed Bogwitt up the iron holds in the wall to the entrance of the pipe, high above. Unlike all the others, no foul water spewed from it. Cowlquape and Tarp followed them close behind. Then, pushing back a heavy hide curtain at the other end of the pipe, they found themselves in a wide chamber.

Wingnut Sleet stood to one side, his face half turned away. 'Welcome,' he said softly.

Cowlquape looked round in amazement. The place was a veritable smuggler's cave, stacked from top to bottom with boxes and crates overflowing with an array of costly items. There were rugs on the floor and hangings on the walls. There was furniture: two armchairs, a table, cupboards – and a small, ornately carved writing-desk. There were pots and pans, bottles and jars, crockery, cutlery, cruet . . . and the mouthwatering smell of tildermeat sausages.

'It used to be a water cistern,' Sleet explained. 'Now it is where we are forced to live.'

Twig nodded. 'I feared you might not be living at all,' he said.

'Aye, well, perhaps it would be better if I weren't,' Sleet muttered under his breath as he turned and crossed the cistern to where a skillet was sizzling on a stove.

'But Sleet . . .' Twig began.

'Oh, him and me get by all right down here,' Bogwitt broke in. 'We've been here weeks now. We forage and

filch – and you'd be amazed at the stuff we find in the
nets some days . . . though we always take any creatures
back to the surface after relieving them of any valuables
they may be carrying. And with light no problem . . .' He
nodded towards Wingnut Sleet's back, hunched over the
stove. 'So long as the two of us stick together.'

'The glowing, you mean?' said Twig.

'It was the same with us two when the cap'n found
me,' said Tarp. 'And now here's the four of us all aglow.'

'Something must have happened out there to cause it,'
said Twig. 'But I remember *nothing*. How about you,
Bogwitt? Can you remember what happened to us out
there in open sky?'

The flat-head goblin shook his head. 'No,' he said. 'We
set off after the caterbird in search of your father, we
entered the weather vortex – and then, not a thing.' He
grimaced as he pointed to his right leg. 'All I know is
that I was injured somehow.'

'And you, Sleet?' said Twig. The hunched figure
remained silent. Twig frowned. The quartermaster's
surliness was beginning to irritate him. 'Sleet!' he said
sharply.

Sleet stiffened. 'Not a thing,' came the sullen reply. He
lay down his spatula and turned slowly round. 'I know
only that it did this to me.' He removed his tricorn hat.

Cowlquape gasped. Tarp Hammelherd turned away.
Twig, eyes wide with horror, started back. 'Y . . . your
face!' he breathed.

The hair was gone, as was the left ear – and the skin
down that side looked as if it had melted like wax.

A white, sightless eye nestled in the molten folds. The quartermaster's hand moved up to the hideous scarring.

'This?' he scowled. 'This is how I found myself on my return from open sky. Not a pretty sight, eh?'

'I . . . I had no idea,' said Twig.

Sleet shrugged. 'There is no reason why you should,' he said.

'But you blame me for taking you inside the weather vortex?'

'No, captain,' said Sleet. 'I agreed to accompany you. It was my choice.' He paused. 'Though I confess to being disappointed that you don't know how we made it back to the Edge either.'

'I know only what I was told,' said Twig regretfully, 'that we looked like eight shooting stars as we sped back across the night sky. At least, that's how the Professor of Darkness described it.'

Sleet's one good eye narrowed. The scarred flesh quivered. 'The Professor of Darkness?' he said.

Twig nodded. 'Some he saw landing in Undertown – you, Bogwitt, Tarp Hammelherd; perhaps one other as well. The others travelled further. They came down somewhere in the Deepwoods. I vowed to find you all. And look, I've found three of you already. It's more than I'd ever dared hope for.'

'Hope,' said Sleet bitterly. 'I've learnt to live without it. After all, hope isn't going to heal this.' He ran his fingertips gently down the terrible scars.

Cowlquape turned away.

'I could bear neither the staring eyes . . .' Sleet glanced at Cowlquape and Tarp Hammelherd, 'nor the averted gazes of those who are repelled by my appearance. So I came down to the sewers, to hide myself away. And Bogwitt – to his credit – accompanied me.'

'Where he goes, I go,' Bogwitt growled loyally.

'We look out for each other,' said Sleet. 'It is necessary down here,' he added darkly.

'Like the professor – sorry, Twig – looks out for me,' said Cowlquape, turning back. 'It's sometimes necessary, even in Sanctaphrax.'

'Sanctaphrax,' said Sleet, more softly. His eyes misted over. 'I too once nurtured dreams of finding a position in the floating city of academics. But then, with that place, it isn't *what* you know, but *who* you know.' He sniffed bitterly. 'And I knew no-one.'

From the back of the chamber came the smell of burning. Bogwitt limped across the floor and seized the skillet from the stove. 'Supper's ready,' he announced.

'Tildermeat sausages,' said Sleet.

'My favourite,' said Twig, suddenly realizing how hungry he was.

Bogwitt shared out the sausages, sliced up a loaf of bread and returned with five plates balanced in his arms. He handed them out.

'And there's a flagon of excellent sapwine I've been saving for a special occasion,' said Sleet. 'Bogwitt, our finest goblets if you please.'

'To the crew of the *Edgedancer*,' Twig announced when each of them had a brimming glass in his hand. 'To those found and to those still to be found.'

The others chorused the toast in hearty agreement and everyone sipped at the sweet, golden liquid.

'*Aaah!*' sighed Tarp Hammelherd, wiping his whiskers on the back of his hand. 'Exquisite!'

Even Cowlquape appreciated the warm spicy flavours of the sapwine and a little later, when they were all tucking into the succulent tildermeat sausages he too realized just how hungry he'd become.

'Delicious,' he spluttered, tearing off a chunk of sausage and a hunk of bread. 'Absolutely deee-licious!'

Twig turned to his scarred quartermaster. 'I must say, Sleet, you've done well given the awful situation you found yourselves in. And you, too, Bogwitt. Very well. But you can't stay here in this terrible place, especially as you have both been injured on my behalf. One day I shall have a new ship and you shall be my crew again. But for now I must find out what has happened to the others.'

'We will go with you,' said Sleet.

Bogwitt nodded enthusiastically. 'Where you go, we go, Captain Twig,' he said.

'Not this time, Bogwitt,' Twig replied gently. 'Your leg needs time to heal, too.'

'Then we must stay here,' said Sleet sullenly. He nodded towards the vaulted roof. 'For there is nothing for us *up there*.'

'On the contrary,' said Twig. '*Sanctaphrax* is up there.'

'S . . . Sanctaphrax?' said Wingnut Sleet. 'But . . .'

'As you so rightly said, Sleet, it isn't what you know, but who. *I* know the Professor of Darkness. And *you* know me.'

Wingnut Sleet's mouth dropped open.

'I shall write you a letter which you will deliver to the professor himself.' He glanced round. 'I assume you have the means to do so,' he said.

'Oh, yes,' said Sleet. 'Paper and ink of the highest quality, and the finest snowbird quills. Something I picked up on one of our foraging trips.'

Twig smiled. 'You will stay in my study in the School of Light and Darkness and await my return,' he said. 'I would guess that the professor might wish to conduct a couple of experiments on you, concerning the way you glow – but otherwise, you will be left alone. How does that sound?'

'It sounds very good, captain,' said Wingnut Sleet. 'Very good indeed.'

'Indeed,' Bogwitt echoed.

'Yes, Bogwitt,' said Twig. 'As you once worked there as a guard, you must know Sanctaphrax like the back of your hand. Take the hidden alleys and secret passages on your way to the Professor of Darkness. Let's try and keep those gossipy academic tongues from wagging.' He turned to the slaughterer. 'Tarp,' he said, 'you must go with them.'

'Me?' Tarp cried out. 'Accompany them to Sanctaphrax?' He shook his head in disbelief. 'But I want to go with *you*, cap'n. I'm fit. I'm strong. You need someone like me on such a perilous quest.'

'I'm sorry, Tarp, but only Cowlquape can travel with me.'

'But why, cap'n?'

'Think about it, Tarp,' said Twig gently. 'How far do you think we'd get, glowing like tilder lamps? Whenever it is dark, we would begin to glow if together – and the fear of others would not help in our search.'

'But we could cover up,' Tarp persisted. 'We could wear thick hooded cloaks to conceal the light and . . .'

'And end up more conspicuous than ever!' said Twig. 'No, I must do this without you. Together, we would only fail – and that is something I must not do.'

The slaughterer nodded understandingly. 'You're right, Cap'n Twig,' he said. 'I should have thought.'

'Thank you, Tarp,' said Twig gratefully. He turned to Bogwitt and Sleet. 'It is agreed then. You three will await my return in Sanctaphrax, while Cowlquape and I journey on to find what has become of the rest of my missing crew.' He frowned with pretend impatience. 'So where is that paper and pen?'

·CHAPTER ELEVEN·

THE WESTERN QUAYS

Two weeks later, Cowlquape and Twig found themselves on the dockside of the western quays. Their previous night's lodgings had been infested with vicious dustfleas and, having been bitten half to death, they'd decided to cut their losses before sunrise and leave the filthy dormitory. Outside now, the first deep red feathers of sunrise were tickling the horizon. Twig yawned, stretched and rubbed his eyes.

'May this new day bring us the information we require,' he said, and sighed. 'Oh, why is the fourth crew member proving to be so elusive?' he wondered out loud.

'Mm-hmm,' mumbled Cowlquape. He was sitting on the jetty by Twig's feet, his legs dangling over the side. His nose, as always, was buried deep in one of the precious scrolls he kept in the bag slung over his shoulder.

Twig looked around him. Unlike the rundown boom-docks to the east, where only the lowliest of tug ships moored, the western quays were well-heeled. This was where the leaguesmen's sky ships were docked, and the shore behind was lined with their buildings – solid constructions with façades that were more than merely functional. Each one bore the coat of arms of the league it housed: the crossed sickle and chisel of the League of Gutters and Gougers, the piebald rat and coiled rope of the Gluesloppers and Ropeteasers, the pot and pliers of the Melders and Moulders . . .

Behind them all stood the lofty Leagues' Chamber, where the High Council of the Merchant League of Undertown sat. Always the most impressive building in the boom-docks, it looked more striking than ever at the moment, surrounded as it was by an intricate framework of scaffolding. Twig nodded towards it.

'They must be seeing to the roof,' he said.

'Mm-hmm,' Cowlquape mumbled again. He licked his finger and, without looking up, turned to the next barkscroll.

Twig turned back and stared at the river, flowing weakly past. The rising sun bounced oozy blobs of red over its crumpled surface.

The trouble was, their search for the fourth crewman in the leaguesmen's district had proved as unrewarding as their searches everywhere else in Undertown. The bustling streets, the noisy markets, the industrial quarter, the northern heights – Twig and Cowlquape had visited them all. Yet no matter how many taverns they visited, how many individuals they spoke to, how many enquiries they made, they had discovered nothing whatsoever about a falling shooting star or the sudden appearance of someone acting oddly.

'Perhaps the time has come for us simply to abandon our search here in Undertown and set forth for the Deepwoods,' said Twig.

'Mm-hmm,' said Cowlquape, his brow furrowed.

'Cowlquape!' said Twig. 'Have you heard a single word I've been saying to you?'

Cowlquape looked up, his expression puzzled, his eyes gleaming with excitement.

'Ever the studious academic, eh?' said Twig. 'You've been lost in those barkscrolls ever since we got here.'

'Oh, but it's . . . they're . . . just let me read you this,' he said. 'It really is absolutely fascinating stuff.'

'If you must,' said Twig resignedly.

'It's more about *The Myth of Riverrise*,' said Cowlquape eagerly. 'About the Mother Storm . . .'

Twig started as, for a fleeting moment, a memory from the fatal voyage into open sky flashed inside his head. 'The Mother Storm,' he muttered, but even as he said the words the elusive memory slipped away again. He looked up. 'Go on then,' he said. 'Tell me what it says.'

Cowlquape nodded and found the place with his finger. '*For as I write, it is now the commonly held belief that the Mother Storm has struck the Edge not once, but many times, destroying and recreating with each return,*' he read out. '*I* . . .'

'*I*?' said Twig. 'Who wrote these words?'

Cowlquape glanced up. 'They are a transcription of the original bark-writings that date back to the Time of Enlightenment in the Ancient Deepwoods,' Cowlquape explained. 'This version,' he said, stroking the scroll affectionately, 'was written down by a lowly scribe several hundred years ago. But the originals were much, much older.'

Twig smiled. The lad's enthusiasm was infectious.

'The Time of Enlightenment!' said Cowlquape. 'Oh, it must have been such a wonderful time to be alive. A glorious age of freedom and learning – long before our magnificent floating city of Sanctaphrax was even dreamed of. The Deepwoods emerged from darkness under the visionary leadership of Kobold the Wise. How I would love to have known him! He banished slavery. He united the thousand tribes under the lordly arms of the Trident and the Snake. He even oversaw the invention of the written word . . .'

'Yes, yes, Cowlquape,' said Twig. 'Very interesting. Is there a point to all this?'

'Patience, Twig,' said Cowlquape. 'All will soon be revealed. The Time of Enlightenment was abruptly snuffed out like a candle, Kobold the Wise's Union of a Thousand Tribes broke up, and the whole region descended into the barbarity and chaos that has reigned in the Deepwoods to this day.' He returned his attention to the barkscroll. 'Listen,' he said, 'this is what the scribe writes.'

Despite himself, Twig remained silent and listened attentively as Cowlquape read from the curled and yellowed scroll.

'*Kobold the Wise grew old and weary. Madness walked the market glades and deep meadows. Tribe turned upon tribe, brother upon brother, father upon son, for the Sky had grown angry and stole the reason of all who dwelt beneath it.*

'*Thus did representatives of the Thousand Tribes gather at Riverrise, and say, "Kobold, you who see further into Open Sky than the greatest of us, tell us what to do, for, in our madness, we are devouring each other and the sky turns our hearts black."*

'*And Kobold raised himself up from his sick bed and said, "Lo, the Mother Storm returns. Her madness shall be our madness. Prepare yourselves, for time is short . . ."*'

Cowlquape paused. 'There's a bit of a gap in the text here,' he explained. 'Wood-weevils have devoured the original bark.' He looked down again. 'This is how it continues.

'*. . . The Mother Storm, she who first seeded the Edge with life, shall come back to reap what she has sown, and the world shall return to Darkness,*' he said, emphasizing every word. 'Do you see, Twig? Kobold the Wise was describing *The Myth of Riverrise* and predicting the return of the Mother Storm – a prediction that came all too true, for the Deepwoods did indeed return to darkness. And now it is happening all over again.'

Twig turned away and stared up into open sky where

the Mother Storm had held him in her terrible grasp.

'The madness described is with us again,' Cowlquape said solemnly, 'blown in on the weather from beyond the Edge. The mad mists and heart-breaking rains – the terrible violence. What was it I read out?' He found the place again. '. . . *in our madness we are devouring each other*. Don't you see, Twig. It isn't a myth at all. The Mother Storm is returning.'

'The Mother Storm is returning,' Twig repeated quietly. The words chimed with familiarity. But how? Why? He shook his head with frustration. Something important had undoubtedly happened to him out there in the weather vortex far away in open sky. Why couldn't he remember what it was? Would he ever remember?

He looked at his troubled young apprentice. 'Come, Cowlquape,' he said. 'I think we can safely leave such matters to the academics of Sanctaphrax. For ourselves, it is time we abandoned – or at least postponed – our search for the fourth crew-member of the *Edgedancer*, and set forth into the Deepwoods. Let's go to the posting-pole and find ourselves passage on board a sky ship.'

Somewhat reluctantly, Cowlquape rolled up his precious barkscrolls, pushed them back into the bag and climbed to his feet. Then, together, he and Twig headed off along the quay to the central embarkation jetty. It was there that the posting-pole was situated.

The posting-pole was a tall, stout pillar of wood to which those sky ship captains with spare berths to announce would nail advertisements, written out on

squares of shimmering cloth. It was
the easiest way for those with no
means of transport of their own to
travel from one part of the Edge to
another.

As Twig and Cowlquape
reached the end of the embarkation
jetty, the sun wobbled up above the
horizon, crimson and majestic. Ahead
of them, silhouetted against the sky,
stood the posting-pole. With the
countless fluttering pink-tinged
scraps of material nailed along its
length, it looked like a curious
tree, its bark covered in blossom.

'I only hope that one of them is
offering something suitable,' Twig muttered as he
walked forwards.

Cowlquape went with him. 'How about this one?' he
said a moment later, and read from the square of cloth.
'*Raggers and Royners Leagueship. Departing for the
Deepwoods this afternoon.* They've got a double berth
spare. And the price seems fair.'

But Twig shook his head. 'No,' he said. 'No, it's not
quite . . .' His voice drifted away as he raised and read
announcement after announcement.

'What about this one, then?' said Cowlquape. 'A tug-
master bound for the ironwood copses of the barktrolls
is leaving later this morning and needs an extra two
pairs of hands.'

But Twig paid him no attention as he continued to read down the list of vessels and their destinations. The *Stormfinder*, destination: the slaughterer camps.

A voice in his head said, '*No.*'

The *Cloudeater*, destination: the Great Hammelhorn Fair.

'*No.*'

The *Luggerbrill*, destination: the Goblin Glades.

'*No.*'

On down the list he went. *No, no, no,* until . . .

'*Yes, this is the sky ship you must take,*' the voice said, softly but clearly.

'Of course!' Twig exclaimed. 'Cowlquape, this is it. This is the one. Listen.

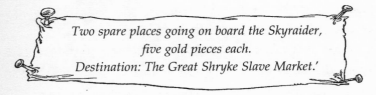

Two spare places going on board the Skyraider,
five gold pieces each.
Destination: The Great Shryke Slave Market.'

Twig looked up. 'What better place to resume our search?'

Cowlquape nodded uncertainly. His father, Ulbus Pentephraxis, had told him terrible stories about the Great Shryke Slave Market. 'Won't it be a bit dangerous?' he asked warily.

Twig shrugged. 'Undertown can also be dangerous,' he said. 'We must visit a place where creatures from all over the Deepwoods congregate.'

'Yes, but . . .' Cowlquape said. 'I mean, couldn't we go to that Great Hammelhorn Fair you mentioned. Or, look, there's a sky ship heading for the Timber Clearings of the woodtrolls. Wouldn't that do instead?'

'Cowlquape,' said Twig, 'there is no place in the Deepwoods like the Great Shryke Slave Market. Its denizens travel from every corner to be there. It is the obvious place to start our search.' He glanced down at the announcement once again and smiled. 'Thunderbolt Vulpoon,' he said. 'Now there's a name to conjure with.'

Cowlquape shivered. 'He sounds horrible,' he said. 'Isn't a vulpoon one of those vicious birds with a serrated beak?'

'It is,' said Twig.

'And Thunderbolt!' said Cowlquape. 'What kind of a monster would take the name of a bloodthirsty bird of prey *and* the most terrible and unpredictable feature of the weather?'

Twig snorted. 'A vain and foolish one,' he said. '*Name wild, captain mild*, as my father used to say. Those who select the most ferocious of names are without exception the ones least worthy of them.' His eyes misted up. 'Whereas the more gallant and valiant call themselves by less ostentatious names.'

'Like Cloud Wolf,' said Cowlquape quietly.

'Yes,' said Twig, 'like my father, Cloud Wolf, the most gallant and valiant sky pirate captain of them all.' He glanced back down at the announcement. 'Sky above!' he exclaimed.

'What?' said Cowlquape, alarmed.

'The departure time!' said Twig. 'The *Skyraider* is due to set sail in less than a quarter of an hour.'

*

'This is hopeless!' Twig cried out. 'Where is it?'

Ten minutes had passed since he'd stuffed the cloth announcement into his back pocket – ten minutes spent dashing along the quay, racing up and down the jetties, looking at the names of the sky ships. An old lugtroll had just assured them that the sky ship they were searching was at the second jetty, but they were there now and, despite looking twice, had drawn yet another blank.

'You don't think it might have left early, do you?' said Twig breathlessly.

'If the two spare places have already been filled, maybe so,' said Cowlquape, secretly hoping that it had.

'But it *can't* have,' said Twig. He paused and looked up and down the docks.

There were so many sky ships there – elegant league ships, sturdy merchant tug ships, streamlined patrol ships, as well as the occasional sky pirate ship – yet the *Skyraider* itself was nowhere to be seen.

'Perhaps we should return to the posting-pole and . . .'

'No,' said Twig. 'There isn't time.' He called to a group of dock-workers standing with their backs turned, deep in conversation. ''Scuse me,' he yelled. 'Do *you* know where a sky ship by the name of *Skyraider* is berthed?'

Without even deigning to turn round, one of them shouted back. 'Nineteenth jetty. Bottom right.'

Cowlquape turned to Twig. 'But we've just come from that end of the quays,' he said.

'I don't care,' said Twig. 'This could be our last chance.' He grabbed Cowlquape by the arm and dragged him forwards. 'Come on, Cowlquape,' he shouted. 'Run!'

Along the quayside promenade, they dashed. With Cowlquape close on his heels, Twig barged blindly through groups of haggling merchants, upending boxes of fish and barrows of fruit. Cowlquape glanced back over his shoulders. 'Sorry,' he called. On they sped, past jetty after numbered jetty which stuck out into mid-air, high above the Edgewater River. The eighth, ninth and tenth jetties flashed past.

'Faster, Cowlquape!' Twig shouted breathlessly, as the voice in his head urged him on.

Twelfth . . . thirteenth . . . Cowlquape's heart was pounding, his lungs burning, yet still he drove himself on. Seventeenth . . . Eighteenth . . .

'The nineteenth jetty!' Twig exclaimed. He skidded round, jumped down the five stairs in one leap and pounded along the wooden platform. 'And look!' he cried. 'How in Sky's name did we miss it before?'

Cowlquape looked up and followed Twig's pointing finger to a magnificent sky pirate ship tethered to the end of the raised jetty on the left.

'The *Skyraider*!' said Twig. 'We've found it, but . . . Oh, no!' he gasped.

The mainsail was up, the grappling-hooks had been raised and a small figure was crouched over the tether-ring, unfastening the tolley-rope. The sky ship was about to depart.

'STOP!' Twig roared, as he doubled his speed and hurtled headlong along the jetty. Although he could not explain it, something told him he *had* to board the *Skyraider*. No other ship would do. 'WAIT FOR US!'

But the crew-member – a mobgnome – paid him no heed.

'STOP!' Twig shouted again.

He could hear the mobgnome muttering irritably as he tugged at the snagged rope, then sigh with relief as it came free.

Nearly there . . .

The mobgnome tossed the rope onto the deck and, in the same movement, jumped aboard himself. Tantalizingly slowly at first, the sky pirate ship began to float up and away from the jetty.

'NO!' screamed Twig.

The gap between jetty and sky ship widened.

'Are you with me, Cowlquape?' he cried.

'I'm with you,' came the reply.

'Then, jump!' yelled Twig and, as the pair of them reached the end of the jetty at last, they launched themselves at the departing sky ship. Together they flew through the air, arms outstretched, willing themselves on.

'*Unkhh!*' Cowlquape grunted as his hands gripped the safety-rail and his body slammed into the hull. The next instant, Twig landed beside him.

Winded, the pair of them clung on for grim death. They would have to catch their breath before pulling themselves up on to the deck. But it didn't matter. The important thing was that they had made it, just in the nick of time.

'*Well done,*' whispered a voice in his ear.

'We're on our way, Cowlquape,' Twig murmured. 'To the Deepwoods and the Great Shryke Slave Market.'

'Twig, I . . . I . . .'

'Cowlquape?' said Twig, twisting his head round. 'What is it?'

'My hands . . . all slippery,' Cowlquape mumbled, and Twig watched helplessly as his young apprentice struggled desperately to pull himself up. 'Can't . . . can't hold . . . *aaaargh!*' He was falling. Away from the *Skyraider*, out of the sky and down to the pleated mud below . . .

CHAPTER TWELVE

THUNDERBOLT
VULPOON

Twig heaved himself up, swung his leg over the safety-rail and rolled over onto the deck. Then, without pausing, he jumped to his feet and peered back down, over the side.

'Cowlquape!' he bellowed. Certainly he had heard no splash and, though he peered closely at the muddy river-bed below, he could see no sign of his young apprentice. 'Cowlquape!' he cried out again. 'Where are you?'

'Down here,' came a weak voice.

Twig's heart gave a leap. 'Where?'

'On the hull-rigging,' said Cowlquape. 'But I don't know if I can hang on for much longer.'

'Yes, you can!' Twig urged him. 'You've got to, Cowlquape.'

Far below now, the Edgewater River gave way to the Mire.

'It . . . it's no good,' Cowlquape whimpered. 'I can't get a foothold and my arms . . . so weak . . .'

Twig looked round desperately for help, but the *Skyraider* was oddly deserted. The mobgnome had disappeared, and there was no-one else in sight apart from a squat and somewhat flamboyant figure standing up at the helm.

'Help!' he bellowed. 'Help! Someone's fallen overboard!'

Lost in the mechanics of skysailing, the helmsman seemed unaware of the drama unfolding behind him. The sky ship soared higher.

'There must be someone here!' Twig roared. 'HELP ME!'

'What, what, what?' came a nervous, twittery voice by his side. It was the mobgnome, back again. An ancient-looking gnokgoblin with bow-legs and white whiskers stood behind him.

Twig groaned. Neither of them looked up to much. 'My companion fell,' he explained hurriedly. 'He's clinging on to the hull-rigging. Get me a rope and a stave-hook. Now!'

The two crew-members nodded and disappeared. A moment later, they were back. Twig tied one end of the rope to the main aft winding-cleat and tossed the rest over the side. Then, with the stave-hook under his arm, he lowered himself down the rope.

'*Whoa,*' he gasped, as the sudden rush of wind snatched his breath away. 'Keep your nerve,' he told himself. 'Easy does it.'

With the rope twisted between his feet, Twig carefully

let himself slip down. Hand over hand, he went, past the portholes, past the winched grappling-hooks. Further and further. As the hull curved in and away from him, he found himself dangling in mid-air.

'Don't look down, whatever you do,' Twig heard.

He twisted round. And there was Cowlquape, half-way down the side of the sky ship, clutching hold of the hull-rigging for dear life. He'd managed to loop one leg through the criss-cross of ropes, but there was blood all round his fingers from his blistered palms. Every second he remained there the rope dug in deeper.

'Hold tight Cowlquape!' Twig yelled across the airy gap. 'I'm going to try swinging closer.'

By constantly shifting his weight Twig set himself in motion – not back and forwards as he'd hoped, but in a series of widening circles. The sky ship soared higher still. Far below him, the bleached mire glistened like the surface of an ocean of milk. As the circles grew wider still, Twig passed closer and closer to the hull-rigging until finally, with the stave-hook outstretched, he managed to hook a piece of rope and pull himself in.

'There,' he grunted, as he grabbed hold of the rigging to Cowlquape's right. 'We'll have you back on board in no time.'

He twisted round, and tied the rope firmly around Cowlquape's waist. As he was securing the knot, he saw just how badly the lad's hands had been chafed. The blood was dripping from his shaking fingertips.

'Hang on, Cowlquape,' he said. 'I . . .'

The stave-hook slipped from his grasp and tumbled down to the ground below. The sky ship was by now too high for them either to see or hear it landing. Twig squeezed Cowlquape's shoulder.

'I'm going to climb back up on deck,' he said. 'When I give the word, let go. We'll pull you up.'

Cowlquape nodded, but could say nothing. His face was white with fear.

Twig darted up the hull-rigging and leapt back onto the deck. The mobgnome and the old gnokgoblin were still there.

'Grab the rope and take the strain,' he ordered. The two crew-members did as they were told. Twig joined them.

'Let go, Cowlquape!' he shouted down.

The rope lurched and grew heavy.

'Right,' Twig grunted to the others. 'Now, pull! Pull as if your lives depended on it.'

Slowly – painfully slowly – the three of them tugged and heaved, inching their way back across the deck. Suspended below them, Cowlquape felt as if nothing was happening. It was only when he twisted round and looked back at the hull that he saw he was indeed rising up towards the deck.

'Nearly there,' Twig said encouragingly. 'Just a little bit more and . . . Yes!' he exclaimed, as the tousled head of his young apprentice abruptly came into view. While the mobgnome and the gnokgoblin braced themselves, Twig secured the end of the rope to the tether-post, rushed back to the balustrade and seized hold of Cowlquape's wrist. 'Got you!' he grunted.

Cowlquape tumbled down onto the deck. Twig slumped down beside him, exhausted.

'Well, well, well, what have we here?' came a syrupy voice. 'Scurvy stowaways, is it?'

Twig looked up. It was the squat figure he had seen at the helm. He climbed to his feet. 'We're no stowaways,' he said, and pulled the small piece of cloth from the posting-pole out of his pocket. 'We wish to travel with you to the Great Shryke Slave Market – I take it you are Thunderbolt Vulpoon.'

'*Captain* Thunderbolt Vulpoon,' came the reply, as the fastidious little person tugged at the ruffs around his wrists and twirled the points of his waxed moustache. A great ring of keys jangled at his belt. 'Indeed I am.' His eyebrows arched and curled like the sound holes on a wood-lute. 'But this is against all the laws of skysailing,' he said. 'Surely you must know that nobody may board a sky ship without its captain's permission. How else can a potential passenger be vetted before setting sail? I don't even know your names.'

'I am Twig,' said Twig and, ignoring the puzzled flicker of half-recognition which passed across the captain's ruddy face, he turned to his apprentice. 'This is Cowlquape.'

The captain sniffed dismissively. 'Riff-raff by any other name would smell as rank.' He turned. 'Grimlock!' he bellowed.

The towering figure of a brogtroll, clothed in filthy rags, emerged from a trapdoor in the floor behind them. 'Grimlock be here, master,' he rumbled.

'Grimlock, seize these wretches!'

With awful purpose, the captain's brutal sidekick strode towards Twig and Cowlquape, arms outstretched. Twig held his ground.

'We are not riff-raff, *Captain* Vulpoon,' he said. 'We apologize for our rather hasty boarding, but yours was the only ship bound for the slave market, and we didn't want to miss it. Call your minder off.'

Grimlock lurched closer.

'We can pay,' said Twig, reaching inside his shirt for the leather pouch the Professor of Darkness had given him. 'Five gold pieces each, wasn't it?'

The captain paused. He looked them up and down.

'Perhaps I've been too hasty,' he said with a smile. 'You have the look of academics about you. From Sanctaphrax, no doubt – I'm sure you could manage fifteen.'

'But . . .' Twig began.

Grimlock seized Cowlquape by the shoulders and lifted him off his feet.

'All right!' shouted Twig. 'Fifteen it is.'

Captain Thunderbolt Vulpoon smirked as the coins jangled down into his pudgy hand. 'Put him down, Grimlock,' he said.

Cowlquape sighed with relief as he felt the reassuring solidity of the deck beneath his feet once more. He watched the flabby captain spit into his right palm and shake hands with Twig, then turn and grab his own hand and . . .

'*Aaa-oww!*' he howled, and pulled away.

The captain looked down. 'Oh, would you look at that,' he said as he saw Cowlquape's upturned palms. 'Like two raw hammelhorn steaks! We'll have to get you patched up.' His dark eyes gleamed. 'A fine specimen like you.'

Cowlquape squirmed uneasily. 'A specimen?' he wondered out loud.

'Did I say *specimen*?' said the captain. 'Sorry, I meant to say, a fine figure of a lad.' Cowlquape recoiled as the captain scrutinized him closely. 'Bright eyes, strong teeth, broad shoulders . . .' He smiled. 'And bound for the Great Shryke Slave Market.'

Twig nodded. 'We have important business there,' he said.

Thunderbolt Vulpoon smiled all the more broadly. The sun glinted on his silver teeth. 'Indeed you have,' he said softly. 'But first things first.' He turned to the old gnok-goblin. 'Jervis,' he said sharply, his face hardening. 'Show our guests to their quarters. And Teasel,' he barked at the mobgnome. 'Tell Stile there will be two extra mouths to feed – and get something from the medical supplies for the lad's wounds.'

Jervis and Teasel jumped to it nervously.

'And you,' he shouted at the brogtroll. 'Go down and still the . . . the cargo.' He nodded up at the main-mast, which was swaying precariously from side to side. 'They're getting too restless.'

'Grimlock go,' the brogtroll muttered, and lumbered off.

Vulpoon raised his eyes theatrically to the sky and swept a limp hand across his powdered forehead. 'Worst crew I've ever captained,' he complained. 'Still,' he went on, affable and charming once again, 'we shall endeavour to ensure that your voyage is a comfortable one.'

The rolling from side to side grew more and more extreme until everyone on deck – the captain included – had to grab on to something or risk being tossed off the side of the sky ship. Vulpoon grinned sheepishly.

'Live cargo!' he said, and snorted. 'Trouble is, once they get the jitter up, the whole boat's thrown out of kilter.'

'Live cargo?' Twig queried, as the sky ship leaned sharply to port, and then lurched back again.

'Hammelhorns,' said Vulpoon, his eyes flickering round his swaying ship. 'To satisfy the catering needs of the slave market.'

Twig nodded, his thoughts already elsewhere. At that moment a plaintive howling went up. It cut through the air and sent shivers of unease darting up and down Cowlquape's spine. The sky ship righted itself. The howling abruptly ceased. And, with the mainsail billowing, the *Skyraider* soared forwards.

'*That's* better,' said Thunderbolt Vulpoon, his fat face creasing into a smile as he rubbed his pudgy hands together. 'So, Jervis, jump to it.' He turned to Twig and Cowlquape. 'And if there's anything you need, don't hesitate to ask. Supper will be served in an hour's time.'

*

Their quarters were comfortable enough, and the days passed with a frustrating sameness – the two companions seldom leaving their cabin. But Cowlquape still felt uneasy. Lying on his front one day, unable to concentrate on the barkscroll in front of him, he looked up from his hammock. 'I just don't trust him,' he said.

'What's that?' said Twig.

'Thunderbolt Vulpoon,' said Cowlquape. 'I don't trust him. Or that hulking great bodyguard of his.'

Twig turned from the porthole of the cramped cabin and looked at the anxious lad.

'What's more,' Cowlquape continued, 'I still don't understand why he's taking a cargo of hammelhorns to the slave market. It can't be profitable.' He frowned. 'I reckon I know what his live cargo is.'

'What?' said Twig.

'Slaves,' said Cowlquape darkly.

'Out of the question,' said Twig. 'Sky ships from Undertown don't carry slaves, you know that.'

'But . . .'

'Undertown is a free town, Cowlquape,' said Twig. 'And the punishment for attempting to enslave the least of its inhabitants is death. No-one would willingly serve on such a ship.'

Cowlquape shrugged. 'I still think hammelhorns is an unlikely cargo,' he said stubbornly. 'Anyway, we'll see when we get to the market, won't we? Though when *that* will be, Sky alone knows! Nine days we've been sailing now. Nearly ten . . .'

'The Deepwoods is vast,' said Twig. He gazed back

through the porthole at the never-ending carpet of green leaves stretching out before them. 'Endless! And the great slave market moves through it, constantly.'

'So, how will we find it,' said Cowlquape, 'if it shifts from place to place?'

Twig smiled. 'The Great Shryke Slave Market stays in one place for many months, sometimes years, then suddenly, overnight, it packs itself up and sets off on prowlgrin-back for a new location in a clamouring, raucous flock.'

'Then, how . . . ?'

'Nothing is impossible to track, Cowlquape,' said Twig. 'It is simply a matter of reading the signs correctly.'

Cowlquape pushed the scrolls away and drew himself up on his elbows. 'Signs?' he said.

'Do you mean to tell me there's nothing about the Great Shryke Slave Market in those scrolls of yours?' asked Twig, his eyes twinkling.

Cowlquape reddened. 'Nothing that I've come across so far,' he said. 'Though my father once told me about the fearsome bird-creatures that run the place – and who give it its name. Shrykes. Flightless. Vicious. With unblinking eyes . . .'

'The Bloodoak tavern back in Undertown is owned by such a bird-woman,' said Twig. 'Mother Horsefeather is her name.' His eyes went dreamy for a moment, then he continued. 'What you've got to understand is that the Great Shryke Slave Market is like one huge living organism, moving across the vast Deepwoods, seeking out fresh pastures in the Deepwoods to "graze". But in time the market consumes everything around it and the area it has occupied dies. Then it must move on – or die itself. The burnt-out villages it leaves behind offer vital clues to the informed as to where the market has travelled on to. An experienced trader – or a keen-eyed sky pirate captain – can spot and follow the dead groves like footprints, until the great market itself is found.'

Cowlquape shook his head. 'Thank Sky we're on a sky ship, then,' he said. He sat up and peeked beneath the bandages around his hands.

On his first night on board, Jervis had spent ages carefully rubbing hyleberry salve into the wounds and wrapping them in padded gauze. Each night since then, he had returned to change the dressing, though he barely spoke a word to the two travellers. Twig saw the lad scrutinizing his hands.

'How are they?' he asked.

'Itchy,' said Cowlquape.

'That means they're healing,' said Twig. 'Do you fancy a bit of a walk? Stretch your legs up on deck?'

Cowlquape shook his head. 'I'd rather get back to my reading if it's all the same to you,' he said, picking up the barkscrolls once again.

'As you wish, Cowlquape,' said Twig. 'But if you ever get bored with ancient history,' he added with a smile, 'you know where to find me.'

The moment he heard the door of the cabin click, Cowlquape set the barkscrolls aside again, lay back in the hammock with his bandaged hands across his chest, and closed his eyes. He'd had no intention of reading. All he wanted to do was shut out the terrible feeling of nausea which had held him in its grip ever since he had first leapt on board the *Skyraider*. Nine days and nine nights he'd been on the ship and he still hadn't got his sky-legs.

The sounds of flight echoed round the cabin as the sky ship sailed on. The creaking of the bows. The slapping of the sails. The soft, hypnotic whistling of the wind in the ropes and rigging. Cowlquape grew drowsy, and fell asleep.

He dreamt that they had landed in the Deepwoods and that he and Twig were on their own. The forest was green and gloomy, like nowhere he had ever seen. The air screeched and twittered with unseen, unknown animals. There was a trail of footprints, scorched into the ground beneath their feet.

'*Welcome*,' came a voice.

Cowlquape looked up. Standing in the shadows of twelve massive lintlepines was a tall, crowned figure.

There was a trident and snake embroidered into his robes. His plaited beard almost touched the ground. His eyes were kindly, but also inexpressibly sad. His whole body seemed to glow. Cowlquape gasped and fell to his knees.

'Kobold the Wise,' he said. 'Oh, sire, you c . . . cannot imagine w . . . what a pleasure . . . w . . . what an honour . . .' His trembling voice gave way to a whisper.

'*You look cold,*' said Kobold, stepping forward. '*Take my mantle,*' he said, swinging it round Cowlquape's shoulders.

'But . . .' Cowlquape protested.

'*Take it,*' said Kobold. '*It is yours now.*'

He turned away and disappeared back into the shadows.

'But, sire!' Cowlquape called after him. 'I cannot . . . I could not . . . I am not worthy.'

His words were drowned out by the insistent sound of a woodpecker hammering its head against the bark of one of the lintlepines.

'Sire!' Cowlquape shouted again.

Bang! Bang! Bang!

Cowlquape's eyes snapped open. The cabin was in darkness. He looked round blindly.

Bang! Bang! Bang! BANG!

'Yes?' Cowlquape shouted.

The cabin door opened and there, silhouetted against the light in the corridor, was the dishevelled figure of Jervis. 'Come to see to your dressings,' he said.

'Oh, yes,' said Cowlquape. 'I didn't realize it was so late.'

Jervis closed the door behind him and crossed the floor. He set a small box down on the ledge, closed the porthole and lit the lamp. Cowlquape sat up and swung his legs down the side of the hammock. Jervis stood before him, then began unwinding the first bandage. The peppery scent of the hyleberry salve grew more intense.

'I think they're almost better,' said Cowlquape.

The scab came away with the final twist of lint. Below it, the skin was smooth and soft. Jervis examined the hand critically in the lamplight before pronouncing it 'good as new'.

'Are we approaching the Great Shryke Slave Market yet?' Cowlquape asked, as Jervis set to work on the second bandage.

'Not approaching, as such,' said Jervis, responsive for once. 'But we're on-track, sure enough. Look-out spotted a market burn-out at sundown, so he did. Signs indicated the great market had flocked north-north-west. That's where we're heading.'

The left hand had healed just as well as the right,

Jervis was pleased to see. He ran a horny finger over the soft, pale skin. The sky ship listed abruptly to port and a beam of moonlight streamed in through the porthole. It passed over Cowlquape's outstretched hands.

'S'posed to be lucky, that is,' said Jervis. 'The moon crossing your palm with silver. Back where I come from they say it means you'll live a long and prosp . . .' He stopped, and Cowlquape thought he could see sorrow in the ancient goblin's expression. Abruptly he rose and left, fear obvious in his eyes, as if he had been about to say something unwise.

Cowlquape stared at the closed door nervously. Why had Jervis seemed so fearful? What had he been too afraid to say?

The soft oil lamplight bathed the cabin in shadowy orange. Cowlquape climbed to his feet, crossed to the porthole and flung it open again. Warm, luscious air – heavy with pinesap and lullabee mist – flooded inside. Cowlquape breathed in deeply and poked his head out through the circular window.

Below him, the canopy of trees stretched out as before like a vast sparkling sea in the bright moonlight. Cowlquape didn't know how far they had travelled nor how far there was still to go. He knew only that, if Jervis's pronouncements proved correct, he would soon be down there in the suffocating darkness beneath its leafy surface – in a place he'd never imagined he would ever visit. A shiver of fear and excitement ran through him. The dream was still fresh in his mind.

'I can't wait to leave this great rolling sky ship,' he

muttered to himself, 'and get my feet back on solid ground. It's . . .' He fell still, and squinted into the distance.

Before him, gleaming in the moonlight far ahead like a great bleached canker in the luxuriant green of the forest canopy, was a ragged patch of land where everything was dead. Cowlquape trembled. He had never before witnessed such barren desolation.

As the *Skyraider* drew closer, Thunderbolt Vulpoon bellowed out his orders to 'fly in low'. Sails were lowered, hull-weights realigned, and the sky ship slowed to a woodslug's pace.

Cowlquape poked his head out of the porthole and looked down uneasily. The line separating the living forest and the lifeless clearing was crossed. 'Sky above!' he exclaimed.

Every single tree beneath him was dead. Some had been burned, some had been hollowed – others looked as if they had simply died, and stood now with their skeleton leaves clinging to their branches. Vast tracts had been scorched back to bare earth. Nothing lived there; nothing grew.

With the *Skyraider* flying down so close to the scarred, bleached forest, the area seemed unimaginably immense. All round, as far as the eye could see, the terrible desolation continued.

'So the Great Shryke Slave Market has done all this,' Cowlquape whispered tremulously.

When the sky ship was passing over the remains of a forest settlement, the captain commanded that they go in especially close, for it was in the decimated villages such as this – in the stonefall and woodburn – that clues to the market's next resting place were to be found.

Cowlquape trembled with horror. Every tree had been felled, every well destroyed, every building had been razed to the ground. As for those who once inhabited the place – the gnokgoblins, mobgnomes, woodtrolls, or whatever – they were now all gone, captured by the bird-creatures and sold on as slaves. Now, only piles of rubble and heaps of charred wood indicated that a thriving village had once been here: that and the network of paths which radiated out from its former centre.

It was there – at the central-most point and sticking up out of the scorched ground like some giant black insect – that a gibbet of burnt timber stood, a bleached white skeleton strapped to its black crossbeam. A bone finger

pointed towards the moon, low on the horizon.

All at once a cry went up. 'East-north-east!'

'East-north-east!' Cowlquape heard the captain repeat, and the *Skyraider* abruptly swung round to port and soared back up into the sky.

Beneath him, as the sky ship gathered speed, the dead area of forest receded and was finally left far behind. Cowlquape shuddered miserably. Having seen for himself the awful devastation it caused, the Great Shryke Slave Market was the last place in the Edge he now wanted to visit.

'I think I'd sooner stay on board the *Skyraider*,' he muttered. Just then, the sky ship hit a patch of squally air and dipped sharply, rocking from side to side as it did so. Cowlquape groaned. His stomach gurgled ominously. 'Then again . . .' he murmured queasily.

BANG! BANG!

The two heavy thuds on the door sounded as though someone was trying to batter it down. Cowlquape jumped and, remembering the look in Jervis's eyes, drew his dagger.

'Wh. . . who i . . . is it?' he asked.

The door was flung wide open. The great ragged brogtroll was standing in the corridor.

'Oh, it's you,' said Cowlquape.

'Grimlock it be,' came the reply as, stooping low, he shuffled into the cabin. He was carrying a tray, with an earthenware jug and two goblets on it, dwarfed by his massive hands. He looked round the cabin. 'Where's the other one?'

'Just stretching his legs,' said Cowlquape, concealing the knife behind his back, but not returning it to its sheath. 'He'll be back in a minute.'

Grimlock nodded. 'Is good,' he said. 'The master said this be for the pair of you.' He held the tray out. 'Finest woodgrog gold can buy. Help you get a good night's sleep, he says.'

'Th . . . thank you,' said Cowlquape, eyeing the murky brew suspiciously. It was the first time Thunderbolt Vulpoon had concerned himself with the quality of their sleep. 'If you just put it on that shelf over there I'll tell Twig directly he returns. As I say, he shouldn't be . . .'

At that moment Twig himself appeared in the doorway. 'Cowlquape,' he said breathlessly 'We've got to talk . . .'

'Twig!' Cowlquape interrupted. 'Just the person I was

hoping to see. Grimlock here,' he said, flapping his hands towards the figure standing in the shadows, 'has just brought us a jug of the captain's finest woodgrog.' Twig nodded towards the bogtroll and smiled. 'It's to help us get a good night's sleep,' added Cowlquape meaningfully.

'I'm sure it is,' said Twig brightly.

'Shall Grimlock pour some?' the lumbering creature asked hopefully.

'No,' said Twig. 'No, I think I shall save it for when I'm about to turn in. But thank you for offering, Grimlock.' He crossed the cabin and sniffed at the jug. 'Mmm, I'll look forward to that,' he said, and looked up at the brogtroll. 'The captain is too kind.'

Grimlock shook his head glumly. 'Oh, no,' he said, 'the master's not kind. Not him. He starves Grimlock, he does. Won't let him eat the cargo – not even the little-'uns.'

Twig looked at the great mountain of muscle in front of him. 'You don't look starved,' he said. 'Could do with a new set of clothes maybe . . .'

'Grimlock's always cold,' the brogtroll complained. 'The master sells the cargo's clothes.'

Cowlquape's jaw dropped. He turned to Twig, who nodded and frowned; he should remain silent.

'Grimlock never gets them,' the brogtroll continued. 'Grimlock likes pretty clothes, he does. Nice pretty clothes to keep Grimlock warm. Grimlock likes your clothes.'

He reached out a meaty paw to brush Twig's hammelhornskin waistcoat. It bristled defensively.

'*Ouch!*' Grimlock wailed, and clutched his finger where the spiky hair of the waistcoat had drawn blood. 'Not pretty!' he exclaimed.

'No,' said Twig, smoothing down the ruffled fur. 'This wouldn't suit you at all. In fact, I'd have thought a nice embroidered coat and a hat with a feather would be much more suitable.'

'Yes, yes!' said the brogtroll excitedly.

'Grimlock!' roared the captain's voice from above. 'The cargo's getting restless again. Go and sort it out!'

'Grimlock's starving,' said the brogtroll. 'Grimlock's cold. Grimlock would like a hat with a feather. Pretty.'

'You'd better go,' said Twig. 'Thank the captain for the woodgrog.'

The bogtroll shuffled out. The door shut. Cowlquape turned immediately to Twig. 'Clothes!' he exclaimed. 'He talked about the cargo's clothes. And how many hammelhorns do you know that wear clothes?'

Without answering, Twig picked up the heavy earthenware jug and emptied its contents into the two goblets. Then he tipped them both out of the porthole. 'Full of powdered sleeping-willow bark,' he muttered. 'Cowlquape, we are in great danger . . .' He placed the empty jug back on the shelf. 'I overheard a conversation

between Teasel, that mobgnome, and Stile,' he continued. 'That dead grove we recently passed over had a
black gibbet with a skeleton strapped to its crossbeam. It
meant one thing and one thing only. Our next stop will
be the Great Shryke Slave Market itself.'

'B ... but that's good, isn't it?' said Cowlquape
uncertainly.

Twig sighed. 'It should have been,' he said. 'Oh,
Cowlquape, I feel so bad about bringing you into all
this.'

'What do you mean?' said Cowlquape anxiously.
'What else did you overhear?'

'I've been stupid. Stupid and blind,' Twig said. 'All I
could think about was finding my lost crew, and
now ...' He gripped his young apprentice by the
shoulder. 'You were right all along, Cowlquape,' he said.
'The cargo we're carrying is not hammelhorns. It *is*
slaves.'

Cowlquape took a sharp intake of breath. 'I knew it,'
he said.

Twig sighed. 'Just our luck to have stumbled across
the most villainous of sky pirate captains ever to have
taken to the air. Five dozen or more wretches he's got
chained up in the lower hold of the ship,' he said.
'Mobgnomes, flat-head goblins, cloddertrogs ... All
bound for the market where they will be sold on to the
highest bidder.'

'And us?' said Cowlquape. 'Why didn't the captain
simply have us thrown into the hold and clapped in
irons with the rest?'

Twig looked away. 'We're too valuable for that,' he said quietly. 'He doesn't want us damaged – the moment he saw us he must have made up his mind. He's a crafty one, I'll give him that.' He turned back to Cowlquape. 'We are to be sold to the roost-mother herself.'

'The roost-mother?' said Cowlquape.

'The leader of the bird-creatures which rule the market,' Twig replied. 'She goes by the name of Mother Muleclaw. Apparently she is offering to pay highly – *very* highly – for specimens such as us. It's not every day that a Sanctaphrax academic is sold in the slave market!'

'That was why he was so interested in our well-being,' said Cowlquape. He stared down gloomily at the pale new skin on the palms of his hands. 'And why he was so keen that my wounds should heal.'

Twig nodded. 'And why the food has been so excellent,' he said, and shuddered. 'He's been fattening us up!'

· CHAPTER THIRTEEN ·

MUTINY

Twig stared out of the porthole as the *Skyraider* lurched and swayed onwards, tacking against the wind in the east-north-easterly direction the gruesome sign had pointed them in. A breeze got up. The moon sank low in the sky, sparkling on the forest canopy as the wind rippled its leafy surface. There was no sight of the slave market.

All round him, he could hear the sounds of the sky ship in flight. The whispering of the sails. The rhythmical tapping of the tolley-ropes. The creaking boards. The whistling rigging. The squeak and scurry of the rat-birds, deep down in the bowels of the ship. And something else . . . A deep, sonorous sound . . .

'Listen,' he said, turning away from the porthole.

Cowlquape looked up from his hammock. 'What?'

'That noise.'

'What noise?'

Twig motioned Cowlquape to be silent. He crouched down on the floor and placed his ear against the dark varnished wood. His face clouded with sorrow. '*That* noise,' he said.

Cowlquape rolled off the hammock and joined Twig on the floor. As his ear touched the wooden floor, the sounds became clearer. Groaning. Howling. Hopeless wailing.

'The cargo?' Cowlquape whispered.

'The cargo,' said Twig. 'The mobgnomes, the flat-head goblins, the cloddertrogs ... the sound of misery and despair – the sound of slavery. Thank Sky we are fore-warned and know what the captain is planning ...'

His words were shattered by a bare-knuckled rapping at the door.

'Quick,' said Twig. 'Into your hammock. Pretend to be asleep.'

A moment later, Twig and Cowlquape were curled up in their hammocks, eyes shut and mouths open, snoring softly. The rapping at the door came a second time.

'We're asleep, you idiots,' Cowlquape muttered under his breath. 'Just come in.'

'*Sshhh!*' Twig hissed.

The door-handle squeaked as it was slowly turned. The door creaked open. Twig rolled over with a grunt and continued snoring, though he sneaked a peek into the cabin from the corner of one eye.

Two heads peered round the cabin door. One was Teasel's. The other belonged to an individual Twig had not seen before: a burly cloddertrog. The pair of them were frozen to the spot, anxiously watching to see if

Twig was about to wake up. He
obliged them with a snoozy
murmur, and settled back
down.

A cloddertrog, he
thought unhappily.

'I think they must
have drunk it,' said
Teasel, crossing the
room. He sniffed at
the goblets, and

peered into the jug. 'Yeah, all gone.' He looked at the two
hammocks. 'Sleeping like babies, so they are,' he gig-
gled. 'Right, then, Korb. You tie up the little'un. I'll see to
this one.'

The pair of them pulled lengths of rope from their
shoulders and advanced to the two hammocks.
Cowlquape trembled as the foul-smelling cloddertrog
came close. He quaked as the great looming creature
tossed the end of the rope over his feet. He was about to
be tied up inside the hammock. Rigid with fear, he felt
the rope bite as it was pulled tight around his ankles.

'Easy there,' said the mobgnome. 'The captain said *no
marks*. And you know what happens if you cross the
captain . . .'

The cloddertrog scratched his head. 'I don't want him
wriggling free when he wakes up though.'

'Don't worry,' the mobgnome assured him, as he went
to secure his own rope around Twig's neck. 'He'll be out
till . . . *Aaaaargh!*' he wailed as a sharp elbow slammed

into the base of his nose with a sickening crunch. Blood gushed in a torrent. The mobgnome clutched his hands to his face and staggered backwards.

Twig sat up, swung round and leapt forwards, sword drawn. 'Drop your knife first,' he shouted at the cloddertrog. 'Then your cutlass.'

The cloddertrog stumbled back in surprise. The mobgnome was still on his knees, clutching his nose. Cowlquape loosened the rope around his legs, climbed off his hammock and stood by Twig's side.

'Knife, Cowlquape,' said Twig, nodding to the hammerhead's dagger. Shakily, Cowlquape drew it from his belt. 'And you,' Twig told the cloddertrog. 'Just use your thumb and forefinger.'

'Thumb and forefinger it is,' he said.

Twig watched. The blade of the knife appeared from its sheath. 'Now, drop it!' he said.

The cloddertrog glanced down at his hand.

'Drop it!' shouted Twig.

'All right, all right,' said the cloddertrog. His knuckles

whitened. 'I just . . .' As he spoke, he flicked his wrist and the knife spun through the air.

Twig recoiled. Too late! '*Aaargh!*' he screamed as the spinning knife sank its razor-sharp point into his side. His sword clattered to the floor.

As Twig toppled backwards the cloddertrog drew his evil-looking cutlass and lunged forwards.

'Twig!' shouted Cowlquape, leaping on the cloddertrog's back.

The heavy cutlass splintered the wooden wall, inches above Twig's head.

'Geddoff me!' roared the cloddertrog, tearing the lad from his shoulders and tossing him aside.

Cowlquape went flying back across the cabin and crashed into the still kneeling Teasel. The mobgnome was knocked senseless.

The cloddertrog sneered. 'I don't care what the captain says,' he said. 'You're going to get what's coming to you!' He raised the fearsome cutlass high above his head and . . .

BOOF!

Cowlquape brought the heavy earthenware jug down with all his strength on the cloddertrog's skull. The cloddertrog keeled forwards, landed heavily
on the floor and
lay still.

'Now that's what I call a sleeping draught,' said Cowlquape with a shaky smile.

'Thank you, lad,' said Twig, as he struggled to his feet. Although his hammelhornskin waistcoat had prevented the knife penetrating too far, the wound was throbbing. He hobbled across to his sword, picked it up and turned to Cowlquape.

'Come, Cowlquape. We have an appointment with Captain Vulpoon.'

Taking care not to make a sound, Twig and Cowlquape made their way through the sky ship. They passed store-rooms and stock-cupboards, the galley, the sleeping berths. At each door and corridor they came to they paused, looked round furtively and listened for any sound. Apart from a low snoring from the crew's quarters – where Jervis and Stile were sleeping – there was nothing.

They were about to make their way up to the helm itself when Cowlquape noticed a narrow, black and gold lacquered staircase set back in an alcove. He looked at Twig questioningly.

Twig nodded and stepped forwards. He began climbing the narrow stairs. 'Well, well, well!' he exclaimed a moment later as he stepped into the room above. 'We've struck lucky.'

Cowlquape joined him. He looked round the ornate chamber with its gold trappings, luxurious carpet and inlaid woodwork, its huge mirrors and crystal chandeliers – its vast, sumptuous four-poster bed.

'We must be in Vulpoon's quarters,' he said. 'It's . . . magnificent!'

'There's certainly profit to be had from the misery of others,' said Twig sourly.

He began opening the mirrored doors to the many wardrobes which lined the room, and rifled through the gaudy clothes which packed every inch within. From the third wardrobe, he pulled out a particularly foppish jacket. Long and quilted, it was a deep magenta colour with navy and gold brocade. There were feathers around the collar and at the cuffs. Semi-precious stones, set into the embroidered threads, sparkled enticingly. Twig slipped the jacket on.

'What do you think?' he said.

'Well, it's . . .' Cowlquape started. He shook his head. 'I don't know what we're doing in here.'

Twig laughed. 'You're right, Cowlquape,' he said. 'It's time we left. Come on.' And with that he strode across the room and back down the stairs. Cowlquape followed close behind.

Up on deck at last, Twig breathed the crisp, cold air deep down into his lungs. A broad grin spread across his face.

'Ah, Cowlquape,' he said. 'Fresh air. A following wind. The sheer exhilaration of soaring across the endless sky.'

Cowlquape laid a hand on Twig's arm and pointed up the wooden staircase to the helm. The captain and the brogtroll, Grimlock, were silhouetted against the greyness of the sky. Twig nodded and raised his finger to his lips.

They advanced, keeping to the shadows cast by the low moon on their port bow. Around the skirting-deck, they went. Up the stairs. Slowly. Stealthily. All at once, the whole sky ship was bathed in purple light.

'*Waah!*' Grimlock cried out.

Twig and Cowlquape froze.

'*Fire!*' the brogtroll bellowed. 'Grimlock see fire!'

'Be still, you fool!' the captain cried. 'It's not fire. It's the signal flare.'

'Signal flare?' said Grimlock blankly.

The captain groaned. 'Oh, Grimlock, Grimlock, there really isn't a lot going on in there, is there?' he said, waving his lace handkerchief at the brogtroll's head. 'The signal flare alerts the guards at the slave market that there are slaves on board!' He rubbed his plump pink hands together. 'And what a lot of slaves we've got. Mother Muleclaw will be so pleased with me.'

'Mother Muleclaw,' Grimlock growled. He remembered her well enough. Beaten him, she had. Beaten poor Grimlock when he'd once strayed from the ship.

'Aye, the roost-mother herself,' said Vulpoon. 'She's the one our two fine young gentlemen are going to.' He chuckled. 'I wonder if they'll last any longer than the last lot?'

Twig's eyes rested on the finery of the captain's clothes – the elegant embroidered silk frock coat with its intricate pattern of costly marsh-gems and mire-pearls, the highly-polished knee-length boots, the ruffs at his collar and cuffs, the fluffy purple vulpoon feather in his tricorn hat. He was a dandy. A fop. Twig had never seen a sky pirate captain like him before, and it turned his stomach knowing how this unpleasant individual had come by such wealth. 'So when is our estimated time of arrival in the slave market?' he asked, stepping from the shadows.

Vulpoon spun round, his face a picture of horrified shock. 'You!' he blurted out. 'What are you doing here? Where are Teasel and Korb?'

'Sleeping soundly,' said Twig, a smile playing over his lips.

'But this is an outrage!' the captain roared. His eyes bulged. His face turned crimson in the purple light. 'You're meant to be . . .'

'Asleep?' said Twig. He drew his sword. 'Bound and gagged? All trussed up for market?' He began to circle the captain.

'I . . . You . . . It's . . .' Thunderbolt Vulpoon blustered. 'And that's *my* jacket you're wearing!' he shrieked. 'GRIMLOCK! SEE TO THEM!'

Grimlock blundered forwards.

Twig calmly ran his hand up and down the jacket, his fingers hovering over the jewels. 'See, Grimlock,' he said.

Grimlock halted in his tracks. 'Pretty clothes,' he said, his eyes lighting up.

'Grimlock!' bellowed Vulpoon furiously.

But Grimlock did not hear him. Mesmerized by the dazzling beauty of the wondrous jacket, he drooled.

'It could be yours, Grimlock,' Twig said. 'All yours.' He slowly slipped an arm out of a sleeve and let the jacket drop down his shoulder. 'Would you like it, Grimlock?' he said. 'Shall I give you the pretty jacket? Shall I?'

Grimlock's eyes widened with confusion. He looked at the captain. He looked at the jacket. His brow furrowed. Twig slipped off the second sleeve and held the jacket in his left hand.

'Grimlock, obey!' Vulpoon screamed. 'Do as you're told!'

A smile spread over Grimlock's clodden features. He

took a step forwards. Twig held the jacket out. 'Take it,' he said.

Grimlock reached out, snatched the jacket and slipped his arms down inside the sleeves. 'Pretty jacket!' he said, grinning from ear to ear. 'Grimlock pretty!'

Twig pointed his sword at Vulpoon. 'It would have taken so little to ensure the loyalty of your crew,' he said. 'And after all, you have so much.' He turned away in disgust. 'Remove his keys and tie him up, Cowlquape.'

'Please, please,' the captain pleaded. 'No, don't do that, I implore you. I didn't mean anything. Really . . . It was all a misunderstanding . . . *Please!*'

Twig grimaced. 'And gag him, Cowlquape!' he said. 'I'll listen to no more of this creature's spineless whining.'

While Cowlquape bound and gagged the former captain of the *Skyraider*, Twig took to the helm and raised his telescope to his eye. Far in the distance and slightly to starboard, a patch of the unending Deepwoods seemed to be glowing with an oily yellow light. He focused the glass.

'We've found it, Cowlquape,' he breathed. 'We've found the Great Shryke Slave Market.'

With nimble fingers, Twig raised the mainsail a fraction, realigned the studsail and lowered the port hull-weights. The great sky ship swung gently round until the faint, but growing, yellow glow was directly before them. He raised the port hull-weight, lowered the stern-weight and shifted the rudder-wheel a tad to starboard. The *Skyraider* was on course.

Cowlquape joined Twig at the helm and, as the slave market drew ever closer, the pair of them were overwhelmed by the sounds, the smells, the sights emanating from the curious agglomeration of life stretching over a vast area of the forest. For if the places the market had left behind were dead, then this – this raucous, pungent, seething mass of activity – was more vibrant than any place either of them had ever experienced before.

A thousand odours filled the air: pine-smoke and pole-weasel perfume, mothballs and woodgrog, and hammelhorns spit-roasting over roaring flames. Below it all, however – noticeable only when the currents shifted the more pleasant scents away – was the omnipresent

stench of rotting, of decay: of death.

Cowlquape shuddered involuntarily.

Twig turned to him. 'You're right to be apprehensive,' he said. 'For all its glitter and dazzle, the Great Shryke Slave Market is a terrible place. It claims for itself the unwary, the foolish . . .' He placed his hand reassuringly on Cowlquape's shoulder. 'But not us, Cowlquape,' he said. 'We shall not fall into its clutches.'

'A thousand strides, and closing,' the look-out called down from the caternest.

Twig readjusted the hull-weights and shifted all the sail-levers down a fraction. The sky ship glided downwards through the sky.

'Five hundred strides!' the look-out announced. 'Landing-stage on the port bow.'

Cowlquape squinted ahead. In front of them he saw an aerial jetty, jutting out from the top of a stripped tree. At the far end, closest to them, stood one of the bird-creatures: a stocky individual with dowdy feathers and a beak and claws which glinted in the purple light of the flare it was waving as it guided them in. Cowlquape swallowed.

'A shryke,' he murmured softly.

Twig raised the neben-hull-weights and lowered the stern-weight. The sky ship slowed and dipped. He lowered the sails, one by one: the flight-rock would do the rest.

'One hundred strides!'

As if in response to the look-out's cry, Jervis and a gangly individual with a markedly twisted spine – Stile the ship's cook, Cowlquape presumed – appeared on the deck. They looked round, eyes wide, mouths open. The sky ship docked.

There were the passengers, sailing the ship. Grimlock was primping and preening by the bowsprit in a frock-coat. And the captain was trussed up on the floor . . .

'What in Sky . . .?' Jervis muttered.

Just then, there was a loud thud behind them as the end of the gangplank dropped down onto the stern. Twig and the others turned to see a dozen or more of the formidable shrykes marching across the board and advancing towards them.

'What have you got to trade?' their leader – a stout

bird-creature with multi-coloured beads plaited into her drab, tawny feathers – asked as she reached the bridge.

'Not much, I'm afraid,' said Twig. 'Bit of a mix-up in Undertown. We ended up carrying hammelhorns instead of slaves.'

The shryke narrowed her cold, glinting eyes and tilted her head to one side. 'Do you mean to tell me there are only free citizens on board?' she squawked indignantly.

'Except for one,' said Twig. He prodded Captain Vulpoon in the back with his foot and smiled at the shryke. 'A prime specimen,' he said. 'Links with academics, or so I understand.'

'Really?' said the shryke, her neck feathers ruffling up. She turned to her second in command. 'The roost-mother might be interested.'

'My thoughts entirely,' said Twig.

'How much are you asking?' asking the shryke.

Twig's head spun. 'A hundred and fifty,' he said, plucking a figure from the air.

The shryke's eyes narrowed. 'Roundels or docklets?' she demanded.

'R . . . roundels,' said Twig. The shryke tutted and turned away. 'I mean, docklets. A hundred and fifty docklets.' He smiled. 'I'm sure Mother Muleclaw won't be able to resist getting her claws into him.'

The shryke hesitated for a moment. Then, she turned back and stared at Twig with one yellow eye. 'The price is still high,' she said. 'But . . . it's a deal.'

The crew of the *Skyraider* gathered on the main deck all gave a cheer as the shryke grasped the bundle before her. Captain Thunderbolt Vulpoon had treated them all like slaves. There were no tears for the avaricious tyrant as – wriggling like a barkslug – he was hefted up onto the feathery shoulders of his captors and carried away.

'*Mffll bwfll blmmf!*' His muffled oaths were lost to the gag.

'The same to you!' Jervis called after him. 'And good riddance.' He turned to Twig. 'What's to become of us now, though?'

'Of you?' said Twig. 'You're all free. You can do what you want, go where you want . . . Back to Undertown for a start, then who knows?'

'Please, young master, take us back,' pleaded Jervis, his gnarled hands reaching out and clutching Twig's. 'We need a captain if we are to sail the ship.'

'No, I . . .' Twig muttered. 'It's not possible. We . . . that is, Cowlquape and I have business to attend to . . .'

Cowlquape leant across, raised his hands and whispered in his ear. 'The cargo, Twig. Don't forget the cargo.'

'Don't worry, Cowlquape. I haven't forgotten,' said Twig. He raised his head and addressed the motley crew before him. 'When I said "you're all free", I meant it. *All* those on board the *Skyraider* – each and every one – are free.'

'You mean . . . ?' Jervis began. 'The . . . the slaves?'

'Yes, old-timer,' said Twig. 'Those you helped to way-lay and transport to this terrible place are as free as yourself. And I warrant that there'll be creatures amongst them who have some skill in skysailing.' He turned to his young apprentice. 'Come, Cowlquape. Let us go and release Vulpoon's prisoners.'

Cowlquape followed Twig back below deck, and down deep into the dark bowels of the sky ship. He couldn't help but feel a warm glow of pride inside him. Twig could simply have walked from the *Skyraider* and left its occupants to their fate. But no. Even now, though they were on a quest to search for Twig's lost crew, the young captain could still spare the time to assist others. Cowlquape remembered his dream, and winced with embarrassment. If anyone was fit to wear the mantle of Kobold the Wise it was the young captain, not himself.

As they clattered down the final flight of stairs – their boots echoing on the bare boards, the air, fetid and foul, chinks of light penetrating the gloom from broken hull planks – a cry went up from the chained prisoners. With a shudder, Cowlquape recognized the sound he'd heard earlier.

'Is there someone there?' they shouted. 'Water! Water!'
'Something to eat.' 'Korb! Korb, is that you?' 'Have
mercy on us, I beg you!'

Twig shook his head. There was no knowing when the
poor wretches had last eaten or drunk anything and
Twig's blood boiled at the monstrous injustice of it all.
He strode towards the door, took the ring of keys from
Cowlquape, selected the largest and pushed it into the
keyhole. The key scraped in the lock like an angry ratbird. Inside, the voices fell still.

'*Pfwooah!*' Cowlquape gasped as Twig pushed the
door open and a blast of foul air struck him full in the
face.

'Hide your revulsion,' Twig whispered back at him. 'It
is not the prisoners' fault that their conditions are so disgusting.' He stepped inside. 'It is the greed that led to
their imprisonment that is to blame for this foul place.'

A raucous clamouring immediately began. 'Where's Korb?' 'Where's our food and water?' 'What's going on?' 'Why aren't we sailing any more?'

Twig looked around at the miserable assembly of flat-heads and gnokgoblins, cloddertrogs and woodtrolls, and raised his hands for quiet.

'Friends, your ordeal is over!' he called. 'The *Skyraider* is to return to Undertown! And you will travel with it, to be reunited with your families!'

The prisoners looked at one another in confusion.

'You are going home!' Twig announced. He raised the ring of keys above his head and shook them. 'As free citizens! You, and the crew that tyrant enslaved. There will be no slaves at all on board this sky ship ever again!'

For a moment, there was absolute silence. Then a flat-head goblin gave a mighty cheer, and the hold exploded in whoops and cries of tumultuous joy. The sky ship trembled and lurched as the trolls, trogs and goblins – their chains clanking – danced round with delight.

Twig waited for the noise to subside before continuing. 'Now, I need volunteers to crew this ship,' he said. 'How many of you have experience of skysailing?'

Half a dozen arms shot up into the air.

'We've done our bit, Cowlquape,' said Twig with a smile. 'They'll be able to get back safely to Undertown. Our quest lies in the slave market.' He turned back to the prisoners. 'You will all be unshackled,' he said. 'Be patient. Your turn will come.'

Twig divided the keys up between himself and Cowlquape. One by one, the pair of them matched key to lock, unfastened the manacles and set the prisoners free. They streamed out of the dark, filthy hold, away from their prison and up on deck to taste the clear air and look at the stars. There was laughter and much hand-shaking; there were tears and heartfelt thanks. At last, wiping sweat from his brow, Cowlquape peered into the gloom of the farthest corners of the hold.

Only two shackled prisoners remained. A young pinched-looking gnokgoblin with an eye-patch and, at the opposite end of the cavernous chamber, a small figure bundled up in a ragged cloak.

Cowlquape approached the bundle. It let out a faint sigh as he fumbled with the key in the lock of the manacle around its leg. The mechanism failed to click.

He tried again, but it was no good.

'I can't seem to unlock this one,' Cowlquape called across the room. 'It must be the key – or the rusty lock. Or something.'

'Let me try my key,' Twig called back. 'I won't be a minute,' he said to the gnokgoblin as he pulled himself up and crossed the filthy straw which covered the floor. 'Let me see,' he said to Cowlquape, putting the key in the lock. 'Ah, yes, I think I've got it.' He frowned. 'Cowlquape?' he said. 'What's the matter?'

Cowlquape shook his head. 'I don't believe it!' he gasped. 'Look, Twig, look!'

'What is it, Cowlquape?' said Twig. 'Tell, me . . .'

But Cowlquape was not listening. 'It's fate, Twig! It's fate!' he babbled excitedly as he stared unblinking at the young captain's outstretched hand. 'Fate itself must have brought us to this place!'

'Cowlquape,' said Twig sharply. 'What are you talking about?'

And then he saw. His hand, his arm – they were glowing. His entire body was aglow with the same bright light that had illuminated him before. When he had met up with Tarp Hammelherd, and Bogwitt, and Wingnut Sleet . . .

He turned and looked at the bundle of rags cowering immediately before him, his raised arm shielding his sensitive eyes from the sudden light. 'It can't be. Can it? Spooler?' he said. 'Can it really be you?'

The oakelf started back. He lowered his arm – an arm that was also glowing. 'Captain Twig?' he whispered.

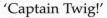

'Captain Twig!'

'Spooler!' Twig exclaimed, and he embraced the oakelf tightly, lifting him up off the ground in his excitement. 'It *is* you!' He turned to Cowlquape, beside himself with joy. 'It's Spooler!' he exclaimed. 'The fourth missing member of my crew. Oh, Spooler,' he said, releasing his grip on the oakelf and looking him deep in his eyes. 'I hoped ... but I never dreamed ... But tell me, how did you end up in this terrible place?'

The oakelf looked down. His brow furrowed. 'I ... I'm not sure, Captain. It's all a blur,' he whispered.

'We were on board the *Edgedancer*,' Twig reminded him gently. 'Tethered to the caterbird. We set off into open sky in search of my father, Cloud Wolf.'

'Yes, yes,' said Spooler. 'That I remember.' He shuddered. 'And I remember seeing the weather vortex from the top of the caternest, coming closer and closer ...'

'Yes?' said Twig eagerly.

'And then, nothing,' said Spooler. 'The next thing I knew I was lying in the gutter in the Undertown fish market.'

Twig hid his disappointment.

'A mobgnome found me,' Spooler continued. 'He

offered me somewhere to spend the night; he gave me something to drink. Woodgrog . . .' His face clouded over. 'And then . . . And then, *this*!' he wailed, and sobs of misery wracked his frail body.

'It's all right, Spooler,' said Twig softly. 'You're safe now. We've found you – though Sky alone knows how. And now this sky ship will take you back to Undertown.'

'But what is there for me in Undertown?' the oakelf wailed.

'You must make your way to my study in Sanctaphrax,' Twig said. 'The others are waiting for me there: Tarp, Bogwitt, Sleet. They will be delighted to see you. You can wait with them. Cowlquape and I shall return when we have discovered what has happened to the rest of the missing crew.' He took the oakelf's bony hands in his own. 'And we must travel on alone, Spooler. We can't take you with us. It was the same with the others. The glow that we create when we are together makes us too conspicuous.'

Spooler pulled away with surprising force. 'No,' he said firmly. 'No, captain. I cannot spend another moment on this evil vessel.' There was a desperate urgency in his voice.

'But Spooler,' said Twig, 'I've explained . . .'

'I can be useful to you,' Spooler persisted. 'On the long voyage here I gleaned a considerable amount of information – vital information – about the slave market from some of my fellow-prisoners.'

'But, Spooler . . .' Twig began again.

'Besides,' Spooler went on, 'I am an oakelf. Observant. Sensitive. My faculties are sharp. And like all other oakelves I know how to read the signs in the behaviour of others. I will be able to determine how the slave market operates.'

Twig shook his head.

'And as for the glowing,' Spooler continued without taking a breath, 'apparently, there are all sorts in the market. *All* sorts! Including creatures that glow – the glimpelt when its fur gets wet, the fritts when they're frightened, the lumhorn when it's attacked . . . No-one will give us a second look.'

Twig glanced up at Cowlquape, who shrugged.

'If you transgress just one of the unwritten laws of this place, then you're done for,' said Spooler, drawing a finger across his exposed throat. 'Believe me, captain, without my help in the Great Shryke Slave Market, you won't last ten minutes.'

'He's got a point,' said Twig.

Cowlquape nodded vigorously. 'He certainly has!' he said. The thought of falling into the clutches of the cold, glinting-eyed shrykes filled him with horror.

'Then it's decided. We shall continue as three,' said Twig.

'I think this was meant to be,' said Cowlquape. He looked down, suddenly serious. 'I read something in the barkscrolls the night before last, something that I think is important. It is what Kobold the Wise said to his followers as they gathered at Riverrise to await the Mother Storm. *"We are all but puppets, waiting for our strings to be tweaked. Our lives are nothing more than the workings of the unseen hand that holds those strings."'*

Twig smiled. 'And you think someone or something tweaked *our* strings, do you?'

'I'm just telling you what I read,' said Cowlquape.

'I know,' said Twig. 'And perhaps you and your Kobold the Wise are right. After all, here we are – we've found the fourth member of my crew. It's more than I'd ever thought possible. If this is the work of an unseen hand, Cowlquape my friend, then I hope its grip is strong, for I feel the greatest test lies ahead of us out there.'

'In the slave market,' said Cowlquape, with a shudder.

'The slave market!' said Spooler darkly. 'And I shall be your guide.'

'Good, well, if that's decided,' came a weary voice from the opposite end of the dank hold. It was the gnok-goblin, still manacled and quite forgotten. 'Then will someone please release *me*.'

·CHAPTER FOURTEEN·

INTO THE GREAT SHRYKE SLAVE MARKET

Having kitted themselves out with fully-equipped longcoats and new parawings from the storeroom of the sky pirate ship, Twig, Cowlquape and Spooler bid a final farewell to the motley company and crew of the *Skyraider*. The sun was rising as they made their way to the end of the gangplank and Cowlquape was relieved to see that, away from the dark hold, neither Twig nor Spooler were glowing.

Twig squinted through the dense foliage at the slave market beyond. Everything was lit up by the oily yellow glow of the lamps, and it was just possible to make out the extraordinary architecture of this hidden city in the forest through the gaps in the leaves. There were tiled cabins and canopied platforms clinging to the trunks of the massive trees; turret-like constructions and curious spheres woven from woodwillow and sallowdrop twigs which hung from their branches, while wooden walkways, slung from tree to tree and strung with smoking oil lamps, formed a network of paths. The noise was cacophonous and unbroken; the stench, repellent.

'*This is the place,*' a voice in Twig's head whispered. '*Let Spooler guide you.*'

Twig turned to the oakelf. 'Spooler,' he said, 'do you really think you can guide us safely through this terrible place?'

Spooler nodded. 'I shall do my best,' he said. 'First of all, we must see about some white cockades. Come, let us go. And Sky protect us all.'

Twig's heart missed a beat as he followed Spooler over the wobbling plank of wood. He hadn't realized how high up they were for, although docked, the *Skyraider* was still some fifty strides above the forest floor.

'The whole market is raised up,' Spooler was saying. They had reached the other side and were stepping through the outer canopy of leaves. 'Everything is fixed to, or suspended from, the great trees.'

Twig stared ahead of him, open-mouthed. 'It's stranger than I ever imagined it would be,' he whispered.

'And vast,' said Spooler. 'Searching for an individual in this lot . . .' His voice faded away and he flapped his hands at the thronging walkways, creaking and groaning under the weight of the crowds that snaked their way along them.

'We'll manage,' said Twig. 'Somehow. Eh, Cowlquape?' There was no reply. Twig spun round.

'Cowlquape?' he called. 'Where are you?'

'*Wuurgh!*' came a small groan from back the way they'd come.

'Cowlquape!' shouted Twig. He ran back through the curtains of foliage and along the landing-stage. And there was his young apprentice, down on his hands and knees in the middle of the bouncing gangplank, eyes tightly closed, shaking like a leaf and unable to move. 'It's all right,' Twig said. 'I'll come and get you.'

'NO!' Cowlquape wailed. 'I can't get up. I'll fall. I know I will.'

Born and raised in Undertown, the youth had never liked heights. Living on the floating city of Sanctaphrax had been fine because it was so vast – though he'd avoided the higher walkways and always shut his eyes in the baskets. Skysailing had scared him at first, but again the ship had been large and, when up on deck, he'd taken care not to look down. But this – wobbling about on a thin gangplank in mid-air – this was almost as petrifying as dangling on that rope from the *Skyraider*. In some ways it was worse. At least boarding the sky ship had been over rapidly; he'd just had to hold on. But here, the walkways went on for miles.

How would he ever cope with them?

'Crawl,' he heard Twig instructing him. 'Grip the sides of the plank and crawl forwards.'

Cowlquape's head spun. His breath came in short, sharp gasps. 'I can't,' he muttered. 'I just can't.' Even though his eyes were still clamped shut he could *feel* the space between him and solid ground.

'You can!' said Twig. 'You can't stay here! Besides, if you fall, what would become of your precious barkscrolls?'

Cowlquape groaned. He felt for the sides of the board with his hands, then shuffled forwards on his knees. His toes dragged along the rough surface of the plank.

'That's the way!' Twig shouted encouragingly. 'Just a little bit further.'

Arms trembling and teeth clenched, Cowlquape moved forwards again. And then again. Moving without thinking. All at once, hands gripped his jacket and he felt himself being dragged forwards. His legs turned to jelly and he fell with a thud on something hard – the walk-way shuddered. He opened his eyes. Twig was crouching down beside him.

'This is a fine place for me to discover about your head for heights, Cowlquape,' he said. 'The whole market's strung up in the trees.'

'Just give me a moment ... I'll be all right,' said Cowlquape bravely, climbing shakily to his feet. He followed Twig along the landing-stage. 'It was just that gangplank. No sides.' He shuddered. 'Nothing to hold on to ...'

At that moment, an ear-piercing squeal ripped through the air, followed by a torrent of curses. Twig, Cowlquape and Spooler ran across to the wooden rail and looked down. Cowlquape gulped nervously.

The noise was coming from a small platform with a red and white striped canopy some way below them. A bandy-legged goblin was leaping around and brandishing a massive fist at the air below him. Beside him was a blazing stove suspended on chains from the branch above.

'Blast you to open sky for wriggling free like that!' he was screaming. 'You've ruined me! Ruined me, do you hear?'

Cowlquape squinted below. There was something there – silent now – bouncing from branch to branch down to the ground. He turned to Twig. 'What is it?' he said.

Twig shrugged.

'A woodhog, probably,' said Spooler. He nodded towards the goblin, still jumping up and down on the platform in uncontrollable fury. 'There are hundreds of vendors like him all over the slave market, living from hand to mouth . . .'

Suddenly, there was a sharp creak and, with a splintering of wood, the platform broke away from the tree-trunk it was anchored to. The goblin screamed and clutched wildly at the hanging stove. For a moment he swung wildly. Then – his fingers hissing and smoking with the intense heat – he let go.

Cowlquape stared in horror, appalled, yet unable to tear his gaze away as the second creature tumbled down after the first. Screaming with terror, the goblin struck a thick branch with a thud, the body – limp now and twisted, with arms and legs akimbo – continued down, down, down . . .

'Sky above!' Cowlquape cried out. 'What are *they*?' He pointed down at the ground, where dozens of fluffy orange creatures were gathering, their bear-trap jaws agape.

Twig and Spooler peered down. 'Wig-wigs,' they said in unison.

Twig shuddered. 'Terrible creatures. They hunt in packs and devour their victims, dead or alive.'

'Here, they don't even need to hunt,' said Spooler. 'They live well enough off the discarded waste from the slave market . . .' The body of the goblin crashed down onto the ground and was immediately pounced upon by the ferocious wig-wigs. 'And anything else that drops down. Accidentally or otherwise,' he added.

'And when they've finished, there's nothing left,' said Twig. 'Not a scrap of fur or a splinter of bone.'

Cowlquape blanched. 'They . . . they can't climb trees, though,' he said anxiously. 'Can they?'

Twig shook his head. 'No,' he said. 'No, they can't.' And from the look which came into his eyes, Cowlquape guessed that the young captain was speaking from experience.

'Come,' said Spooler urgently. 'We must find a tally-hen and buy our white cockades at once. Without them we could be seized by a slave-trader and put on sale at any moment.' His huge black eyes darted round the shadows. 'I heard that there's usually one near the end of each landing-stage,' he said. 'Yes, look.' He pointed to a tall, narrow hut secured to a tree. 'There's a tally-lodge.'

Twig looked. It was one of the turret-like constructions he'd seen earlier. 'What are we waiting for then?' he said.

Together, the three of them crossed the gently swaying hanging walkway. Too terrified to look either left or right, Cowlquape kept his gaze fixed on the hut as he shuffled across. They approached the door.

Close up, the building was a small triumph of Deepwoods architecture. Constructed from buoyant lufwood, it was sturdy yet almost weightless, and art-fully curved to minimize wind resistance. A lantern above the door illuminated a gold-lettered plaque: *Tally-Hen Mossfeather*. Twig raised his fist and knocked.

'Enter,' came a raucous voice.

As Twig went to lift the latch, Spooler stayed his hand. 'Be sure to wait for her to speak first,' he hissed. 'It is the way here.'

Twig nodded and opened the door, and the three of them walked into the dark room. Acrid smoke from the tilder-oil lamps around the walls immediately caught in their throats and made their eyes water. A swarthy shryke with metallic grey-green feathers and ivory-white talons stood before them, her back turned, busily moving coloured discs around a numbered tally-board.

Twig stepped forward and waited.

'Fifty-seven, fifty-eight, plus time-penalties,' the shryke muttered to herself. 'Can't you see I'm busy?' she snapped.

'We wish to buy white cockades,' Twig replied boldly.

The shryke paused. '*Buy*, did you say? Not beg, borrow or barter?' She spun round. 'And what do you intend buying them with? We don't take tokens or vouchers. It's two gold pieces per person.'

Twig reached inside his jacket, undid the leather pouch and counted out six gold pieces. He handed them over. Without saying a word, the shryke took one of the coins and bit into it with her savage-looking hooked beak. She looked up.

'Three cockades, you say?'

'One for each of us,' said Twig.

The shryke nodded sullenly and turned towards a locked door in the back wall, which she opened to reveal a dark safe carved into the living tree itself. She lifted the lid of the box inside and removed three woodthistle-shaped white rosettes.

'Here,' she said. 'The cockades ensure free right of passage for three days and three nights. After that, the material rots away. If you are caught without cockades you will be seized and sold as slaves.'

'Three days in this place will be more than enough,' said Twig.

The shryke snorted unpleasantly. 'That's what they all say. But I'm warning you,' she said, 'the days and nights bleed into one another in the Great Shryke Slave Market. Our visitors are always complaining about the un-common haste with which time passes . . .'

'Which is why we must thank you and bid you farewell,' said Twig promptly. 'We have much to do.' With that, he spun round and left the room, the others following after. The door slammed shut.

'Surly creature,' Cowlquape commented.

'Shrykes aren't exactly known for their graciousness,' Spooler scowled. 'Yet those who are made tally-hens generally act with more integrity than most.' He frowned. 'Attach your cockade to the front of your jacket where you can keep an eye on it. The slave market is full of light-fingered individuals, and hats with cockades upon them have a horrible habit of going missing.'

With the white cockades positioned and secured to

Spooler's satisfaction, the oakelf turned and set off into the slave market. The others followed.

'And keep close,' Spooler instructed. 'Even as cockaded free citizens you risk being picked off by some unscrupulous merchant who would lock you away till the cockade rots and then claim you as his – or her – own.'

Twig's top lip curled with contempt. 'Is there no honour at all amongst slave-traders?' he said.

'You can't buy and sell honour, captain,' said Spooler. He smiled ruefully. 'And money is the only thing that matters here.'

Twig frowned. If any of the crew they were searching for *had* ended up in the slave market, what chance would they have stood in so mercenary a place?

'There is an auction in the slave market,' Spooler was saying. 'The Grand Central Auction. I thought we might try there first.'

Twig nodded. 'Come on, then,' he said wearily. 'But let's keep ourselves to ourselves – and our eyes and ears open.'

Back in Sanctaphrax, a ferocious storm was raging. High winds and driving hail battered the floating city. Above it, the sky was a cauldron of seething, swirling clouds tipping down bolt after bolt of jagged lightning. Up in Twig's study in the opulent School of Light and Darkness, the purple glow from the stove played on the fidgety faces of three sky pirates.

'It's all this waiting around that I can't stand,' Wingnut Sleet complained as he paced up and down the small room.

Bogwitt, who was sprawled out in a chair trying to dislodge some meat from his teeth with a fingernail, looked up. 'It's all them academics ever seem to do,' he growled. 'Idle bunch of slackers the lot of them.'

'Mind you,' said Sleet, wincing uncomfortably with every flash of lightning, 'I wouldn't fancy being out on a night like this. You know, I swear the weather's getting worse.'

Tarp Hammelherd shivered and crossed the room to warm his hands at the stove. 'Goodness knows what it must be like in the Deepwoods,' he said. 'I hope Captain Twig's safe.'

Sleet turned to him, his scarred flesh quivering. 'And what if he never returns?' he said. 'Are we to be expected to spend the rest of our lives in this poky little room?'

'The captain looked after us,' said Tarp. 'The least we can do is wait for him.'

'Yes, but for how long?' Sleet persisted.

'As long as it takes,' said Tarp firmly. A volley of hailstones drummed against the pane of glass, drowning him out. Tarp shuddered and looked out through the window. 'Sky protect you, Captain Twig,' he murmured. 'May you be successful on your quest to find those other crew-members less fortunate than ourselves . . .'

'And get back here as quickly as you can!' added Wingnut Sleet.

The Great Shryke Slave Market was like nothing either Twig or Cowlquape had ever experienced before: a sprawling labyrinth that extended further than any creature could walk in a day and a night – not that such terms had much meaning in a place lit by glowing lamps and sputtering torches, where the sunlight never penetrated.

Over aerial bridges, up rope-ladders and down, they hurried. This way and that. Onwards and inwards. It was as though they had been swallowed up by a huge and monstrous beast, and were now lost within its cavernous innards. Above, below and on every side, there was feverish activity as life coursed through its veins. The air was stale, orange-red, and throbbed like a beating heart. Chaotic, it had seemed at first, yet a closer look revealed that underlying it all was order, purpose.

They passed business after small business – shops, stalls, makeshift trestle-tables – each one with its owner shouting out never-to-be-repeated bargains, trying to catch their eye. One that did was up on a platform just above their heads – a solitary lugtroll, her white cockade pinned to a tall plumed hat, hawking glittering jewellery.

'Look,' Cowlquape gasped. 'It's *alive!*'

Twig looked closely. The lad was right. Each of the necklaces, bracelets and brooches was sparkling, not with precious stones, but with live firebugs which had been fixed into position with filaments of wire twisted round their glowing abdomens.

Spooler nodded at their own bodies, glowing ever so faintly in the dimly-lit gloom. 'Best get out of here before she decides to use us two!' he said.

And on they went. Past hanging cages laden with huddled birds, crates of reptiles and insects, and dying hollowed trees with bars at the gaping holes, forming

cages to woodbears and white-collar wolves; past rows of sleeping oakbats, their ankles tethered to the branches with leather jesses.

A while later, Twig stopped at a food stall, where a vendor – like the hapless goblin he'd seen earlier – had tilder sausages and woodhog steaks sizzling on a hanging stove. He bought three steaks and three hunks of oak bread, handed them round and they continued walking, eating as they went.

'Something to satisfy your thirst, too?' came a voice soon after.

Twig paused. Cowlquape and Spooler stopped beside him. The creature who had spoken to them was a gabtroll. She was stooped, with warty skin, drooping pink ears and, most bizarre of all, bulbous green eyeballs swaying at the end of long eye-stalks, which her long slurping tongue kept moist and clean. She looked up from her steaming pot.

'I've the finest herbal teas in the whole of the slave market,' she told them, her eyes swaying on their rubbery stalks. 'You,' she said, the eyes focusing in on Cowlquape, 'for you, I would recommend an infusion of hairy charlock and oak-apple. It emboldens the timid of heart. And is excellent for vertigo.' She smiled at Spooler, and her tongue slurped noisily over the peering eye-balls. 'For you, wood-comphrey, I think. It's a general pick-me-up.' She smiled and slurped again. 'And you certainly look as though you could do with one.'

She turned to Twig. Her face twitched with surprise and her eyes bounced in and out on their stalks.

'What?' said Twig, somewhat taken aback. 'Do you not know what *I* should drink?'

'Oh, I know all right,' the gabtroll said softly. Her eyes stared directly into his own. 'Bristleweed,' she said.

'Bristleweed,' Twig repeated. He turned to the others and laughed. 'Sounds delicious.'

The gabtroll's eyes retracted. 'Its name sounds common enough, I'll grant you,' she said. 'Yet bristleweed is one of the rarest herbs in all the Deepwoods.' Her voice lowered to a hushed whisper. 'It grows in purple clumps among the skulls and bones at the base of the flesh-eating blood-oak tree. Harvesting it is a nightmare,' she added, and her eyes peered closely into Twig's once more. 'As I'm sure you can imagine.'

Twig nodded. He'd had first-hand experience of the monstrous tree, as the gabtroll seemed to sense.

'You are a seeker, a searcher,' the gabtroll continued, without taking a breath. Her rubbery brow creased with concentration. 'Looking for others . . .'

'Perhaps,' said Twig.

'Yet there is someone else you do not realize that you seek,' said the gabtroll, and smiled. 'And bristleweed will help you.'

'It will?' said Twig.

The gabtroll nodded. She sprinkled a spoonful of the powdered purple herb into a wooden mug, ladled in warm water from the pot and stirred it round with a wooden spoon. 'Here,' she said. 'Take it. Don't expect immediate results, but in time it will help you find the one you are looking for.' She paused. 'Yourself.'

'Find myself?' said Twig, disappointed. 'But *I'm* not lost.'

The gabtroll, busying herself with Cowlquape and Spooler's drinks did not look up. 'Are you sure?' she said softly. 'Is there not *something* missing?'

Twig fell still. The curious creature was right of course. Something *was* missing. That memory of his time spent on board the *Edgedancer,* in the middle of the weather vortex. *That* was what was missing.

What *had* happened to him there?

Twig raised the cup to his lips and drank the sweet, fragrant tea down in one go. The others did the same and, having paid for their drinks, they set off once again into the vast three-dimensional maze, slung out between the trees.

'So how's that timid heart of yours, Cowlquape?' Twig said with a chuckle as they were crossing a hanging walkway some while later.

Cowlquape smiled. 'Believe it or not, Twig, I reckon the tea must have helped.' He stopped, clutched hold of the rope hand-rail and looked down. 'My fear of heights isn't nearly so bad as it was.'

Twig nodded. Gabtrolls were renowned for their understanding of herbs and roots. 'And you, Spooler?'

he said to the oakelf, scuttling on ahead of them.

'Never felt better, captain,' came the cheery reply.

Cowlquape turned to Twig as they continued after him. 'And what about you?' he said. 'Has the bristle-weed tea helped you to find yourself?'

Twig shook his head. 'Not yet, Cowlquape,' he said. 'Not yet . . .'

All round them the air grew more and more stifling and the noise louder. Howling. Wailing. Chatter and squawk. Whipcrack and chain-rattle. The hopeless moaning of a band of waifs, wraiths and the lesser trolls, roped to tether-rings. Roars of triumph. Cries of defeat. And orchestrating the whole terrible cacophony, the raucous flocks of flightless bird-creatures who inhabited the slave market: the shrykes.

They came in all shapes and sizes, from the hefty patrol

leaders to the scrawny little snitches and snoopers. All were female – the few miserable male shrykes there were kept penned and treated like slaves themselves.

The colour of the shrykes' plumage also varied. Most of the guards were tawny; the tally-hens, metallic slate-grey. But there were others. Mottled and striped, piebald and spotted. Some woodnut brown, some ironwood grey, some snowbird white. And some were brightly coloured.

Greater in stature than the others and with a certain air of nobility about them, the roost-sisters, as those with real power were called, were answerable only to Mother Muleclaw herself. Despite the apparent frippery of their dress – the gaudy aprons, the ornate headdresses, the golden rings through their beaks – the roost-sisters were greatly feared. Cold and ruthless, they were also terrifyingly unpredictable.

Twig looked up to see one of them now, strutting arrogantly across a crowded upper parapet, wings swinging, beak in the air, and striking out with her leather flail at random as she went. Twig turned away in disgust.

'The whole accursed place should be razed to the ground,' he said angrily. 'Wiped out. Burned down.'

Cowlquape's expression clouded over. 'I dare say it will be, one day,' he said. 'But not before those beyond the slave market decide they have no more need for pets and servants and bound workers. In the Deepwoods. In Undertown. Yes, and in Sanctaphrax, too.'

Twig turned towards his young apprentice. 'Cowlquape, are you saying that it is in some way *our* fault that this place exists?'

Cowlquape shrugged. 'Perhaps,' he said. 'We demand, they supply. And as Kobold the Wise said . . .'

'Mind your backs!' came a chorus of shrill voices. 'Make way! Make way!'

Twig turned to see half a dozen tawny shryke guards, flails and clubs drawn, marching along a walkway parallel to their own. They were split up into three pairs. Each pair was dragging along a protesting prisoner, beating him savagely as they went.

'We didn't notice!' one of them moaned.

'We can explain!' protested another.

'What's happening?' Cowlquape asked Spooler anxiously. 'What have they done wrong?'

Spooler nodded towards them. 'No cockades, see?' he said. 'They've rotted away. And now they're about to pay the penalty.'

'I wouldn't like to be in their shoes,' said Twig with a shudder.

'Neither would I,' said Cowlquape, nervously checking his own cockade. It was reassuringly fresh. 'I do wish we'd hurry up and find that wretched auction place.'

Twig looked round him. 'Me, too, Cowlquape,' he said. 'Me, too.'

They were passing through a section of the slave market where the more exotic Deepwoods creatures were kept. There were fromps coughing and quarms squealing from behind the bars of the hollowed trees, and razorflits, bound by the legs and suspended upside down from hooks, screeching with fury. A rotsucker, imprisoned in a cage far too small for it, oozed a green bile from the end of its tubular mouthpiece that hissed where it dropped and gave off coils of foul-smelling vapour; a muzzled halitoad crouched in a mist of its own noxious breath.

'It . . . it's disgusting here,' said Cowlquape, his voice muffled by the hand he'd clamped over his mouth.

'Yet no less popular for that,' Twig commented with a weary sigh.

He'd already noticed that the whole area was bustling with particularly eager buyers. The sound of their haggling reached fever pitch as they all tried to secure deals which would, in turn, make them a pretty profit.

'Come on,' he said, lengthening his stride. 'Let's find that auction once and for all. I don't want to stay in this vile, parasitic place a moment longer than we have to.'

An hour later – just as they were about to give up – they saw it: the Grand Central Auction.

Situated on a large, terraced platform, the auction consisted of a long windowless building, a raised stage and a lectern. The whole lot was lit up with heavy hanging glass balls, each one containing a live firebug which gleamed like a candle-flame as it flew round its tiny prison, looking for a way out. They illuminated the auction area so brightly that Twig and Spooler's faint glow faded away completely.

'Twenty-five? Do I hear twenty-five?' The auctioneer – a tall noble-looking shryke with pink and purple plumage – clutched her blackwood hammer and scanned the crowd. 'I'm asking twenty-five for this trio of flat-head goblins. At the peak of their physical con-

dition, they are. Ideal bodyguards or mercenaries. Twenty-five? Thank you. Thirty. Do I hear thirty?'

Twig stared at the scene, his heart beating furiously. Could any of his missing crew be here? The three ragged flat-heads, shackled to one another, stood morosely at the front of the stage. Four tawny shryke guards stood with them, flails and clubs drawn and ready to punish any misdemeanour. The auctioneer stood at the lectern to their right.

'Forty,' she said. 'Do I hear forty?' She nodded. 'Forty-five?'

Below her, on a log, sat a stooped, slate-grey tally-hen with a clipboard clutched in her claws. Between licks at the end of her crayon, she was noting down the rising amount.

Cowlquape nudged Twig. 'Recognize anyone?' he said.

Twig shook his head. 'No,' he said. He peered back into the dark shadows at the back of the stage where an assortment of Deepwoods creatures stood huddled together, waiting their turn to come under the hammer. There were cloddertrogs, mobgnomes, a gnokgoblin with a young'un at her breast, a gangly lugtroll and a couple of unfamiliar wiry, matted-haired trolls from the darkest reaches of the Deepwoods where Twig had never ventured.

'No-one,' he said disappointedly.

'Going once,' the auctioneer cried out 'Going twice . . . Sold!' she announced, and the blackwood hammer cracked down heavily on the top of the lectern. 'Sold to the flat-head with the crimson jerkin.'

Twig snorted. Flat-heads buying flat-heads! What kind of a place was this where free-citizens and slaves could only be told apart by cockades? He turned to Cowlquape and Spooler. 'Come,' he said. 'It was worth a try, but we're clearly wasting our time here. Let's go.'

Cowlquape turned to leave. He was as disappointed as the others. In fact the longer he remained in the slave market, the more uneasy he was becoming. If it were up to him, they would cut their losses and depart at once.

'Lot Nine,' the auctioneer cried. 'A waterwaif.'

Twig started. A waterwaif? He'd seen no waterwaif. He turned round and stared back at the stage. And sure enough, there – cowering behind the cluster of clodder-trogs – was a slight, scaly creature with fanned ears and a darting, reptilian tongue. One of the tawny shrykes jabbed him sharply in the back. The waterwaif groaned and hobbled wearily to the front of the stage.

'I thought we were going,' said Cowlquape.

'Wait,' said Twig.

He stared at the individual before him, then at Spooler, then back at the waterwaif – then back at Spooler.

'Well?' he said.

'I ... I'm not sure,' the oakelf replied. There was excitement in his voice. 'It *could* be ...'

'Could be what?' said Cowlquape.

'Not what, but *who*,' said Twig. 'It could be Woodfish.'

'From your crew?' said Cowlquape.

Twig nodded.

Just then, the auctioneer's bidding got underway.

'Ten!' she announced. 'Who'll offer me ten.'

Twig raised his hand.

The auctioneer glanced at him. She nodded and turned away again.

'Fifteen,' she said. 'Do I hear fifteen?'

'Fifteen,' came a gruff voice.

'Twenty?' said the auctioneer, turning back to Twig.

Twig glanced round at the character who had bid against him – an evil-looking individual with a metal eye-patch, who was leering at the waterwaif with his one good eye and licking his lips ominously.

From the emblem embossed into his heavy leather coat, Twig could see he was a leaguesman – though the symbol was none he recognized. He raised his hand a second time.

The auctioneer nodded again. 'Twenty-five?' she said. 'Do I hear twenty-five.'

Twig glanced around again. This time, his gaze met that of the one-eyed leaguesman, who was glaring back at him furiously. 'Twenty-five!' he bellowed.

'Thirty!' shouted Twig.

'Thirty-five!'

'Fifty!'

The leaguesman hesitated for a moment, then – as Twig looked round – his mouth cracked open and his gold teeth glinted in the glow from the imprisoned fire-bugs. ''S all yours,' he sneered.

'Sold to the individual in the hammelhornskin waist-coat for fifty,' the auctioneer announced. 'Come forward to pay the tally-hen and lot number nine is yours.'

Twig stepped up onto the stage. Cowlquape held his breath. Was the waterwaif the crew-member Twig was searching for or not? The next moment, the air resounded with a screech of surprise.

'You want to do *what*?' the tally-hen demanded, her voice loud and incredulous. 'You want to buy it a cockade?'

Cowlquape's heart leapt. So it *was* Woodfish after all! He moved closer to the stage, the better to hear what was going on.

'I think you'll find the amount correct,' Twig was

saying as he handed over a cluster of gold pieces. 'Fifty for the purchase and an extra two for a white cockade.'

The tally-hen glanced up at the auctioneer questioningly.

'If he wants to waste his money on fine gestures . . .' she sniffed, and her beak clacked with contempt.

The tally-hen shrugged. Fifty-two gold pieces were fifty-two gold pieces after all. She slipped the money into the chest, reached inside the pocket of her pouch and removed a white cockade.

'Here,' she said.

Twig took it and handed it over to the waterwaif. He smiled. 'For you, fellow free-citizen,' he said.

'Th . . . thank you,' the waterwaif said uncertainly.

'Even though you are not the one I hoped you would be,' said Twig quietly.

Cowlquape gasped. *Not* the one? What did he mean?

The waterwaif frowned, and listened in on Twig's thoughts. 'Oh, I see,' he said. 'You thought I was your missing crew-member, Woodfish.' His fan-like ears fluttered. 'I'm sorry to disappoint you.'

Twig shrugged. 'It's not your fault,' he said. Then, smiling grimly, he reached out and shook the scaly hand of the waterwaif.

'Lot number ten!' the auctioneer bellowed above the rising swell of angry voices in the crowd. She looked down impatiently. 'Will those involved in the previous sale kindly leave the stage.'

Cowlquape and Spooler helped the still somewhat bewildered waterwaif down onto the platform. Twig jumped down after him. The four of them slipped back through the crowd.

On the other side, Twig turned to the waterwaif. 'Anyway,' he said, 'I'm glad to have been of help. Live long and fare well,' he said formally, and turned away – to be confronted with the furious face of the thwarted leaguesman pressed closely into his own.

'What do you think you're playing at?' he said.

'Playing at?' said Twig.

The leaguesman seized him by the shoulder and pulled him close. 'You heard me,' he spat. 'Do you realize how long I've been searching for a waterwaif?' the leaguesman hissed into Twig's ear. His breath was warm, moist and made fetid by the rotten meat trapped between his gold teeth. 'Thirty-six cockades-worth!' he said. 'Thirty-six dumping cockades-worth! This was the first I'd found. And then you come along!'

With that, he drew his dagger. Twig stumbled. The blade glinted. Crying out, the waterwaif leapt between them. The knife plunged into his chest.

A curious look of serenity passed over the waterwaif's face as he tumbled back to the wooden platform. It had all happened so quickly, but he had read the leagues-man's murderous thoughts in an instant. His eyes misted over; his ears fell still.

Astonishment turning to rage, Twig drew his own sword. But as he stepped forwards, half a dozen of the tawny shryke guards brushed him aside and fell upon the leaguesman.

Shrieking with fury – eyes glinting and feathers erect – they tore the cockade from his lapel and seized him in their vicious claws. The leaguesman struggled in vain as he was bundled away.

'It was him!' he protested. 'Let me go!'

'Oh, we'll let you go, all right!' came the gleeful reply. 'We'll let you go under the auctioneer's hammer.'

'No, not a slave,' the leaguesman shouted, and struggled all the more desperately. 'You can't sell me as a slave. Do you not realize who I am . . . ?' His voice was drowned out by the sound of scornful laughter as the shrykes dragged him away.

Twig shakily approached the dying waterwaif. He crouched down. 'I'm so sorry,' he said tearfully. 'Ending up a slave would have been better than . . . than this.'

The waterwaif's ears fluttered weakly. 'No,' he whispered. 'Nothing is worse than that,' he said. 'You saved my life, and I am happy I was able to save yours . . .' His eyes widened abruptly as a spasm of pain racked his body. 'And there is one last service I can do you . . .'

As Cowlquape and Spooler watched on, Twig lowered his head and listened intently.

'You are looking for the missing crew of the *Edgedancer*,' the waterwaif whispered hoarsely. 'I read it in your thoughts.'

'Yes,' said Twig.

The waterwaif clutched at him weakly. 'One of those you remember in your thoughts, well . . . I have seen him here . . . in the market.'

'You have?' Twig exclaimed. 'Who is it? And where can I find him?'

'He . . . he . . .' His voice gurgled. Twig held the waterwaif up and put an ear to his mouth. 'The Wig-Wig . . . Arena,' he whispered, and his body juddered. There was a gasp. A whimper. And the light in his eyes flickered and died.

Twig laid the waterwaif back down and closed his eyelids. Cowlquape and Spooler crouched down beside him.

'It wasn't your fault,' said Cowlquape.

'Yet he's dead, for all that,' said Twig. He sighed. 'What should we do with the body?'

'The shrykes will take care of it,' said Spooler. 'Come, captain. There's nothing more you can – or may – do here.'

With heavy-troubled hearts, the three of them left. Cowlquape, who was last in line as they crossed over the nearest hanging walkway, glanced back to see that the tawny guard shrykes had returned to the scene. Two of them hoisted the dead body onto their feathery shoulders, and all six of them scuttled off. Cowlquape turned away.

On the far side of the hanging walkway, Twig stopped and looked round him. More than ever, he felt that the Great Shryke Slave Market was nothing less than an evil wood fungus, sucking the life out of its host, the Deepwoods, and all who dwelt in her. He couldn't wait to leave. He looked at Cowlquape and Spooler and knew that they felt the same way. But they couldn't leave. Not yet.

'The Wig-Wig Arena,' he said to Spooler. 'Does that name mean anything to you?'

The oakelf's dark eyes widened with unmistakable fear. 'Oh, yes, captain,' he said, his voice trembling. 'It certainly does. I know all about the Wig-Wig Arena.' He shuddered. 'I only wish I didn't.'

CHAPTER FIFTEEN

THE WIG-WIG ARENA

Cowlquape suddenly looked up, breaking the silence that had followed the oakelf's words. His face was deathly pale. 'Twig,' he trembled. 'It's started.'

'What's started?'

Cowlquape lightly touched his woodthistle-shaped rosette. 'My cockade,' he said miserably. 'The material is starting to wilt.'

'Are you sure?' said Twig. 'It looks all right to me.'

Cowlquape shook his head angrily. 'Look!' he said. 'It's gone all limp at the edges. I can't believe we've been here long enough for that to happen.'

'That tally-hen did warn us to keep track of time,' Twig reminded him.

'Yes, but three days!' Cowlquape exclaimed hotly. 'We can't possibly have been here for three days. It's all a con, a trick to enslave more unsuspecting free citizens . . .'

'Cowlquape, calm down,' said Twig. 'It hasn't rotted away yet. And anyway, what's done is done. We must look forwards.' He turned to Spooler. 'Time's running short,' he said. 'This Wig-Wig Arena,' he said. 'Can you take us there?'

The oakelf nodded and looked round about him slowly, thoughtfully. 'By reading the signs in the market crowds, I can,' he said. 'Look over there at those merchants. See the greed in their faces? Follow them and they'll lead us back to the Grand Central Auction. Whereas over there, those gnokgoblins. See the way they stop, look around, then go on a few steps? They're browsers. They'll lead us to the livestock-traders and trinket-sellers.'

'Yes, yes,' said Twig impatiently. 'But what about the Arena? How do we know who to follow there?'

'Bloodlust,' said Spooler. 'Look for bloodlust in the faces of the crowd.' He continued scanning the milling groups of trogs and trolls, goblins and gnomes, leaguesmen and sky pirates. 'There!' he said at last, and pointed at a gaggle of goblins. 'That looks a likely group. Look at the purpose in their stride. The violence in their gestures. The glint in their eyes?' He sniffed the air and shuddered. 'I can *smell* their lust for blood, oozing from every pore. Oh, they're heading for the Wig-Wig Arena, all right,' he said. 'I'd stake my life on it.'

'That's good enough for me,' said Twig. 'We'll follow them. And Sky willing we will find the crew-member the waterwaif saw there. Come on, Cowlquape. Before we lose sight of those goblins.'

They set off in pursuit. Ahead of them the group of goblins was becoming increasingly rowdy and, as that happened, so the numbers heading in the same direction increased as more and more, attracted by the noise, came to swell their ranks. Twig, Cowlquape and Spooler surrendered themselves to the stream. Past a tattooing-stall they went, a whip-merchant's, a leech-doctor's; past a corral of roosting prowlgrins, a flock of tethered vulpoons – impelled ever onwards by the excited crowd. They couldn't have escaped the forward surge now even if they'd wanted to.

'I'll say this for the roost-mother,' a shrill gnokgoblin piped up. 'She certainly knows how to put on a spectacle.'

His companion nodded vigorously. 'Nothing beats a contest with a banderbear pitted against the wig-wigs,'

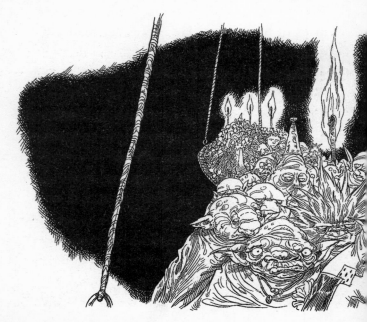

he said. 'It's an absolute classic!'

Twig gasped. A banderbear? Pitted against wig-wigs!

'Wasn't there a banderbear on board the *Edgedancer*?'
Cowlquape said in Twig's ear, whilst all the time fighting to keep up in the jostling scrum. 'You think it might
be the one that the waterwaif saw, don't you?'

'Perhaps,' said Twig. 'I cannot leave until I know one
way or the other.'

'Still,' Cowlquape went on, as he stumbled forwards.
'A big strong creature like a banderbear can defend itself
against wig-wigs, surely?'

Twig shook his head seriously. 'I once saw what a pack
of wig-wigs can do to a banderbear.' He pulled a pen-
dant from the folds of his jacket and held it up for
Cowlquape to see. It was a tooth. 'This is all that is left of
that banderbear,' he said.

'But . . . *Whoooah!*' Cowlquape exclaimed as the crowd abruptly squeezed in on him from all sides and surged forwards. He was carried towards a narrow archway. THE WIG-WIG ARENA, he read, in gold letters, as he was swept beneath the arch and on to a broad platform. He looked round. His mouth fell open.

'Amazing, isn't it?' said Twig.

'Unbelievable,' said Cowlquape. 'The architecture, the planning – the *size* . . .'

They were in a bright clearing, encircled by huge trees. Tier upon tier of curved terraces had been suspended from the branches above to form a vast amphitheatre. At its centre, far below them, lay a deep torch-lit pit, ringed by mesh-like netting.

'Move along there,' came an irritated voice from behind them. 'Move right down into the arena.'

Cowlquape recognized the shrill tone of a guard shryke at once. His head buzzed with fear as, without turning round, he did as was told, stepping down off the platform and onto the first of the circular terraces that extended far down below them. Twig and Spooler followed him.

Down, they went; one terrace after another. Cowlquape took it all in, as they picked their way through the countless groups of chattering goblins and trolls.

The Wig-Wig Arena was like a giant funnel rising up from the forest floor at the bottom, where the bloody contests would take place, to the forest canopy at the top. One tree, even more massive than its neighbours, dominated the arena. It was directly opposite the terrace where Twig, Cowlquape and Spooler found themselves jostled into seats – a colossal ironwood tree, its black, spade-like leaves in sharp relief against the blondwood steps rising up behind it. Cowlquape looked more closely.

Attached to the tree's sturdy branches were several constructions: square platforms for the armed guard shrykes dotted here and there; a small, squat building beside a raised stage; cogs, pulleys and winding gear; a plank jutting out from the main trunk, leading nowhere. Further up the tree was a broad podium, with the brightly-coloured roost-sisters standing along its balustrade in a row. And above this – suspended from a network of heavy ropes – was an ornate royal-box. Inside it sat a solitary figure.

It was the roost-mother herself: Mother Muleclaw. She was resplendent in her crested head-dress, her firebug jewels and a diaphanous silver cloak which hung loosely over her rainbow plumage. No finery, however, could conceal the wickedness in her eyes. From her box, she had a perfect view of every inch of the arena.

As she cast her malevolent gaze round Cowlquape quaked, and his hand shot up to conceal his wilting cockade. Twig noticed the movement.

'Cowlquape,' he said gently. 'Calm yourself.' He swung his arm round in a wide arc. 'There are hundreds, perhaps thousands, of individuals here,' he said. 'They're not interested in us when there's so much money to be made.'

He nodded towards the slate-grey tally-hens already scuttling about taking bets from the growing swell of spectators. Cowlquape watched them for a moment.

'No, I suppose not,' he said hesitantly. 'All the same . . .' He looked across the arena and shuddered. 'There's someone in there,' he said, pointing to the squat construction below the podium.

Twig looked. He saw fingers clutching the bars at the locked door. Some poor wretch was about to meet his death – yet it was not a banderbear . . .

At that moment, a fanfare of trumpeting cut through the air. A roar of approval went up round the crowd. Cowlquape looked up into the ironwood tree to see a dozen striped shrykes perching in the upper branches, with long tasselled horns at their beaks. The fanfare was repeated. This time, the crowd fell still. All eyes fell on the royal-box.

Mother Muleclaw arose slowly. Her beak clacked noisily. 'We are gratified to see so many here,' she announced. 'We know you will not be disappointed by this evening's contest. It isn't every night we get to see a banderbear in battle.'

The crowd roared its agreement. Mother Muleclaw raised her multicoloured wings for quiet.

'Before the main event, we have a little surprise for you. The appetizer, so to speak,' she said, and her beak clacked with amusement. She leant down from the box. 'Release the prisoner,' she demanded.

The guard shryke saluted with its tawny wing and stepped forward to unlock the door of the prison

beneath the podium. A portly individual appeared at the doorway and looked round with obvious confusion.

'What? What? What?' he blustered.

Cowlquape stared in disbelief – at the ornate jacket with its marsh-gems and mire-pearls, at the tricorn hat with the purple vulpoon feather, at the waxed moustache, the arched eyebrows, the pink, pudgy hands. 'Thunderbolt Vulpoon,' he breathed, and clutched hold of Twig's arm. 'This is what he had planned for us!' he whispered, his voice low with dread.

'If I'd known,' said Twig, 'I'd never have handed him over to the shrykes. Not even a slave-trader deserves this.'

The crowd watched in silence as the guard shryke cracked her flail and drove the sky pirate captain towards the plank jutting out over the pit below. The yellow torchlight gleamed on his quivering features as he looked up at the hanging royal-box. 'Why?' he cried out. 'For the love of Sky, why are you doing this?'

Mother Muleclaw squawked with irritation, and the shryke's heavy flail cracked Vulpoon around the head.

'We had promised you a leaguesman from Undertown for your delectation,' said Mother Muleclaw, addressing the crowd.

The crowd cheered happily.

'Or perhaps even a Sanctaphrax academic,' she said.

The cheering of the crowd grew louder still.

'Unfortunately, due to circumstances beyond our control, this will not now be possible . . .'

The crowd booed and hissed. Mother Muleclaw

glared down at Vulpoon. 'All I can offer you is this miserable specimen. Still I am sure he'll put on an excellent show for you.' Her voice became a raucous screech, that echoed round the arena. 'I give you Thunderbolt Vulpoon, the sky pirate captain.'

A deafening roar went up. Cowlquape looked round in disgust at the rapt expressions on the spectators' faces as they watched the hapless Vulpoon being prodded forward with a sharp pike onto the plank. A chant started up, and was soon echoing all round the arena.

'Down! Down! Down! Down!'

Vulpoon stumbled forwards. For an instant, his body hung there at the end of the plank as if held by invisible ropes. Then there was movement again, and Thunderbolt Vulpoon was toppling forwards –

rolling over

and over

as he fell,

before landing in a bed of soft moss at the bottom of the pit. The crowd roared its approval.

For a moment, the sky pirate captain didn't move. Then, with a shake of his head, he climbed to his feet and drew his sword and dagger. He looked round – at the heavy curtain of netting that enclosed the pit; at the small holes cut into it every ten metres, allowing access from the forest floor outside. The crowd looked too, scrutinizing the shadowy openings for that first tell-tale flash of orange.

'There!' someone screamed. 'Over there!'

It was the first of the wig-wigs. It dashed across the arena floor, looking no more frightening than an orange floor-mop. Until the creature opened its mouth! The crowd gasped as one as the powerful jaws snapped wide open to reveal the rows of razor-sharp teeth.

All round the arena, the arrival of the first wig-wig had prompted a flurry of betting. Tally-hens and tote-fledgers darted among the crowds, shouting out ever-changing odds and exchanging gold pieces (each one, checked with a sharp clack of the beak) for betting-slips.

'Twenty-five on twelve minutes!'

'Fifty on forty-seven dead wig-wigs.'

'A hundred that he's got a maximum of ten seconds left!'

Sickened, Cowlquape turned away and buried his face in his hands.

At last, a roar went up.

'YES!'

Louder and louder it became, until the terraces them-selves were trembling with the noise. Above the uproar came the trumpeting of the horns. And still the clamour did not abate. One of the tally-hens trotted to the iron-wood tree and a message was passed up to the roost-mother.

Mother Muleclaw rose to her feet once more. A hush fell.

'The sky pirate captain managed to kill forty-three wig-wigs before his demise,' she announced. 'And twenty-seven more were wounded.'

The winners cheered. The losers – of whom there were many more – groaned.

'The contest lasted for precisely ten minutes and . . .' she hesitated. The spectators clasped their betting-slips tightly. 'Ten minutes and forty seconds. That's four-o. Forty.'

Again, the few excited whoops of delight were drowned out by a general groan of disappointment. Mother Muleclaw clacked her beak.

'But now, my friends, we must proceed,' she announced. 'It is time for the evening's main event.' She nodded at the shryke guard on the platform below her, who began turning a great handled wheel. The pulleys creaked. The ropes shifted. From above the hanging royal-box, the bottom of a heavy, ironwood cage began slowly to descend from the dense grey-black foliage.

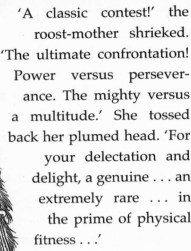

'A classic contest!' the roost-mother shrieked. 'The ultimate confrontation! Power versus perseverance. The mighty versus a multitude.' She tossed back her plumed head. 'For your delectation and delight, a genuine . . . an extremely rare . . . in the prime of physical fitness . . .'

The crowd went wild with feverish anticipation; waving their arms, stamping their feet. And, as the cage came lower – revealing the fierce, furious beast pounding at the bars of its hanging prison – their bloodthirsty cries became more and more tumultuous. Mother Muleclaw smirked with self-satisfaction, and when the cage was hanging directly next to the royal-box, she nodded down at the shryke for a second time. The turning stopped. The cage juddered to a halt. Mother Muleclaw raised a great taloned hand.

'I give you . . . a BANDERBEAR!' she screeched.

Twig gasped. It wasn't just *a* banderbear. It was Goom.

There wasn't any doubt. Even if he hadn't recognized his face, the tell-tale scars from the spiked pit that had once trapped him gleamed on his left flank.

Clucking softly, Mother Muleclaw reached out and stroked the claws of the banderbear which stuck out between the bars of the hanging cage. 'I know he's going to give those wig-wigs a run for their money,' she said, her voice oily.

The crowd – whipped up to a frenzy by the thought of the ensuing confrontation – had begun chanting once again.

'Down!' they demanded. 'Down! Down! Down!'

Cowlquape's whole body shuddered with revulsion.

'We must act quickly,' said Twig urgently. 'Go back to that prowlgrin corral we passed. Buy four prowlgrins,' he said, giving Cowlquape a handful of gold coins. 'The largest and strongest you can find. Then meet me round the other side of the arena, on the walkway directly beneath the branches of the ironwood tree.'

'But Twig . . .' Cowlquape began.

'*Now*, Cowlquape,' said Twig firmly and, before his young apprentice could say another word, he dashed off through the crowd.

Cowlquape stared after him for a moment, then turned to Spooler.

'We'd best see about those prowlgrins,' the oakelf said.

Cowlquape nodded. He only hoped Twig knew what he was doing.

The arena was thick with feverish betting as Twig made his way towards the ironwood tree.

'Thirty gold pieces on twenty-eight minutes and nine seconds.'

'Fifty each way on at least two hundred and fifty wig-wigs copping it.'

'Seventy-five gold pieces!'

'A hundred!'

Ignoring the yelps of pain and cries of anger as he elbowed his way through the jostling crowd, Twig finally arrived at the point where the trunk of the great tree emerged from behind the top terrace. He stopped, pulled the sky pirate grappling-hook from the front of his heavy longcoat and glanced round.

The atmosphere was now approaching fever-pitch and no-one – neither shryke nor spectator – noticed the young sky pirate standing in the shadows. Taking the rope in his hand, Twig swung the hook into the branches above and, when it took securely, scrambled up.

'And now,' Mother Muleclaw screamed above the din, 'the moment you've all been waiting for!' She nodded down at the shryke guard: she should begin to lower the banderbear into the pit below.

Twig reached a broad, flat branch high in the iron-wood tree and crept carefully along it. He stopped when he was directly above the royal-box and hanging cage. Below him, Mother Muleclaw raised her wings.

'And so,' she announced, 'let the contest begin ... *Whurrggh!*'

As one, the crowd let out a gasp of astonishment at the sight of the young sky pirate dropping down into the royal-box and seizing the roost-mother. An arm grasped

her round the throat; a
hand pressed the glint-
ing blade of a knife
against her ruffled
neck.

'Stop lowering the
cage!' Twig bellowed.
'Bring it up level with
the royal-box again
– or the roost-
mother gets it!'

With a squawk
of indignation, the
tawny shryke paused
and fixed Twig with
an astonished stare.
Then slowly, she
reversed the direction of her turning. The roost-sisters
were in uproar, shifting about on their podium,
screeching and squawking. Other shrykes – tawny
guards and great, serrated-beaked slavers – closed in
on the tree from the walkways menacingly.

'Back off!' Twig roared. 'Tell them,' he hissed into
Mother Muleclaw's feathery ear. 'Tell them now.'

'St . . . stay back,' said Mother Muleclaw, in a strangu-
lated voice.

'And tell them to drop their weapons!' Twig increased
the pressure of the knife.

'Do as he says!' she squawked.

'That's better,' said Twig. Then, still maintaining the

pressure on the knife, he reached over to the cage and unclasped the lid at the top. One of the banderbear's massive paws appeared.

Suddenly, the crowd seemed to realize what was happening. Up until that moment, the spectacle of the youth threatening the roost-mother had held them captivated. Now they saw what he had in mind, and were incensed.

'He's released it!' they roared furiously. 'He's letting it go!'

Twig dragged the cowering Muleclaw to the far end of the royal-box as the banderbear heaved himself up out of the cage. He watched, heart in his mouth, as the great, clumsy creature grasped at a branch above his head for support, and stepped across the yawning chasm below.

As the banderbear fell into the royal-box, the crowd exploded with anger. 'It's getting away!' they raged.

The roost-sisters below craned their necks round to see what was happening.

Twig watched the banderbear climbing to his feet. 'Goom,' he said. 'I knew it was you.'

'Wuh?' the great beast asked. 'T-wuh-g?'

'Yes, Goom,' said Twig. 'Didn't I promise that I'd never abandon my crew.' He glanced upwards. 'Pull yourself up onto that branch above our heads. Then pull me up beside you.'

The banderbear shuddered nervously, making the royal-box shake. Mother Muleclaw cried out as Twig's knife nicked the scaly skin beneath the feathers. The crowd howled with dismay as the great lumbering creature reached up, sunk its claws into the overhead branch and swung its tree-trunk legs up into the air.

'A hundred and fifty says he doesn't make it,' a voice rang out above the din.

'Two hundred says we'll be looking at a new roost-mother before the night is out!' yelled another.

The crowd went wild.

At his third attempt, Goom managed to swing his legs over the edge of the branch and drag himself up. He crouched down on the broad branch and lowered a great arm.

'Wuh!' he said.

Twig grabbed hold of the banderbear's wrist. Goom pulled, and Twig was whisked up clear of the royal-box. The instant her attacker was gone, Mother Muleclaw cried out.

'Seize them!' she shrieked, jumping up and down in the box in a fever of rage. 'No-one threatens the roost-mother and lives! Guards . . . *Aaargh!*' she screamed, as one of the banderbear's razor-sharp claws sliced through several of the ropes that kept the royal-box in place. The box swung wildly. Her sharp talons gripped the wooden sides. 'No,' she whimpered. 'Have pity . . .'

'Pity?' Twig shouted. 'The only pity is that this was not done long ago.' And with that, he reached down and sliced through the last ropes.

The royal-box plummeted down through the air, with Mother Muleclaw screaming all the way.

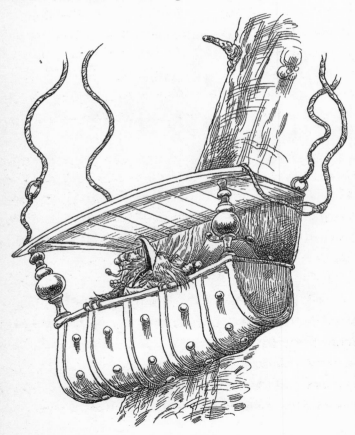

The crowd roared with delight. This was even better than a banderbear. This was the roost-mother herself. As the first of the wig-wigs emerged from the dark openings in the stockade, the noise became deafening. Whooping. Wailing. Cheering and shouting. 'A hundred on . . .' 'Five hundred that . . .' 'A thousand!'

Twig turned to the banderbear. He seized him by a quivering paw.

'Edge your way along this branch,' he shouted, 'then down onto that one, there.' He pointed to a broader, flatter branch growing out of the trunk behind him. 'It's almost as wide as the walkways. And then, when I say jump, jump!'

'Wuh!' the banderbear grunted in alarm.

The noise all around them was deafening: a great screeching from the shrykes and the roar of the blood-thirsty crowd.

'Trust me,' said Twig, struggling to make himself heard. He turned and made his own way along the branch, arms raised to keep his balance as the heavy banderbear anxiously lumbered after him. The leaves quivered. The branch swayed. Below him, Twig saw the boards of the wooden walkway come closer.

'Jump!' he shouted.

'WUH!' cried the banderbear, and the pair of them leapt from the branch and down to the walkway below. Scrambling to his feet, Twig looked around wildly. Angry shrykes on the adjacent walkways were running at them from every side, shoving their way through the crowds who were still thronging towards the extraordinary spectacle unfolding in the pit.

'Twig! Twig!' came an urgent voice.

Twig spun round to see Cowlquape and Spooler on a broad platform just ahead, pushing towards them through the crowd. They both held a tether in each of their hands, at the end of which were four startled prowlgrins.

'Well done, Cowlquape!' he shouted.

Just then, four shryke guards dropped onto the walkway from above. They landed between them, cutting Twig and the banderbear off from escape. In a split second the banderbear was on them. With a mighty blow from his paw, he swept two shrykes from the walkway in a flurry of feathers. The other two dropped their clubs and flails, and fled with terrified screeches.

'They were the biggest ones I could find,' panted Cowlquape, as he and Spooler finally reached the others. The prowlgrins bucked and whinnied from the end of their tethers.

'Ideal,' said Twig. 'Goom, take the biggest. Climb up, all of you.' He grabbed the reins and leapt onto his own prowlgrin.

Goom remained still. 'Wuh-wuh!' he groaned miserably.

'It's the *only* way,' said Twig. 'Come on!'

Already more shrykes were gathering. For the moment they hung back, but when there were enough of them, they would rush forward. There was murder in their yellow eyes.

Reluctantly, the massive banderbear clambered up onto the waiting prowlgrin. The creature groaned under the heavy weight, and locked its bow-legs.

'All right?' said Twig.

The banderbear nodded unhappily.

'Let's get out of here!' Twig shouted.

Gripping the reins tightly, he kicked hard into the prowlgrin's flanks. The others did the same. The next instant – as if in some strange dance – the four beasts reared up, pawed the air with their fore-legs and leapt forwards.

Clutching on for dear life, Twig and Cowlquape, Spooler and Goom found themselves charging along the walkway away from the ironwood tree and the terrible arena. They knocked spectators and shrykes aside. Cowlquape held on for dear life. He'd never ridden a prowlgrin before, and never wanted to again. It was terrifying.

The walkways swayed and shuddered beneath them, market-stalls crashed as they careered past – but the prowlgrins were as sure-footed as they were swift. The market sped by in a hazy blur of colour and oily lamp-light. Suddenly, they were approaching the end of a walkway that gave way to nothing. It was the edge of the slave market. The astonished face of a slate-grey shryke peered out from a tally-booth directly ahead.

Now what? thought Cowlquape, his heart pounding.

Without a moment's hesitation, the prowlgrin beneath him launched itself off from the end of the walkway and into mid-air. Cowlquape sank his heels deep into its belly as the wind whistled past. He gripped the reins, white-knuckled.

Below him, the forest opened up like a gaping mouth. Falling. They were falling. His stomach leapt up into his mouth; he screwed his eyes shut. This was worse than the Sanctaphrax baskets, worse than the sky ship, worse than . . .

Ker-dunk!

His whole body jarred as the prowlgrin grabbed a branch with its fore-paws and, in an instant, kicked off again with its hind-legs. Cowlquape gripped the reins tighter still. Again, the forest opened up. And again, the prowlgrin landed, sure-footed on a branch before kicking down hard with its powerful hindquarters and leaping again.

The prowlgrin was well trained. Even though Cowlquape had never ridden before, all he had to do

was hold on as it forged its way through the forest from tree to tree. *Ker-dunk – whoosh! Kerdunk* . . . Little by little, it became easier. Cowlquape was learning when to tense his stomach and when to relax; when to lean forwards, when to sit back.

But what of the others?

Cowlquape stole a hurried glance back over his shoulders. Twig and Spooler were close behind him. And behind them was the banderbear. Despite the weight on its back, Goom's prowlgrin was managing to keep up. Then, with a jolt, Cowlquape saw a flurry of movement behind the banderbear. Half a dozen or more of the tawny shryke guards, on prowlgrins of their own, were close on their heels.

'What do we do, Twig?' Cowlquape shouted out.

'They're catching up.'

'Courage, Cowlquape!' Twig called breathlessly. 'Prowlgrins are beasts of the Deepwoods. They're used to travelling through the dark forest. But shrykes are roost creatures. They seldom stray far from the flock.'

Quite suddenly, the lights of the slave market disappeared and they were plunged into gloom. Cowlquape cried out with fear and screwed his eyes tightly shut.

'It's all right!' he heard Twig shouting happily. 'Cowlquape, open your eyes. It's all right.'

Cowlquape did as he was told and was relieved to discover that, though the forest itself was indeed pitch black, the sky pirates he was travelling with were glowing brightly in the darkness. Twig, Spooler and Goom; all three of them were bathed in the strange luminous light.

On they went, without easing up for a moment, from branch to dark, looming branch; fleet and sure-footed.

Then Twig called out. 'They've stopped!'

Cowlquape glanced round a second time. He saw the group of prowlgrins with their shryke riders perched on branches in the shadows, some distance behind them. They seemed in no hurry to continue the chase into the depths of the black forest. He saw something else; his cockade had disintegrated completely. All that remained was the pin.

'Thank Sky!' he murmured. 'We've beaten them! We ... *whooah!*' he gasped as he slipped in the saddle.

'Careful, Cowlquape,' said Twig. 'We might have escaped the Great Shryke Slave Market, but there are still wig-wigs below on the forest floor.'

Cowlquape gripped the reins grimly. And as they continued on their flight and the slave market was left far behind, he kept his gaze fixed firmly on the forest ahead.

They did not stop, nor even slacken their pace. Before they could descend to the forest floor to rest up for the night, they had to ensure that they were well away from the voracious wig-wigs that had been attracted by the slave market. Cowlquape grew weary as they pressed on.

'How much farther?' he shouted after Twig.

'Just a little,' Twig shouted back. 'We must . . .'

'Captain!' shouted Spooler. The agitation in his voice was unmistakable. 'Captain Twig, it's Goom's prowlgrin.'

Twig spun round. 'Oh, no,' he muttered. The poor creature was suffering under the burdensome weight on its back. Its strength was all but used up. Each leap was laboured, each landing a gamble. As for Goom himself, the banderbear's glowing face was contorted with fear as his mount struggled on, ever more precariously.

'Wuh,' it was groaning. 'Wuh-wuh.'

Twig sighed. There was nothing for it. Wig-wigs or no wig-wigs they would have to descend. Sky willing, they had already put enough distance between them and the vicious orange creatures.

'Down!' he bellowed, and tugged on the reins of his own prowlgrin. 'We're going down.'

Their slow descent coincided with a thinning of the trees. As they leapt down, from branch to branch, lower and lower, Cowlquape scoured the forest floor for any tell-tale flash of orange.

There was none. He sighed with relief.

They landed in a tussocky glade of greatgrass. First Twig, then Spooler and Cowlquape, and finally Goom. His prowlgrin slumped to the ground, panting with exhaustion. Goom rolled off and lay beside it. The others dismounted, too. Spooler led the prowlgrins to a nearby tree and tethered them to a low branch. Twig crossed over towards the banderbear and crouched down next to him. He wrapped his arm around the creature's great neck and Goom rose, lifting Twig right off his feet.

The two figures lit up the glade with their eerie glow.

Cowlquape ran over to join them.

'You did it!' he exclaimed. 'You did it!'

Twig turned his head and smiled at his young apprentice. '*We* did it,' he said. 'You and me and Spooler, and Goom himself. We all did it!'

·CHAPTER SIXTEEN·

THE WELL-TRODDEN PATH

Having ridden so far and for so long, the four travellers were weary. Twig knew there was no point in forging on any further that night.

'We'll stop here,' he said 'and set off again early tomorrow morning. Cowlquape, Spooler, get a fire going. Goom and I will see about something to eat.'

'Aye, aye, captain,' said Spooler.

Cowlquape shivered as he watched Twig and the banderbear setting off into the darkness of the great forest. They looked so small against the massive trees: so insignificant, so vulnerable.

'Take care,' he muttered, and busied himself collecting sticks and branches from the surrounding undergrowth – taking care himself not to stray too far.

'Good,' said Spooler when he returned. 'Make a pile over there.'

Cowlquape dropped the huge bundle of wood and

watched Spooler coaxing a flame from something grey and fluffy. 'What's that?' he said.

'Barkmoss,' said Spooler, between blows. 'Excellent tinder. Usually.' He blew some more. His face was red and gleaming. 'The accursed stuff's damp though.' He blew harder still. Abruptly, the moss burst into flames. Spooler placed it gently down on a flat rock and turned to Cowlquape. 'Get me some small twigs,' he said. 'Dry ones.'

Cowlquape leapt to the pile and returned with a handful. He handed them to Spooler, who arranged them in a pyramid-shape above the flames. They too caught, and the pair of them stoked up the blaze with larger logs. Soon, they had a huge fire burning.

While Spooler sorted through their provisions for pots, plates and mugs, Cowlquape sat himself down next to the fire. With the night-sounds all around – a screech here, a squawk there – he felt safer there next to its protective flames. He reached into his bag for his beloved barkscrolls.

At that moment, there was a crashing noise to their left, and Goom came blundering back through the forest. Twig followed close behind, keeping to the trail the banderbear had carved out. He approached the fire and emptied a sack of fruits and roots onto the ground. 'Oak-apples, dellberries, yarrowroots,' he said, 'and numerous other delicacies especially selected by Goom with his sensitive banderbear nose, as being both nutritious and delicious!'

'Wuh!' said the banderbear, nodding his head in agreement. He lowered his great shoulder and lifted off the body of a young tilder. An arrow stuck out from its neck.

'Did you shoot that, Twig?' said Cowlquape, impressed.

'With my improvised home-made bow and arrow,' Twig laughed. 'It's been a long time, but I haven't lost my touch,' he said. 'Steaks for us and the rest of the carcass for the prowlgrins.'

A sudden fit of spluttered coughing echoed round the trees just above. Cowlquape ducked down and covered his head with his hands – only to see the others laughing at him.

'It's just a fromp,' said Twig. 'Quite harmless . . .'

'Wa-iiiiiii-kakakakaka . . .'

The mating call of a night-lemuel cut him short. Cowlquape ducked down for a second time.

'Cowlquape,' said Twig softly. 'You're right to be cautious, for the Deepwoods is a dark and dangerous place. But I'm afraid you're just going to have to get used to the sounds it makes.'

Cowlquape nodded sheepishly. He didn't mean to keep reacting the way he did. 'I think I need some more of that gabtroll's special tea,' he said.

Twig smiled. 'Perhaps that could be arranged. We've got the oak-apples.' He turned to Goom. 'Did you find any hairy charlock?'

The banderbear rummaged through the pile of fruit and roots with surprising delicacy for one so huge. He selected a stubby root with a topknot of feathery leaves. 'Wuh,' he announced, holding it up together with a bunch of sugar grass.

'There,' said Twig. 'All the ingredients we need.'

By the time the moon rose, plump and bright, the four of them were sitting round the fire tucking into their tilder steaks and sweet rootmash, while the prowlgrins, apparently none the worse for their long ride, devoured the tilder carcass noisily. Cowlquape sipped at the tea Twig had put together.

'Not bad,' he said. 'The gabtroll's was sweeter, but . . . not bad at all.' All round him, the Deepwoods echoed with the rising crescendo of noise. Coughing, squealing, screeching . . . Cowlquape smiled. 'And what's more,' he said, 'it seems to be doing the trick.'

Twig yawned. 'Glad to hear it, Cowlquape, I . . .' He yawned again.

'Why don't you get some sleep,' said Cowlquape generously. 'I'll take first watch.'

'I'll join you,' said Spooler.

Twig nodded, too tired to argue. 'We'll rest up till dawn,' he said. 'Make an early start.' And with the old, familiar Deepwoods sounds ringing in his ears, he lay down by the fire, curled up and drifted off to sleep. Goom did the same. Spooler got up to check the prowlgrins.

Cowlquape crouched down by the fire and poked the glowing embers into life with a greenwood stick.

'Who'd have thought that *I* would ever end up inside the Deepwoods, the ancient home of Kobold the Wise?' he muttered. He lay the stick down and pulled the ancient barkscrolls from his pack. 'Of all places!'

*

Far away in the floating city of Sanctaphrax, a cold, heavy mist swirled round its avenues and alleyways. Vox, the tall young apprentice from the College of Cloud, shuddered, wrapped his fur-lined gowns tightly about him and lengthened his stride. He was already late for his secret meeting with the newly-appointed Professor of Psycho-Climatic Studies.

'Out of my way, scum!' he cursed, as an unfortunate sub-acolyte blundered into him in the mist.

'S ... sorry, Vox,' the youth stammered, and Vox was gratified to hear the respectful nervousness in his voice. He cuffed him about the head, twice.

'Just watch it in future,' he snarled as, gown flapping in the icy wind, he strode away.

CRASH!

The ground behind him shook. Vox started with alarm, then spun round angrily, sure that the impudent youth had thrown something at him. But he was wrong. He stared down shakily at the huge chunk of shattered masonry which had been dislodged by the treacherous winds high above his head. It had missed him by a hair's breadth.

'The whole place is falling to bits,' he muttered bitterly. 'Time was when an apprenticeship in Sanctaphrax meant a secure future.' Several more pieces of rock and mortar peppered down onto the walkway, sending Vox scuttling away.

These days, nothing was secure in Sanctaphrax; the ferocity of the weather saw to that. Storm after storm had been blowing in from beyond the Edge of late, each one worse than the one before – thunderstorms, wind-storms, fire and ice-storms; great storms and mind storms. No-one had ever known anything like it. Repairs to the damaged buildings couldn't be made quickly enough, while all academic studies had ground to a halt. Something was brewing out there in open sky, that much was clear – yet there wasn't a single academic, not even the Most High Academe himself, who knew what.

'And how can an ambitious young apprentice know who to make alliances with when the conditions are so unpredictable?' Vox asked himself. Was the Professor of Psycho-Climatic Studies likely to prove any more influential than the Professor of Cloud in the end?

He paused on a bridge and, gripping the balustrade, looked at the clouds tumbling in from beyond the Edge.

'That little runt, Cowlquape, had the right idea, disappearing from Sanctaphrax when he did,' he muttered. Refectory gossip had it that the youth had set off with Twig, the wild-eyed madman that the Professor of Darkness had taken under his wing. Even stranger, the professor now had three more peculiar guests . . . Vox gritted his teeth. Despite his words, he had no intention of leaving Sanctaphrax.

'Come what may, I shall turn the current situation to my advantage,' he murmured. He traced his fingers over the scar on his cheek left by the bowl of steaming tilder stew. 'And woe betide Cowlquape if our paths should ever cross again.'

*

A soft drizzle fell in the Deepwoods as the four travellers packed up the following morning. It dampened everybody's mood. Twig, Cowlquape and Spooler mounted their prowlgrins and set off. Goom, to save the strength of his prowlgrin, alternately rode or loped after them, the tether of the fourth prowlgrin wrapped round one massive fore-paw.

They continued through the dense, green forest in silence. It was no coincidence that, as clouds overhead grew darker and the rain fell heavier, niggling doubts began to gnaw at each and every one of them. They'd been lucky so far – very lucky – but now their luck had run out. They all knew that finding any further crew-members in the vast Deepwoods was an impossible task. The best they could hope for now was to find a village settlement, somewhere leaguesmen or sky pirates might visit to trade – then buy their passage back to Undertown. But out here in the perilous forest, even that was a formidable task.

Yet when the sky brightened and the warm sun burst through the canopy, their moods improved. Cowlquape breathed in the rich smells of the surrounding woodland: the dark, loamy soil, the juicy foliage, the fragrant fruit. It was all so different to the stale, smoky odour which tainted everything in Undertown.

'How's it going?' Twig asked him.

'It's all so beautiful,' Cowlquape said, with a sweep of his arm. 'Especially now the sun's shining.'

'Beautiful but deadly,' said Twig in a low voice.

They travelled far that first day, eating the fruit and

berries that Goom sniffed out as edible as they went. (The prowlgrins would have to wait until they put up for the night before their meal.) And as they rode further, Twig pointed out some of the more exotic Deepwoods creatures that he recognized.

To Cowlquape, each one sounded grimmer than the last and the hairs at the back of his neck were soon tingling uncomfortably. There were halitoads, with their foul, choking breath; feline mewmels, with spiky tails and poisonous spit; mannilids – sticky, brain-shaped creatures which hung disguised in bulbul trees and lived off the oakhens who came in search of bulbul berries. A rotsucker flapped slowly across the sky far above their heads, while a skullpelt – with its yellow claws and hooked teeth – dined on a quarm it had charmed from the trees.

Despite everything they encountered, however, by the time evening came around again, they had not seen a single trog or troll or goblin – no-one who might be able

to help them. Twig seemed increasingly worried.

'I know the Deepwoods,' he said. 'I was brought up amongst woodtrolls. They taught me never to trust the forest, always to be on the alert for danger.'

Cowlquape looked up from the oak-mallows he was toasting in the dancing flames of their fire. His mug of tea stood on the ground beside him. 'We are going to be all right, Twig,' he said nervously, 'aren't we?'

'Sky willing, Cowlquape,' Twig replied softly. He turned to the youth and smiled. 'Course we are,' he said reassuringly. 'Now drink your tea.'

On their tenth morning in the Deepwoods though, having still not met any creature who could help, no amount of the hairy charlock and oak-apple tea was enough to raise Cowlquape's spirits. The prowlgrins had gone.

'I just can't believe it,' he groaned. 'I'm sure I checked them before I went to bed. They did seem jumpy – but I thought they'd be all right.'

Twig was alarmed. 'Something must have scared them in the night and they pulled free of their tethers.' He looked at Cowlquape. 'Didn't I tell you to double-knot the tether-ropes?'

Cowlquape stared at the ground. 'Sorry,' he said, in a whisper. He looked up sheepishly. 'So – what do we do now, without the prowlgrins?'

'We go on,' said Twig angrily. 'On foot.' With a sinking feeling in the pit of his stomach, Cowlquape saw fear in his eyes.

Twig set off at a furious pace and Cowlquape was soon puffing and panting.

'Why can't we rest?' he wheezed. 'Or at least slow down a bit?'

Twig laid his hand on the young apprentice's shoulder. 'You've still got a lot to learn about the Deepwoods, Cowlquape,' he said. The fear remained in his eyes. 'They might look peaceful and idyllic, but behind every tree there lurks danger – and we still don't know what may have upset the prowlgrins. We must find a settlement as soon as we can, or we will surely perish.'

'But Twig, a few minutes' rest can't hurt, can it?' pleaded Cowlquape.

All at once, a series of piercing screams cut through the air. 'Aaargh! *Aaaargh!* AAAAARGH!'

Up ahead, the banderbear was leaping about in the middle of a glade of long swaying grass, like a creature possessed. The oakelf was nowhere to be seen.

'Wuh!' Goom bellowed, as he scythed furiously at the waving green fronds.

'What's the matter with him?' Cowlquape gasped. 'And where's Spooler?'

'This is the Deepwoods, Cowlquape!' said Twig. He drew his sword and raced towards the banderbear. 'I told you – there is danger everywhere!'

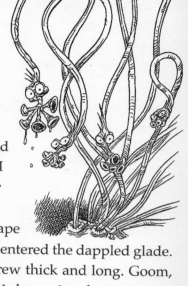

Dagger in hand, Cowlquape followed close behind as they entered the dappled glade. All round them, greatgrass grew thick and long. Goom, up ahead, waved his arms and shouted at them. Even to Cowlquape – who couldn't understand a single word the creature said – the meaning was clear. They should go back. The banderbear was telling them to escape while they still had the chance.

Suddenly Twig began slashing all around him. 'I should have guessed!' he shouted back. 'We're in a bed of reed-eels, Cowlquape. They must nest all round here. No wonder the prowlgrins fled. Protect yourself . . .'

For a moment, Cowlquape couldn't move. Where the tall grass ought to have been, there was instead a great mass of green worm-like creatures protruding straight up from holes in the ground. They had small deep-set orange eyes and, for a mouth, petal-shaped suckers which swayed towards him as he passed by, trying to attach themselves to his skin.

'Get off!' he screamed as, twisting and turning, he stabbed all round with the dagger.

As the blade came close, the lithe reed-eels retracted, sliding from view down inside their holes – only to pop up a moment later. Cowlquape swung his knife backwards and forwards. He couldn't afford to let up for an instant. When he caught up with the others, Goom had the oakelf over his shoulders and was beating a hasty retreat. Twig grabbed Cowlquape by the arm.

'Hurry,' he said, sweeping his sword round in a long low arc. 'We must get out of here. The reed-eels are in a feeding frenzy.'

Cowlquape didn't wait to be told a second time. With his dagger slicing wildly at anything that moved, he dashed ahead. The reed-eels were cunning. They plaited themselves together to bar his way. They slithered across the ground at his ankles.

'Cowlquape, be careful!' Twig shouted, and slashed at a loop of twisted eels.

'Deepwoods,' Cowlquape muttered. 'Danger . . .' He stumbled on. Beneath his feet, there was greatgrass once again. He double over and gasped for breath. 'That . . . was . . . close,' he panted. 'I . . .'

'*Too* close,' he heard Twig saying. He looked up. Twig was kneeling next to Spooler's body, Goom by his side.

'Is he . . .?' Cowlquape said.

Twig nodded. 'Dead,' he said. 'The fangs of the reed-eels have spread their venom through him.'

Cowlquape stared down in horror at the petal-shaped

marks all over the oakelf's exposed skin; at his dis-
coloured face, his swollen body. 'Blast you!' he howled,
and threw back his head. 'Blast you, Deepwoods!'

Twig pulled his young apprentice to his feet. He spoke
softly and urgently. 'Take care, Cowlquape. The
Deepwoods have ears. Believe me, I know.'

Cowlquape looked into Twig's eyes and fell silent. He
had, indeed, so much to learn about the Deepwoods.

Having buried Spooler deep within the roots of a lullabee tree as oakelf tradition demanded, Twig, Cowlquape
and Goom set off once again. Their spirits were lower
than ever. Twig cursed himself for not insisting that the
oakelf return with the *Skyraider*. All round them, the
forest seemed deeper and darker than before.

On and on they tramped. Up steep, grassy banks,
through marshy flats, over hillocks and hummocks and
rocky outcrops. Cowlquape was overwhelmed with an
aching tiredness that made every step an effort.
Brambles scratched his legs, branches slapped his face.
His legs ached. His stomach churned.

Overhead, the sun set on yet another day. The sky
darkened and the moon rose. Suddenly Twig stopped.
He stood stock-still, a look of wonder on his face.

'Shall I get some firewood?' said Cowlquape.

Twig shook his head. 'I don't believe it,' he murmured.

'Wh . . . what?' said Cowlquape, his eyes darting
round nervously.

Twig pointed to the ground at their feet. 'Look! There!'
he said.

'I can't see anything,' said Cowlquape. 'Twig, are you all right?'

'It's a path, Cowlquape,' said Twig. 'A *woodtroll* path.'

Cowlquape frowned. 'A woodtroll path?'

'Yes,' said Twig. 'I'd know it anywhere. The path has been flattened by generations of passing woodtrolls. See there, baked into the mud: it's a footprint. Look at the broad heel, the low arch, the stubby toes. Unmistakable. This is definitely a woodtroll path!' He looked up at Cowlquape, tears in his eyes. 'Once, long ago, I strayed from a path just like this. It was a mistake yet, as I came to learn, my destiny lay beyond the Deepwoods.' He sighed. 'Now I seem to have come full circle.'

'You think *this* is the path you strayed from?' said Cowlquape incredulously.

'All woodtroll paths join up,' said Twig. 'They form a network through the Deepwoods – to the lufwood groves, to the market clearings. They connect village to woodtroll village. If we stick to this path – *the* path – we will come to a woodtroll settlement. And woodtrolls trade with sky pirates! We're saved, Cowlquape! We're saved!'

'Well, what are we waiting for?' said Cowlquape, turning away. 'Let's follow the path!'

'I just can't believe it,' Twig whispered. 'After so many years, I've found the path again!' He looked up. 'Hey, wait for me, you two!' He stepped onto the path and hurried after Cowlquape and Goom.

The path wound and twisted, but never disappeared. With the moon shining down, it glistened brightly like the slimy trail of a barkslug. Often they came to forks in the path, sometimes to junctions where several paths met. At each one, Twig always chose which way to go without the least hesitation.

'All paths lead to other paths that lead to woodtroll villages,' he assured them. 'We can't go wrong.'

Cowlquape nodded. Yet the further they went, the more it seemed to him that the young captain was taking them in a specific direction.

Suddenly Twig stopped. 'Smell the air,' he said. 'That aromatic smoke is from scentwood. It's what woodtrolls burn in their stoves when they want to dream, and when . . .' He paused and cocked his head to one side. 'And can you hear that?' he whispered.

Cowlquape listened, and yes – there, behind the sounds of the night-creatures, was something else. 'Music,' he said, surprised.

'We must be very near a village,' said Twig.

They walked on a little further. The sound of sad singing voices filtered through the trees. Then the wind changed, and the lament faded away – only to return, louder than ever, a moment later. Deep voices, high voices, singing their own tunes yet all bound together by the sad underlying melody.

'Wuh-wuh!' said Goom.

'I know this music,' said Twig, a strange, haunted look on his face. 'Someone has died.' He turned to Cowlquape. 'They are performing their Ceremony for the Dead.'

Drawn on by the mournful song, the three of them continued along the path. Left, they went. Then left again. Then right. Abruptly, through the dense under-growth, the flickering yellow of torchlight appeared. Twig stopped in his tracks and trembled.

Cowlquape had never seen him like this before. Young. Uncertain. The years seemed to have fallen away, leaving the inexperienced woodtroll-lad within, exposed. His eyes glistened with tears and there was a sad smile on his face.

'Twig,' said Cowlquape, concerned. 'Is there some-thing the matter? Do you want to turn back?'

Twig shook his head. 'No,' he said. 'I'll be all right. It's just that I'd forgotten so much. I grew up in a village like this one, Cowlquape.' He peered ahead at the familiar woodtroll cabins secured high up in the trees. 'I lived in a lufwood cabin just like those . . . Still, enough!' Twig seemed to pull himself together. 'Keep close to me. And

if anyone stops us, I'll do the talking. Woodtrolls can be
very suspicious about uninvited arrivals – especially on
so solemn an occasion.'

They were on the edge of a clearing dominated by a
huge lullabee tree from which hung a caterbird cocoon.
It was in such cocoons, hatching places of the great cater-
birds, that the wise ones of the village – oakelves
normally – took up residence. Sleeping in the warm,
aromatic cocoons enabled them to share the dreams of
the widely-travelled birds.

It seemed as if every single woodtroll villager was out
there in the clearing, flaming torch in hand, as they
gathered round the tree. The music was coming from the
midst of the crowd directly beneath the cocoon.

As Twig and the others stepped forwards, the
ceremonial song reached its climax – a discordant howl
of grief that rose higher and higher. Twig hesitated. Row
after row of woodtrolls stood before him, their backs
turned, their heads bowed. The song came to an abrupt
end. The silence which followed was broken by a voice.
It came from the caterbird cocoon.

Twig gasped. He'd know that rich, cracked voice
anywhere. 'No,' he murmured. 'No, it can't be.' He
strained to get a better look over the bowed heads in
front. An ancient oakelf was sitting in the suspended
caterbird cocoon, high up in the great, spreading lullabee
tree.

'Taghair!' he breathed.

'You know him?' Cowlquape said.

'I . . . I can hardly believe it,' said Twig. 'It's like a

dream, Cowlquape. I have indeed come full circle. This isn't any old woodtroll village. This . . .' He swallowed away the painful lump in his throat. 'This is *my* village, Cowlquape. I've come home.'

'*From the sky we come and to the sky we go,*' the oakelf was reciting. '*Descending and ascending. This night we are here to commend to open sky, that his unencumbered spirit might once again fly free, the body of our beloved Tuntum, husband, father, friend . . .*'

'Tuntum? Did he say, Tuntum? No, it can't be true!' Twig wailed.

The woodtrolls spun round to see a tall, gangly individual with matted hair and a furry waistcoat hurtling

towards them. Outraged by the intrusion, yet too timid
to confront the wild-eyed stranger in their midst, the
crowd parted to let him pass.

Twig stopped in front of the lullabee tree, beneath the
cocoon. Before him stood the bereaved family. Huddled
together in their grief, they turned angrily as one to face
the unwanted intruder. Twig hardly dared believe it but,
yes, he knew them all – Snodpill, Henchweed, Poohsniff
– the half-brothers and sisters he never imagined he
would ever meet again. And there, looking smaller than
he remembered, was Spelda, the kindly woodtroll who
had taken him as a foundling-infant into her home and
raised him as her own.

'Mother-Mine!' he sobbed and ran towards her, arms open wide.

Spelda's jaw dropped. Her eyes grew wide. 'Twig?' she said. She gaped at his longcoat and parawings, the accoutrements of a sky pirate. 'Can it truly be you?'

Twig nodded, tearfully, bending to clasp her hands between his own.

'You came back,' Spelda whispered.

They stayed silent for a long time: the tall, young sky pirate and the little old woodtroll. At last Spelda drew back.

'I know you and he didn't always see eye to eye,' she said, 'but he never stopped loving you, Twig.' She sniffed and wiped her rubbery button-nose. 'Right to the very end.'

Twig looked down at the platform of bound scent-wood logs by his feet; the sky raft of buoyant lufwood which, when lit, would rise up into the sky. He looked at the shrouded bundle which was tethered to it.

'Can I see him?' he asked.

Spelda nodded. Twig stepped forwards and pulled aside the shroud of woodspider silk at Tuntum's head.

'He looks so peaceful,' said Twig quietly. 'How did he die?'

'In his sleep,' said Spelda. 'He'd been ill for several moons.' She smiled bravely. 'He was a good husband, and father . . .'

'The time is upon us,' came the oakelf's voice from above them.

Twig bent over and kissed Tuntum's forehead lightly, then fastened the shroud.

'Who will touch the pyre with the celestial flame?' asked the oakelf.

Snodpill stepped forwards and handed a burning torch to Spelda. She looked at it for a moment then, with a soft sigh turned to Twig. 'Can you still remember the words?' she said.

Twig nodded. He took the torch from Spelda's hand and raised it to the sky. Behind him the woodtrolls pressed their hands together in prayer.

'From the first lightning bolt you came, O, Sky flame!' Twig said.

'O, Sky flame!' the others murmured.

'Sky fire, light the pyre, return to open sky again, O, Sky flame!'

'O, Sky flame!'

Twig stooped and touched the burning torch to the base of the sky raft. There was a crackle and hiss; the next instant the entire construction was engulfed in sheets of purple flame.

'Return to open sky,' he murmured, as the blazing platform rose and hovered in front of them. The flames blazed all the more fiercely and the buoyant sky-raft with its precious cargo soared up towards the forest

canopy and away into the endlessness of open sky.
Twig watched it become a ball, a dot, a speck,
unable to tear his eyes away as it flew –
like a shooting star – across the
sky and away.

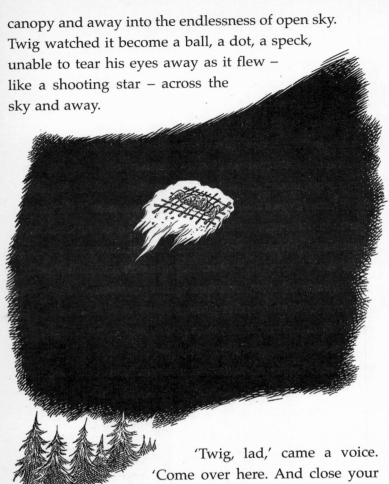

'Twig, lad,' came a voice.
'Come over here. And close your
mouth if you don't wish to swallow a
woodmidge.'

Twig looked up. The ancient oakelf's wise and kindly
ancient face was smiling down at him. He turned to
Spelda, who nodded. 'Go to him, Twig,' she whispered.

'Greetings to you, Taghair,' Twig called back, and
bowed low.

'Oh, such polite phrases and pretty graces,' Taghair replied. 'Let me get a closer look at you, lad.'

Twig stepped forwards.

'Come, we must talk,' he said, and nodded towards the suspended sling-chair. 'I take it you still remember how to use it.'

'Of course,' said Twig. He'd done it a hundred times or more as a youngster. He fastened himself into the hanging seat, pulled the rope and raised himself up into the air until he was high above the ground and face to face with the ancient oakelf himself, peering out of his caterbird cocoon.

'So,' said Taghair, slowly. 'You have come a long way, Twig. I've been expecting you.'

Twig's eyes lit up. 'You dream caterbird dreams, don't you?' he said. 'Was it the caterbird who told you to expect me?'

'No, Twig,' said Taghair. 'It was not your caterbird who informed me that you were on your way.' He leant down and touched Twig's glowing hand. His eyes twinkled. 'It was another who has been calling you – ever since his return from open sky.'

Taghair shifted across to one side of the opening. As he did so, an eerie luminous light streamed out from the depths of the cocoon.

'Captain Twig,' said a voice.

Twig peered in. His jaw dropped. 'Woodfish!' he cried out. 'It's you! But how ...? When ...? Where ...?'

Taghair chuckled. 'Always were a one for questions, weren't you?' he said.

Woodfish the waterwaif leant forwards. His fan-like ears fluttered. 'At your service, captain,' he said. 'I knew you'd make it!'

'B ... b ... but how is this possible?' Twig spluttered. He looked from one to the other.

Taghair breathed in noisily. 'I believe it was no accident that Woodfish's *shooting star* fell so close to the woodtroll village where his beloved captain grew up. He was drawn to it, you might say,' he explained. 'The woodtrolls found him and brought him to me. He has been here ever since. Waiting.'

'Waiting?' said Twig.

'Waiting for you,' said Taghair.

'I can read thoughts, as you know,' Woodfish broke in. 'All waifs can. But Taghair, here, taught me how to dream.'

'And he proved an excellent pupil,' said Taghair solemnly. 'He dreamt of you lying, broken, in the Stone Gardens below faraway Sanctaphrax.'

'You did?' said Twig.

Woodfish smiled. 'Yes, Captain Twig,' he said. 'And I dreamt of the others, too: Tarp in the taverns, Wingnut Sleet and Bogwitt in the sewers, poor Spooler on the slave ship, and Goom in the hands of the shrykes. My dreams touched all of them.'

'He guided you to them, Twig,' said Taghair. 'With a

whisper here and a word there, he told you which way to go. And then he guided you here.'

Twig's jaw dropped. 'You!' he said to Woodfish. He remembered the little sibilant whisper he'd heard so many times – urging him into the Lullabee Inn, drawing him away from the cloddertrogs, helping him to select the *Skyraider* from the numerous sky ships on offer at the posting-pole, guiding him along the woodtroll path. 'It was *you* all the time!'

Woodfish nodded. 'Every step of the way, captain,' he said. 'Though I couldn't have done it by dreaming alone. I needed your courage, your stubbornness and most of all, your loyalty. We *all* needed that.' His rubbery mouth broke into a smile. 'And we still do.'

Twig stared back. 'You discovered *all* the crew?'

'I did,' Woodfish confirmed.

'So the last crew-member,' said Twig excitedly. 'The Stone Pilot. Is the Stone Pilot alive?'

'Yes,' Woodfish said simply.

'Where?' said Twig. 'Tell me where, Woodfish. We must set forth at once.' His head was in a spin. 'And do you remember what happened out there in open sky?' he pressed. 'What happened to the *Edgedancer*? And my father – Woodfish, did we find my father?'

'I don't know,' said Woodfish, the barbels at the corners of his mouth quivering as he shook his head. 'I remember nothing of what happened after we entered the weather vortex. But I know what lies ahead.'

'What does lie ahead, Woodfish? Tell me,' said Twig urgently.

'When I dream of it,' said Woodfish, 'my dreams go dark. We must go into the darkness, Captain, and beyond that. At the very edge of my dreams, the Stone Pilot is waiting.'

'But where, Woodfish? Where?' Twig was almost shouting now.

Woodfish looked at Taghair, then back at Twig. 'On the other side of the deepest, blackest part of the Deepwoods,' he said, 'where all creation began ... *Riverrise!*'

·CHAPTER SEVENTEEN·

THE DEEPWOODS' DARK HEART

Despite Spelda's best endeavours, Twig could not be persuaded to stay in the woodtroll village a moment longer than necessary. He was packed up and ready to leave long before sunrise.

'I shall come back, Mother-Mine,' he said. 'Now that I've found you, I won't lose you again.'

'You promise?' said Spelda.

'I promise,' said Twig.

Spelda nodded sadly, and wiped away a tear. 'Take these,' she said. 'Some extra provisions for your long journey. Food and drink. Warm cloaks.' She sniffed. 'Your father's axe.'

Twig held the familiar axe in his hands. 'Thank you,' he said.

Spelda smiled bravely. 'Tuntum always hoped that you might one day have it.' She rummaged in the pockets of her dress, and pulled out a talisman on a leather thong. 'And this is from me,' she said tearfully. 'A charm.' She reached up and tied it around his neck. 'It will protect you in those dark places you must go . . .' She shivered. 'And guide you safely back to me.'

'Begging your pardon, captain, but we must go,' said Woodfish. 'We have a long journey ahead.'

Twig bent down and kissed Spelda on her forehead. 'Bid farewell to Taghair for me,' he said. 'And don't worry!'

Spelda nodded. 'And don't you go forgetting your promise,' she said. She wiped her tears away. 'Go now,' she said. 'And Sky protect you.'

Twig turned away. The others were already heading out of the village back towards the path. He walked steadily after them. He didn't look back.

'She loves you very much,' said Cowlquape, when he caught up. The glow from the village lanterns and the babble of woodtroll voices faded away behind them.

'Spelda?' said Twig. 'She was the finest mother anyone could hope for. And, looking back, Tuntum loved me also – he just found it harder to show it.'

Cowlquape smiled weakly. He thought of his own bully of a father, Ulbus Pentephraxis, who would beat him as soon as look at him. Yet here was Twig, with *two* fathers – Tuntum and Cloud Wolf – and he was about to tell Twig how much he envied him his memories when Woodfish came to an abrupt halt. They were standing in front of a gnarled tree, festooned with hooks and rings.

'The Anchor Tree,' said Twig. 'This marks the

woodtroll village boundary.'

Woodfish nodded. 'We must strike out on our own from here.'

A single bolt of lightning darted across the sky, followed by an ominous rumble of thunder. Rain – heavy and warm – began to fall. Twig fingered the amulet Spelda had just given him.

'Time for me to stray from the path once again,' he said softly.

The forest grew denser as they went further from the woodtroll path into the Deepwoods. The rain eased off and high up above their heads the sun rose on another day. And another. And another – until they seemed to have been walking for ever. Beneath the forest canopy, it remained dark and gloomy. Cowlquape hated it. The air was close, windless, and he was continually panting to keep up with Twig and the others.

The Deepwoods were as menacing as ever. Flesh-eating pods snapped at him greedily as he scurried past. Scaly tree-creatures bared their teeth at him from the branches overhead, the spikes down their back quivering menacingly. A bulging, yellow wood-python – basking in a shaft of sunlight after a recent meal – slithered into the undergrowth as he stumbled close. And all the time, the forest itself grew more and more impenetrable as the days passed. Cowlquape gritted his teeth and struggled on, deeper and deeper.

Now, up ahead, Goom began having problems

hacking through the undergrowth. The thorny brambles which had been dogging their way for an hour or more were becoming thicker, more tangled; their barbs, the size of daggers. One of the banderbear's shoulders was already matted with blood.

'Ease off, old friend,' said Twig. 'Those thorns are sharp.' He pulled Tuntum's axe from his belt. 'Let Woodfish and me go first.'

Woodfish drew his cutlass. 'And keep your wits about you,' he warned. 'Even this inhospitable forest of thorns is home to dangerous predators.'

Cowlquape shivered, and glanced round nervously. He followed Twig and Woodfish into the tunnel they were hacking out. His senses were on fire – ears listening for any suspicious sound, nose twitching, eyes peeled. Progress was painfully slow. Every step they advanced was a struggle. They rested up increasingly often, and for longer periods of time.

'This is hopeless,' Cowlquape complained as, for the third time in as many minutes, Twig let his axe fall limp at his side. 'We're lost in this terrible thorny place. We'll never find our way out.'

Twig turned to him, his face shiny with sweat.

'Woodfish is our guide, Cowlquape, and we must trust him. We are in his world now.'

The waterwaif shook his head. 'This is merely the beginning of the Nightwoods,' he said. 'True waif country lies beyond the great thorn forests.' He sighed. 'I thought I'd escaped it for good. It is an evil place.'

Cowlquape frowned. 'You speak harshly of the place you were born and raised,' he said.

Woodfish returned his puzzled gaze. 'Life in waif country is a short and brutal affair,' he explained. 'A hand-to-mouth existence with none of the things you take for granted, Cowlquape. Hot meals, comfortable beds . . .' He smiled. 'Ancient barkscrolls. Besides,' he went on, 'I daresay I am not the only one to take little pride in his origins.'

Cowlquape nodded sadly. 'And beyond the waif country?' he said.

'The Dark Heart of the Deepwoods,' said Woodfish. 'And perhaps Riverrise.'

'*Perhaps* Riverrise?' said Cowlquape. 'You mean you don't know.'

'I have never been to Riverrise,' said Woodfish. 'Nor has any soul I've ever heard of. But you know that, Cowlquape. It is written in those barkscrolls you treasure. Riverrise has been lost, forgotten since the passing of Kobold the Wise. Yet it is said that it lies at the very heart of the Deepwoods.'

'But you can't know that for sure, for all your dreaming and waif ways,' wailed Cowlquape.

Twig smiled and lifted his axe over his head. 'Don't let

your courage fail you now, Cowlquape,' he said. The axe came crashing down, slicing through half a dozen of the thick woody brambles. 'After all, we can't abandon our search here. Woodfish did dream that the final member of the crew is at Riverrise waiting for us. It must exist – and now we must find it.' The axe crashed down again. 'And wouldn't you love to actually see Riverrise – to walk where Kobold the Wise once walked?'

'Yes,' said Cowlquape meekly. 'Yes, I would.'

They went on. The sun passed unseen across the sky and set. Later, the moon rose. It was only when the splinters of moonlight pierced through the thorn-bushes that Twig realized how much time had passed. He laid his axe aside, heavy with fatigue, dripping with sweat.

'We'll rest up here,' he panted.

Cowlquape looked round. With the thorn-bush surrounding them and the uneven boulders beneath their feet, it didn't look too promising. But once Twig and Goom had hacked out a larger clearing, and they'd all removed the rocks and laid out their cloaks on the sand below, it wasn't too bad. Of course, a hot, bright fire would have been nice, but with the bushes all round them so dry, they dared not light one. One spark and the whole lot was likely to go up. Thankfully, it was a warm enough night, and the glowing sky pirates themselves provided enough light to see by. Cowlquape wondered once again what it was that made Twig and his crew shine so brightly. Something *must* have happened to them all out there in open sky. But what?

Woodfish heard his thoughts. 'It is a question I have

asked myself a thousand times,' he said. 'Perhaps it is to remind us of something important that happened.' He shrugged. 'Sadly, as I told the captain, I have no memory of what took place after we entered the weather vortex.' He nodded at Goom and Twig. 'And unfortunately, neither have they.'

'We can worry about the past later,' said Twig. 'For now, we must get some sleep.' He laid himself down on the soft sand and wrapped about him the thick cloak, which abruptly extinguished the glow from his body.

Cowlquape turned to Woodfish. 'When will we get to waif country?'

'Sleep, Cowlquape!' said Twig, without looking up. 'The more tired you are, the longer it'll take.'

All round them the thorns clicked as a chilly breeze blew through the surrounding bushes. Cowlquape lay down between Twig and Goom, and pulled his cloak up around his shoulders. Woodfish settled himself last. Awake or asleep, the waterwaif would hear any intruders. As he wrapped his cloak around him, the whole clearing was plunged into darkness.

Refreshed and rested, the four travellers were up early the following morning, and taking it in turns to hack at the wall of thorns once more – first Twig and Woodfish, then Cowlquape and Goom. They made good headway and at midday, Woodfish announced that their ordeal was almost over.

'Let me take over,' said Twig, seizing his axe off Cowlquape. And he began chopping at the thick brambles like a creature possessed. 'Yes!' he called back a moment later. 'I can see it. I can see the end of the thorn-bushes.'

Half a dozen well-positioned swings of the axe later, and Twig was through.

'So far, so good,' he panted.

The others crawled through the narrow gap and straightened up. Cowlquape looked around and trembled with horror. The relief he'd felt at escaping the clutches of the thorn-bushes instantly melted away. Before them lay waif country.

It was a dreary place, marshy underfoot, foul-smelling, and so dark that Cowlquape would have been blind had it not been for his three glowing companions. As he stared about him at the gnarled trees, encrusted with dripping moss and oozing fungus, which loomed from the shadows like fearsome monsters, he almost wished he were.

'Where now, Woodfish?' he heard Twig asking.

The waterwaif was crouching down with his large fluttering ears close to the ground. He looked up and pointed into the darkness of the dismal forest ahead. 'The heart of the Deepwoods lies in that direction,' he said.

It was a hard slog through the cold, dank forest. The

air was brittle with eerie stillness. There was no bird-song. No creature-cry. Every time a twig was cracked by a passing boot, or a pebble kicked, the sound ricocheted from tree to tree, and off into the darkness.

Cowlquape stumbled blindly on. His sodden feet had blistered and swelled. His face and hands were criss-crossed with cuts from spiny creepers he never saw until it was too late. Reduced to eating the bark and fungus that Goom selected as edible, Cowlquape's stomach cried out for food; proper food – yet he did not complain.

By night, they slept in makeshift hammocks fashioned from their cloaks and ropes, strung out between the branches of the trees. By day they walked. And walked and walked. It was on the seventh day that Woodfish discovered running water.

'Look at it,' he said, staring down at the tiny stream trickling through the centre of a broad river basin. 'This used to be a raging torrent. No wonder we've seen no sign of life for so long.'

Cowlquape crouched down at the sandy edge. 'So long as it quenches my thirst, I don't mind how little there is.' He cupped his hands and slurped at the clear water.

Woodfish turned to Twig. 'The running water marks the beginning of true waif territory.' His fan-like ears trembled. 'They are all around us. I can *hear* them.'

'I can't hear anything,' said Cowlquape, looking up.

'Yet, they are there,' said Woodfish nervily. 'Waterwaifs. Flitterwaifs. Barkwaifs. Nightwaifs . . . Put your cloaks on, all of you. Raise the hoods over your heads to dim your glow. We must not draw attention to ourselves.'

'It's so dark,' said Cowlquape nervously. 'How will we find our way?'

'We follow the stream,' said Woodfish. 'She will lead us to the heart.'

'But what if we lose one another?' Cowlquape whimpered.

'We'll rope ourselves together,' said Twig. 'Don't panic, Cowlquape.'

'No, don't panic, whatever you do,' said Woodfish. 'Waifs will be attracted by fearful thoughts.'

Cowlquape groaned. Now, on top of everything else, he had to pretend not to be scared.

'Follow me,' Woodfish told them. 'Stay close. And whatever voices you may hear, ignore them as best you can.'

Gripping the rope that was strung between them, the four of them stumbled on through the darkness, following the water upstream. Cowlquape fixed his thoughts on the stories he'd read in the barkscrolls and imagined what Riverrise might be like.

'*This way,*' whispered a voice. '*It's over here.*'

Cowlquape hesitated. He looked round. Two round eyes glowed in mid-air some way to his left, staring, unblinking. Woodfish tugged his cloak sharply.

'Keep going,' he warned. 'Don't let them into your thoughts.'

But the voices continued. Sometimes tempting, sometimes pleading; always soft and seductive.

'*Come this way,*' they crooned. '*You'll be all right. Trust*

us – *please trust us. If you're not too timid. If you're not too* scared.'

'Ignore them,' Woodfish's voice broke into their minds, calm and reassuring. 'We must keep going.'

The eyes glinting in the invisible branches increased in number. Twenty. Fifty. A hundred pairs stared down at them as they stumbled on through the dark forest.

'*Follow us; follow,*' the voices sighed, and in their soft invitation, Cowlquape heard the promise of something he couldn't ignore. '*Kobold the Wise came this way. Let us show you, Cowlquape.*'

He let go of the rope.

'*Twig, Riverrise is so close. So close, Twig,*' whispered the voices. Twig hesitated.

'Captain Twig!' Woodfish's voice in his ear was urgent. 'Do not listen to them, Cowlquape . . .'

'But they're waifs, Woodfish,' said Twig. 'Like your good self. Like Forficule, a nightwaif I once knew in Undertown . . .'

'We are not in Undertown now. These are *wild* waifs,

and they are hunting us. They're *hungry*, captain,' said
Woodfish sharply. 'They're . . .' He peered back along the
line and grimaced. 'Sky above! Where *is* Cowlquape?'

Twig looked about him, unable to see anything at all,
apart from the gleaming eyes. 'Has he gone?' he said.

'He has,' said Woodfish, scanning the darkness. He
crouched down, ears twitching. 'Wait, I think I hear him.
I . . . Oh, no!'

'*This way, Cowlquape, that's right,*' chorused the unseen
voices.

'Quick!' said Woodfish. 'He's still close by. You stick
with me, Captain Twig,' he said as he seized him by the
arm and dragged him away from the river-bed and off
into the darkness. 'Stay close, Goom,' he called back.

They stumbled and groped their way through the
dark forest.

'Calm your thoughts,' urged the waterwaif. 'I must
listen.'

'*Kobold the Wise once trod this ground, Cowlquape,*'
murmured the voices.

'Yes, there he is!' said Woodfish. 'This way!'

The terrain grew wilder, more treacherous. Black logs littered the forest floor, impeding their progress. Bindweeds and barbed knotweeds slowed them down still more.

'They're getting away with him,' Twig gasped as the light grew dim far in front of them. 'Oh, Cowlquape,' he whispered. 'Cowlquape.'

'Wuh-wuh!' grunted Goom.

'Quiet!' said Woodfish. He stopped to crouch low to the ground again.

'Just a little further, Cowlquape. That's right.'

Woodfish shuddered. 'We haven't much time!' he said.

They bounded on into the darkness, Woodfish now on Goom's shoulders in front, crashing through the undergrowth, carving out a path for Twig to follow. Ahead they could see countless pairs of eyes, dropping down from the trees onto the forest floor and gathering in a circle.

'Kneel down, Cowlquape. Rest your head. You're so tired, so very tired . . .'

'What's going on?' Twig panted.

'I told you,' Woodfish muttered. 'The waifs are hungry, and they're closing in for a kill.'

Goom burst onto the scene. The waifs darted back in alarm and flew into the surrounding trees, hissing and mewling. All, that is, apart from the ones already attached to Cowlquape's twisted body. Woodfish shuddered. 'Flitterwaifs,' he said. 'I might have known!'

Twig stared at the dark creatures. They had stubby legs, broad, membraned wings and flattened faces, with jagged fangs that jutted down at an angle from their top jaw. It was these fangs which were biting into Cowlquape's back, his leg, his neck . . .

'Get off him!' Twig roared. He drew his sword and dashed forwards. He plunged the blade through the flitterwaif on Cowlquape's back and, tossing it aside, slashed at the one on his leg. Spitting and snarling, the creature flapped its wings and flew up into the branches with the rest. The flitterwaif at Cowlquape's neck turned and fixed Twig with its blazing eyes. The jagged fangs glinted. Twig gripped the sword tightly. He would have to be careful not . . .

'. . . *to sever Cowlquape's neck,*' the flitterwaif completed for him. '*You wouldn't want to do that, captain,*' it said, and hissed malevolently.

Twig's eyes narrowed. Since the creature could read his thoughts he would have to act suddenly, to take it unawares . . . No! Don't think, don't think . . . just . . .

With a sudden *swoosh,* the great sword leapt forwards,

flew down through the air and sliced off the flitterwaif's head in one deadly movement. Twig breathed a sigh of relief and sank to his knees. He hadn't even scratched Cowlquape's throat – yet Cowlquape was in a bad way. He seemed to be unconscious.

'Help me move him,' Twig called to the others. 'Goom, can you carry him away from here?'

'Wuh,' the banderbear grunted, and picked Cowlquape up in his massive arms.

'*You can't escape.*' '*You'll never make it!*' '*Leave the boy behind,*' the flitterwaifs hissed furiously as they flapped around in the trees above them. They were ravenous. They smelt blood and sensed fear. Food so succulent was hard to find in the Nightwoods and they weren't about to surrender their prey without a fight. All at once, one of their number tilted its wings and dive-bombed. Others followed suit.

'*Aaargh!*' Woodfish screeched, as three sharp claws slashed at his face. He swung his cutlass. Twig gripped his father's great sword tightly. They took up positions on either side of Goom and staggered on blindly, stabbing and thrusting at the darkness – and as the flitterwaifs continued their frenzied bombardment, so the travellers' heads were filled with the shrill voices of their attackers.

'*Give him up!*' they screeched. '*Leave the boy. He's ours!*'

'What do we do, Woodfish?' said Twig nervously. 'We're never going to outrun them.'

Without saying a word, Woodfish crouched down and began heaping lumps of the claggy mud beneath his feet on top of one another. Then, reaching up to the youth in Goom's arms, he removed his cloak and wrapped it around the large shapeless form he'd constructed.

'Right, let's get out of here,' he whispered. 'And as we leave, I want you all to *think* about how sad it is that we have had to abandon Cowlquape to his fate.'

'Don't go. Not that way,' the flitterwaif complained. *'Leave the boy, or you'll be sorry!'*

As Twig continued into the darkness he did as Woodfish had told him, concentrating on what an awful tragedy it was that his young friend had been left behind. Goom and Woodfish were doing the same. They hadn't gone more than a hundred strides when the flitterwaifs began to fall back.

'It's working,' came Woodfish's voice inside his head. 'Keep it up.'

I'm so sorry to leave you here, Twig thought. But we'll be back for you soon, Cowlquape. I give you my word!

Behind them now – and further behind with every step they took – the flitterwaifs were converging on the cloaked heap of mud. It sounded right. It smelled right. Yet the youth was not there. All at once, a far-off howl of rage echoed through the trees as the waifs realized that they had been tricked.

Woodfish turned and mopped his brow. 'We've lost them,' he said. The waterwaif knelt and listened again, ears close to the ground. 'I hear water. We're very close.'

'Close to what?' Twig asked.

Woodfish gestured ahead. 'The Deepwoods' black heart.'

*

At the top of the Loftus Tower in Sanctaphrax, the Professor of Darkness was close to despair. The barometer needle was rising and falling, seemingly at will. The tacheometer was broken, as were the dynamometer and anemometer, while the fragile woodmoth material of the sense-sifter was hanging in tatters. Every single one of his precious instruments was being battered to bits. And if he was unable to collect the relevant data, then what was he to tell the academics and apprentices who were relying on their Most High Academe to come up with a reason for the sudden change in the weather?

He crossed to the broken window and, shielding his eyes from the searing blast of air, looked down on his beloved floating city. There wasn't a single building which didn't bear the scars of the ravaging storms. Statues had been toppled. Towers had collapsed. Debris littered the ground. And there were gaping holes in every roof where slates had been torn away by powerful twisters which had swept in from open sky the previous night.

It was little wonder that there were whispers going round the dusty corridors about evacuating the floating city. To remain on the great floating rock, so exposed to the incoming storms, seemed more and more foolhardy by the day. Yet, for the Professor of Darkness, leaving Sanctaphrax was unthinkable. It was his sanctuary, his home – his life. And he had the three sky pirates to consider too. Tarp, the slaughterer, and Bogwitt, the goblin, were adamant that they were to stay until Twig returned – even if the weasely Wingnut Sleet did not seem so convinced . . .

'Oh, Sky preserve us,' he muttered unhappily to himself. 'Where is this all going to end?'

*

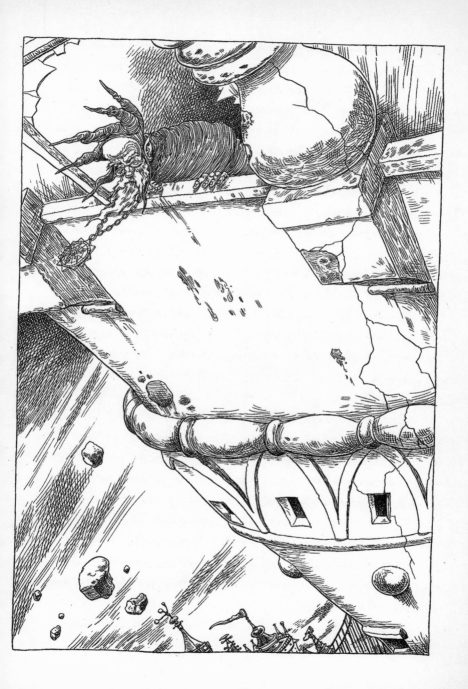

Drawn on by the sound of running water, Woodfish continued through the dark forest with the others following close behind. In Goom's arms, Cowlquape stirred.

'I'm sorry,' he moaned. 'I didn't mean to . . . They said Kobold the Wise . . . They said . . .'

'It's all right, Cowlquape,' said Twig. 'You're safe now. Do you think you can walk?'

'I think so,' said Cowlquape as Goom put him gently down. 'It's all my fault, Twig . . .'

'Quiet!' said Woodfish. His fan-like ears quivered. 'I sense great danger. We're not out of waif country yet.'

They edged forwards step by faltering step, each holding the shoulder of the one in front, with Woodfish leading the way. The forest was black and, with their hooded cloaks masking their luminous glow, the three sky pirates were invisible. Behind them followed Cowlquape, shivering with cold and weakened by the attack on him. Although he had no glow to mask, he missed the warmth of his abandoned outer cloak. A deep silence fell, as impenetrable as the darkness.

Then Twig saw them, just ahead – waif eyes glinting from the surrounding trees. He took a sharp intake of breath. How could they possibly survive another attack?

'This way!' cried Woodfish suddenly, his fan-like ears fluttering. 'Follow the sound of the water. And don't listen to the waifs!'

Stumbling wildly, the four travellers carried on through the lurching forest, the eyes dancing in the trees ever closer, and fearful whispers invading their thoughts again.

'You'll never escape! You'll never get away!'

'Stay! Stay here with us . . .'

'Twig!' Cowlquape moaned. 'I can't . . .'

'You must, Cowlquape!' Twig urged him breathlessly. 'Just a little further . . . I can hear the water now.'

'NO!' came an anguished cry, and the waterwaif disappeared from view.

'Woodfish!' Twig cried.

The next moment he and Cowlquape reached the edge of the dark, boggy ground. The land fell away abruptly before them, steep and strewn with boulders. And there was Woodfish, his faintly glowing figure tumbling down over the scree, far beneath them. Cowlquape groaned with dread.

Behind, the intensity of the whispers grew to a mounting crescendo. The air trembled with flapping wings.

'Wuh?' Goom grunted.

The bell-like sound of trickling water echoed up out of the gloomy abyss.

Cowlquape hesitated. 'This can't be right,' he shouted to Twig. 'This can't be Riverrise!'

'We must go on!' Twig cried. 'We must follow Woodfish!'

Before he knew what was happening, Cowlquape felt his arm being tugged, and he was pulled forwards onto the treacherous slope beside Twig. Down he hurtled, his feet slipping on the sliding gravel scree.

All round them, the desolate howl of the thwarted waifs echoed through the air. Even they would not venture down into the rocky abyss.

'Aaaaiii!' Cowlquape screamed with pain.

His ankle had gone over. He tumbled to the ground, but kept falling down the long, steep slope. Down, down, amid a tumbling mass of rock and stone. Bouncing. Crashing. His knee struck a boulder. His face and hands were cut. His head slammed down against the ground.

Then nothing . . .

'The water, Cowlquape,' came a voice. *'Go to the water, and drink.'*

Cowlquape looked up. There before him, standing next to a deep pool at the base of a mighty waterfall, was a tall, crowned figure with embroidered robes and a long plaited beard. His warm, sorrowful eyes seemed to stare right through into Cowlquape's spirit. Every inch of him ached; his head throbbed and a sharp pain stabbed up from his legs as he tried to move.

'You,' he murmured softly.

'*Yes,*' said Kobold the Wise. '*It is I,
Cowlquape.*' He dipped his finger
in the pool and wiped it along
Cowlquape's lips. '*The water,
Cowlquape,*' he said. '*You must
drink the water. It will restore
you. It is the water of Riverrise.*'
He smiled. '*So much awaits
you, Cowlquape,*' he said, as
he turned and walked off
behind the waterfall. '*But
first, drink the water.*'

The dream ended. Cowlquape stirred. And back came
the pain. Every bone in his body felt as if it had been
snapped in two. His nails were ragged and torn. Blood,
from deep gashes across his forehead, trickled down his
face.

Then he heard water trickling, and opened his eyes.
There *was* a pool there. It was smaller and darker than
the one of his dreams, and the mighty waterfall no more
than a trickle. *Drink the water.* The words of Kobold the
Wise filled Cowlquape's head.

He looked round. The others lay near him. With a jolt, he
saw that their motionless bodies were glowing no more.

Drink the water.

Wincing with agony, Cowlquape rolled onto his front.
Slowly, painfully, he pulled himself along the ground
with his one good arm, inch by terrible inch.

Drink the water.

At the edge of the pool at last, Cowlquape stared
down at his battered reflection in the rippled water – the
gash, the torn ear, the blood . . . He reached down and
scooped at the water with his hand. It was cool and
velvety. He brought it to his mouth, and sipped.

A shimmering warmth coursed through his veins in

an instant. He drank some more. The terrible racking
pains vanished and the wounds stopped throbbing.
When he'd drunk his fill, Cowlquape wiped away the
blood and inspected his reflection a second time. There
wasn't a scratch on him.

'The water of Riverrise,' he gasped.

Once, twice, three times, he cupped his hands in the
pool and carried the cool, restoring water to his
companions. He let it trickle down over their lips, into
their mouths, and watched with unbounded joy as their
eyes flickered and the soft familiar luminosity began to
glow from their bodies once again.

Twig looked up, his eyes wild with fear. 'Cowlquape!'
he gasped. 'Falling . . . falling . . .'

'Don't speak, Twig,' said Cowlquape, as he helped the young captain to his feet. 'Come with me to the pool, and drink.'

One by one, Twig, Woodfish and Goom slaked their thirst with the cool, life-giving waters. They drank away their injuries, their misgivings, their fears.

Twig looked up, and followed the thin trickle of water which threaded down the rock face from a jutting ledge far, far above their heads. 'What is this place?' he said.

'We are at the foot of Riverrise,' said Cowlquape excitedly. 'This, this is her water!'

Twig stared up at the vertical rockface.

'It's this way, Twig!' said Cowlquape, jumping down into the pool and splashing through it. 'Behind the waterfall – or what now remains of it. Yes, there!' he exclaimed. 'Look, Twig!'

A narrow crack in the cliff-face, like a knife cut, sliced back into the rock. Cowlquape scrambled out of the water and stared up into the shadowy gap. The others splashed across the pool to join him.

'You see,' said Cowlquape. 'And look here,' he said, fingering the two symbols carved into the rock at the entrance. 'The trident and snake of . . .'

'Kobold the Wise,' Twig breathed. He turned to Cowlquape. 'But how did you know? Was this also in those precious barkscrolls of yours?'

Cowlquape shook his head, and smiled. 'I dreamt it,' he said simply.

Twig nodded. 'Then let us follow your dream,' he said. 'Lead us, Cowlquape. Lead us to Riverrise!'

·CHAPTER EIGHTEEN·

RIVERRISE

At first, the going was hard. Fallen rock debris littered the ground, and even Goom was forced down onto his hands and knees as he scrabbled up the narrow cutting. The sound of shifting gravel and bouncing pebbles echoed round the steep walls on either side.

'It's getting easier here,' Cowlquape called back. 'The path is firm – like steps.' He looked down. 'They *are* steps,' he whispered.

Twig caught him up, and the pair of them paused for a moment to look ahead. Rising up was a long winding staircase, carved out of the rock by the passing of countless feet.

Cowlquape shuddered with excitement. 'I am treading where *he* trod,' he murmured as he hurried ahead. 'I am walking in the footsteps of Kobold the Wise.'

Higher and higher, Cowlquape climbed. Not once did he falter. Not once was he short of breath. Abruptly, the air grew light. Cowlquape looked round and his heart gave a leap. At last – at long, long last – he was above the terrible canopy of the stifling Deepwoods he had feared he would never leave.

He hesitated, and looked up. White and yellow clouds swirled high above his head, offering tantalizing glimpses of the tall mountain peak beyond. He felt Twig's hand resting on his shoulder, and turned towards him.

'Listen to the water, Cowlquape,' said Twig. Cowlquape cocked his head to one side. The tinkling sound of the trickling stream had stopped. In its place was a soft yet insistent *plink plink plink* as the water dripped down into the pool, far below them. 'It's drying up,' said Twig grimly. 'And when the waters of Riverrise stop flowing . . .' He paused, puzzled by the words he had uttered.

'Yes, Twig?' said Cowlquape.

'When the waters of Riverrise stop flowing . . .' Twig repeated. He clutched his head with his hands. 'Oh, Cowlquape, why can I hear my father speaking these words? I . . . I . . . No, it's no good,' he said, the frustration clear in his voice. 'I just can't remember.'

'Come on,' said Cowlquape. 'Perhaps the answer lies at Riverrise.'

The air grew warmer as they continued upwards. The clouds came closer and closer still. Swirling, wispy, bewildering. All at once, the bright sun burst through, bathing everything beneath it in golden shadows.

'We're above the clouds!' Cowlquape cried out with

joy. 'And look!' He pointed ahead. The end of their climb lay so close.

Cowlquape ran forwards, his heart thumping with anticipation. Twig trotted by his side with Goom and Woodfish following close behind.

Far in the distance, a great caterbird – no more than a ragged dot against the tangerine sky – wheeled round. Its gimlet eyes scanned the high mountain tops for a moment. Then it flapped its broad wings, and soared off.

As the heads of the four travellers emerged above the upper ridge of rock, the dazzling sun filled their eyes. They raised their hands to shade them and squinted ahead.

Cowlquape gasped and fell to his knees. 'Riverrise,' he trembled.

Behind him, the sound of water echoed up from the pool far below them. *Drip. Drip. Drip.*

Side by side, the four travellers stared ahead in awe and elation at the magnificent scene spread out before them. They were standing on a great white marble slab over-looking the wide bowl of a once mighty lake, now no more than a shallow pool, which was fringed with luxu-riant vegetation.

There were emerald green trees, and bushes and shrubs, all laden with heavy fruit; and flowers – red and purple and yellow and orange and blue – which filled the air with a heady mix of perfumes.

'It's a huge garden,' Cowlquape breathed.

Before them, the quivering sun was sinking down

behind the western reaches of the lofty, gleaming pinnacles which ringed the whole area like a great, gold crown. Lengthening shadows raced towards them, down over the fertile gardens of the slopes and on across the shrunken, turquoise spring beneath their feet.

'Look there,' said Cowlquape, pointing. A jutting spur of rock stood out at the lake's furthermost point. 'That's where the water spills over into the pool below.' A single drip echoed up out of the stillness. 'This *is* Riverrise!'

The sun disappeared behind the marble rocks, silhouetting them against the dark red sky like a magnificent temple. Soon it would be dark. Twig turned to the water-waif.

'The Stone Pilot?' he said. 'Where is the Stone Pilot, Woodfish?'

Woodfish raised his hand for silence. His ears pricked up and quivered. He peered into the towering stacks of fluted marble down by the edge of the spring.

'What is it, Woodfish?' said Twig. 'Do you hear some-one . . . ?'

And then he heard it too. A soft rustling stirring the stillness. His breath caught in his throat. He stepped forwards, his body faintly glowing with luminous light. As he did so, a figure appeared on the other side of the spring. And as it came closer – moving in and out of the trees – it became clearer, and also began to glow.

Cowlquape found himself staring at a slim girl with pale, almost translucent skin and a shock of fiery hair. His jaw dropped. Surely this could not be the remaining missing crew-member? Yet, she was glowing . . .

'Wuh-wuh?' Goom grunted.

'Twig?' said Cowlquape. 'Is this girl the Stone Pilot?'

Twig made no reply. The girl came closer.

'Captain Twig?' she said tentatively.

'Maugin,' Twig whispered. 'It *is* you.'

'Yes, captain,' the girl said, running forwards and throwing her arms around him. A single drop of water dripped down from the lip of the rock. 'I knew you would come for me.'

'Didn't I swear I would never abandon any of my crew?' said Twig, and smiled. 'You are the last, Maugin.'

Maugin pulled away. 'The last?' she said.

'Yes, Maugin,' said Twig.

Far below, the drop splashed into the dark pool.

Maugin looked up shyly at Woodfish and Goom. 'But where are the others? Tarp Hammelherd? Spooler?'

Twig looked away. 'Spooler is dead,' he said sadly. 'But Tarp, Bogwitt and Wingnut Sleet are waiting for us back in Sanctaphrax.'

Maugin started back in alarm. 'In Sanctaphrax?' she said. 'But are they all right?'

Twig chuckled. 'They've been resting up in my study in the School of Light and Darkness,' he said. 'Safe and sound.'

'But, captain,' said Maugin. Her face looked tense. Fine lines puckered the corners of her mouth. 'Do you not remember what Cloud Wolf told you?'

Twig froze. 'Cloud Wolf?' he whispered. 'I . . . I don't remember, no.'

Maugin frowned. 'He told you what you must do,' she

said. 'On the *Stormchaser*, far out in open sky,' she added gently, trying to jog his memory. 'Before the white storm struck . . .'

'*Stormchaser*? White storm?' said Twig, shaking his head. 'I don't remember anything. None of us do,' he said, looking round at the others. 'Nothing at all, from the moment we entered the weather vortex . . .' He turned back to Maugin. 'But *you* do. Because you were clothed in your heavy, hooded coat, the storm did not fog your memory . . . Tell me what happened, Maugin. Tell me what you remember.'

The sound of another drop splashing into the pool echoed up through the air. Maugin turned away.

'Tell me!' Twig shouted. 'I must know!'

'Yes, tell him the thoughts in your head,' said Woodfish. 'Or I shall!'

Maugin sighed. 'You leave me no choice.' She breathed in, noisily, and looked up. 'With the caterbird gone – cut from its tethers by your own hand – I feared . . .'

'I cut the caterbird loose?' Twig gasped.

Maugin nodded. 'Do you want me to continue?'

'Yes,' said Twig.

'. . . I feared we would never find the *Stormchaser*. Yet find it, we did, becalmed at the still centre of the weather vortex. Your father, Cloud Wolf was waiting for you there.'

'My father,' Twig whispered, as a distant recollection

stirred deep within his memory. 'He spoke to me.'

Maugin nodded. 'He told you that the Mother Storm – that mighty storm which first seeded the Edge with life – was returning.'

Cowlquape shuffled about excitedly. It was what he had guessed all along.

'He explained how it would sweep in from open sky towards Riverrise, at the highest point of the Deepwoods,' Maugin continued, 'to rejuvenate the dying spring.'

'Yes, yes,' said Cowlquape, unable to remain silent a moment longer. 'Just as it's written in the barkscrolls.'

'Hush, Cowlquape,' said Twig sharply. Fragments of memory were beginning to come together. He looked up at Maugin. 'But Sanctaphrax lies in its path,' he said. 'Yes, *now I remember* . . . Cloud Wolf . . . he told me to . . . to cut the great Anchor Chain, didn't he?'

Maugin nodded. 'If the Mother Storm wastes her energy destroying Sanctaphrax, she will never reach Riverrise to bring new life to her waters,' she said. 'Then the stagnant darkness at the black heart of the Deepwoods will spread out, until every inch of the Edge has been swallowed up!'

'Sky above,' Twig moaned. 'What have I done?' He looked into Maugin's eyes. 'I was *there*, Maugin. In Sanctaphrax. I could have told them. The way our bodies glowed should have reminded me . . . Oh, if only I'd remembered what I had to do.' He turned to the others. 'We'll set off back at once. Maugin, you must come with us.' Then his face paled and he staggered to one side. 'Maugin,' he said desperately. 'Did I tell you *when* this had to be done?'

She shook her head.

Twig moaned. 'You had part of the story, Maugin. And I needed to hear it to unlock my memory, and remember the rest . . .' He faltered. 'The Mother Storm will return when . . .' His father's words came back to him with awful clarity, '. . . when the waters of Riverrise stop flowing . . .'

Maugin suddenly drew away. Her whole body was rigid, her gaze fixed on the spur of rock jutting out from the edge of the Riverrise spring.

'Twig!' said Maugin suddenly, seizing him by the arm. 'Twig, listen!'

Twig fell still. He cocked his head to one side. 'What?' he said. 'I can't hear anything.'

'Exactly,' said Maugin. 'It is silent.'

Twig frowned. 'What do you mean? I . . .' An icy shiver ran the length of his spine. The regular *drip drip* of the Riverrise water had stopped.

'The Riverrise spring has finally died,' said Maugin in a low voice. 'It can mean only one thing . . .'

Twig looked up, his eyes wide. 'The Mother Storm is

on her way,' he said. 'I remember everything now. She should reach here at dawn. But that will never happen. Instead, she will strike Sanctaphrax at the stroke of midnight, expending her energy uselessly – and the Edge will descend into darkness. I've failed,' he said bitterly. 'I've failed Cloud Wolf. I've failed Sanctaphrax. I've failed myself.'

Woodfish stepped forwards. 'Yet, perhaps there is a solution, after all.' He looked at Maugin, and his eyes narrowed. 'I can read it in her thoughts.'

'What?' said Twig. 'What is she thinking, Woodfish?' He turned to Maugin. 'Is there something you're not telling me?'

She looked away.

'Maugin!' said Twig. 'Please!'

'Do you want *me* to tell him?' said Woodfish.

Maugin swallowed back her tears. 'There's only one way of getting back to Sanctaphrax in time,' she said quietly. 'But at terrible risk.'

Twig's jaw dropped. 'By midnight?' he said. 'How?'

'But it's madness,' said Maugin. She glared at Woodfish. 'Just a foolish thought.'

'Tell me!' Twig demanded.

Maugin sighed. And although she stared back at him evenly enough, when she spoke, her voice was no more than a tremulous whisper.

'By sky-firing.'

·CHAPTER NINETEEN·

FLIGHT TO SANCTAPHRAX

Sky-firing! Twig blanched. It was a method the more unscrupulous captains – both sky pirates and leaguesmen – had of dealing with mutinous crew-members. The offending individual was tied to a burning length of buoyant wood and launched off like a rocket on a one-way trip into open sky. It was a horrific punishment, feared by all who took to the skies in ships. Surely Maugin couldn't really mean . . .

'I know it sounds insane, captain,' said Maugin. 'But instead of launching a blazing tree-trunk upwards, it could just be possible to calculate an angle of ascent that would take you in a wide arc over the Deepwoods and on to Undertown. But the risks are appalling. You could fall short and land in the Twilight Woods or the Mire, or overshoot Undertown entirely and disappear over the Edge itself. And even if, by some miracle, you did reach Undertown, the chances are you'd be a charred corpse when you hit the ground.'

Twig looked back at Maugin steadily. 'That's a chance I'm prepared to take,' he said.

'But, Twig,' said Cowlquape. 'You heard what she said. It would be certain death!'

'I must try,' said Twig firmly. 'It'll be certain death for Sanctaphrax if I don't. And for every single creature in the Deepwoods if the river is not rejuvenated. I *must* try.'

Cowlquape grasped Twig's hand. He was trembling; his breath came in gasps. 'Let *me* go in your place. Let *me* be sky-fired to Sanctaphrax. I am younger than you. Lighter. And what's the life of a failed apprentice compared with that of the finest sky pirate that ever lived?' He paused. 'And . . . and you could tie a message to my back addressed to the Professor of Darkness, just in case I didn't make it there alive . . .'

Twig smiled. 'You are not a failed apprentice, Cowlquape; you have served me well.' He shook his head. 'I can't ask you to do this. It is my task.'

'But Twig!' protested Cowlquape, tears in his eyes.

'Thank you,' said Twig, 'but I won't hear another word on the matter . . .'

'And yet the idea of someone accompanying you is not a bad one,' Maugin said thoughtfully. 'A stout tree should bear the weight of two passengers, and it would mean that if one blacked out, the other would still have a fighting chance. *I* shall go with you, captain.'

'You?' said Cowlquape incredulously.

'I am a Stone Pilot,' said Maugin. 'I have the knowledge and expertise. I should be the one to accompany Twig.'

Twig smiled and bowed his head. 'I'm very touched,' he said. 'But I must go alone.'

'But, captain!' protested Maugin.

'I'm sorry, Maugin,' said Twig. 'You and the rest of the crew have followed me faithfully for long enough. I risked all your lives by sailing into open sky. I've already asked too much of you.' He paused. 'Give me your expertise, not your life.'

Maugin took his hand. 'You have my life already,' she said.

They searched the luxuriant gardens of Riverrise for the tallest, stoutest, most buoyant tree they could find. At last, they settled on a magnificent silver-grey lufwood standing proud at the very edge of the still water of the spring.

'It seems almost a shame to cut down such a beautiful tree,' said Cowlquape with a faraway look in his eyes. 'I wonder how long it has stood here, drinking the waters of Riverrise. Why, Kobold the Wise might himself have sat in its shade.'

'It's a fine choice, captain,' said Maugin. 'It'll burn long and bright.'

'Let's get to work,' said Twig impatiently. 'Time is running out. The Mother Storm is on her way – and midnight is drawing closer and closer over Sanctaphrax.'

Goom felled the great tree with massive blows of Tuntum's axe; splinters of ash-grey lufwood peppered the air. At last the tree fell with what, to Cowlquape at

least, seemed like a sad, creaking sigh, followed by a tremendous crash.

While Goom stripped the branches, till all that was left was the trunk itself, Twig and the others – under Maugin's close supervision – set about feverishly lashing together a launching ramp from the stoutest branches.

'We must align the ramp with the east star, for there lies Sanctaphrax,' said Maugin. 'And angle it carefully. The flight's path must not be too high, or you'll never return to earth.'

'But how can you possibly judge the distance?' asked Cowlquape, shaking his head.

'I can't,' said Maugin bluntly. 'But I was a Stone Pilot before you were born. Flight is my trade. It's all I know. I must use all my experience – though even then it only comes down to making a good guess.' She turned away. 'Twig, you will have to keep your wits about you. We'll rope you to the very tip of the trunk with slip-knots that you can pull to release yourself when Undertown appears beneath you.'

'I understand,' said Twig.

As the sky darkened, they set the log against the ramp, angled to Maugin's satisfaction, and bundles of the leafy branches were arranged around the base in a tight cluster. Twig buttoned up his longcoat and tightened the straps of his parawings. Then, at Maugin's insistence, he was smeared all over with a thick covering of the cooling Riverrise mud from the water's edge.

'The mud will protect you from the intense heat from the flames,' she explained. 'And take this,' she added, handing him a small bottle. 'It contains the restorative water of Riverrise – though, Sky willing, you will not have to use it.'

Finally, Twig was lashed to the underside of the great tree trunk. Maugin secured the final slip-knot.

'Farewell, Captain Twig,' she whispered.

Twig twisted his head round and watched as Maugin climbed down the launching ramp and jumped to the ground. He looked along the length of the tree-trunk behind him, straight and streamlined for flight; and at the bundle of leaves bound to its base that, even now, Woodfish was waiting to ignite with the flaming torch in his hand.

'Wait for my signal,' called Maugin. 'Light those leafy branches first, exactly at the places I point out.'

'Stop!' shouted Cowlquape. He was running from the water's edge, his clothes covered in mud, hastily daubed. 'I can't let you go alone, Twig,' he cried. 'I can't!'

He shinned up the sloping lufwood tree and clung tightly to the trunk.

'We don't have time for this!' said Twig impatiently.

'Then move over, Twig,' said Cowlquape. 'Maugin, tie me into place. You said yourself that two stand a better chance than one.'

'You would really do this for Sanctaphrax?' said Twig. 'Even though it could mean death?'

'Not for Sanctaphrax,' said Cowlquape. 'For you, Twig.' He smiled. 'And perhaps also for Kobold the Wise.'

Twig turned to Maugin. 'Do as he says,' he told her.

Finally they were ready. Twig smiled down at his loyal crew-members standing on the ground below him.

'Wuh-wuh, T-wuh-g!' Goom called.

'My dreams will go with you,' said Woodfish. He bent down to the branches Maugin pointed to, one after another, and touched them with the burning torch. The oily leaves exploded into flame.

'I will be back!' Twig shouted above the roar of the blaze.

White hot inside the blazing branches, the base of the trunk caught fire. It hissed. It steamed. It juddered and shook, and then . . .

Tearing away from its tethers, the great burning tree-trunk blasted away from the scaffold and soared up into the sky – leaving a fan of orange sparks in its wake. The top of the tree, with its two tethered passengers, soon disappeared into the darkness, until only the blazing base could still be seen – a dot of light that grew smaller and fainter as it sped off on its perilous journey.

'Sky protect you, Twig!' Maugin whispered.

When the blazing tree launched itself into the air the upward force was so strong that it stole Twig's breath away and left him gasping for air. Face to one side, eyes clenched shut, he gripped the ropes that bound him to the trunk, and prayed they'd hold.

And still they were accelerating. The pressure was intolerable. His stomach sunk down to his toes. The blood rushed from his brain. His mouth was tugged down at the corners. At unimaginable speed, the tree hurtled over the Deepwoods with its living cargo. Any forest-dweller noticing it would have wished upon a shooting star in vain.

Feeling sick and light-headed Twig saw the moonlit canopy of burnished silver blurring past beneath him.

He gritted his teeth. His temples throbbed, his neck ached, his stomach churned with fear.

'Don't black out!' he told himself grimly, and prayed again that the knots would hold.

The caterbird's words of encouragement on board the *Edgedancer* came back to him. Crystal clear, as though his great wise protector had never left him after all, they whispered inside his head. *This too will pass*, they said. *This too will pass*.

Twig closed his eyes. Everything passes. Joy. Pain. The moment of triumph; the sigh of despair. Nothing lasts for ever – not even this . . .

Reluctantly, Twig opened his eyes. Travelling almost horizontally now, they seemed to be at the top of the flaming comet's great arc. The endless expanse of trees flashed past, far below him. Speed. Pressure. Unbearable heat. He heard Cowlquape groaning beside him.

The flames had consumed more than half of the great tree-trunk. Huge chunks of blackened cinder broke off and fell away and, as the flames came closer, the heat grew more and more intense. Neither Twig nor Cowlquape could stand it much longer. Their hearts thumped. Their hands trembled. Their bodies were bathed in sweat.

'Don't give up now,' Twig whispered. His head spun with weakness. 'Keep going . . .'

The great buoyant tree had passed its highest point, that much was certain. Grunting with effort, Twig peered ahead – and his heart gave a leap. Far in front of them, gleaming brightly beneath the silver moon, was the barren wasteland of the Mire. Twig had never been so happy to see the terrible, bleached landscape before. A moment later, they were above it – further off in the distance, the lights of Sanctaphrax glimmered.

Down, they were flying now. Lower and lower. The intense heat was staggering. Cowlquape's boots blistered. The hairs on Twig's hammelhornskin waistcoat shrivelled and fell limp.

Keep going, Twig urged himself again. Just a little longer . . .

Low in the sky, the great towers of Sanctaphrax gleamed in the moonlight. Beneath it, the squalid mess of Undertown sprawled down to and along the banks of the now waterless Edgewater River. It had dried up completely, Twig realized with a jolt. And now that the water from Riverrise had ceased to flow . . .

Cowlquape screamed.

The flames were roaring all round them and, despite the thick, protective layer of Riverrise mud, the pair of them were being baked alive. Twig turned to meet Cowlquape's panic-stricken gaze.

'Hold on,' he rasped. The boom-docks came into view. The farthest outskirts of Undertown passed below them. 'Now, Cowlquape!' Twig cried. 'Pull the ropes!'

The apprentice's eyes rolled back in their sockets and his head slumped forwards.

'COWLQUAPE!'

Beneath him, the great floating rock of Sanctaphrax passed by. Twig's head spun. What should he do? If he released himself, Cowlquape would hurtle on, over the Edge and into open sky. Yet if he tried to rescue him, Sanctaphrax itself might perish.

There was no choice.

Twig drew his knife and sliced through Cowlquape's binding ropes. They frayed and snapped, and the young apprentice was plucked from the stump of blazing wood by the wind. The parawings flew open and Cowlquape floated away.

Without missing a beat, Twig slipped the knot binding himself to the stubby remains of the once great tree, and flew up into the air after him. His parawings opened, and the silken folds billowed out behind him. Twig looked round nervously, half-expecting to see Cowlquape plummeting down to the ground. But no. There he was, gliding below him.

'Cowlquape!' he shouted and, by bringing his knees up and thrusting forwards, he tilted the angle of the parawings and swooped down towards him.

Cowlquape's face was as white as a sheet, but he was alive. And not only alive, but also – thank Sky – conscious once more.

'How do I steer these things?' he wailed.

'Don't even try,' Twig called back. 'You're doing fine. Just don't make any sudden movements!'

As they glided down, the last signs of ramshackle habitation fell away behind them. The land beneath became rocky and inhospitable. It sped up to meet them.

'There's no turning back now,' Twig cried. 'Prepare yourself for landing. Crumple and roll, Cowlquape!' he bellowed. 'Crumple and roll.'

The next moment Twig landed, followed immediately by Cowlquape. As they felt the ground beneath their feet, they let their legs relax and rolled over onto their sides. The baked mud cracked and fell away.

Twig was first up. He crouched down over the motionless body of his friend, unstoppered the little bottle Maugin had given him, and touched the Riverrise water to his lips.

Cowlquape opened his eyes at once and looked up.

'How are you?' Twig whispered.

'Apart from being burned and battered half to death, you mean?' said Cowlquape, sitting up.

Twig smiled. 'Can you walk?' he said.

'I . . . I think so,' said Cowlquape. 'Where are we?'

Twig looked round at the silvery stacks of rocks, each one larger than the one beneath. 'In the Stone Gardens,' he groaned.

Wisps of mist coiled up from the earth where the cold air touched the warm ground. A wind was getting up. Cowlquape shivered.

'The Stone Gardens,' he complained. 'But that's miles from Sanctaphrax!'

Just then, the air all round them filled with a flurry of wings. One by one, sleek white birds landed and loped towards them, forming an unbroken circle around the hapless pair. They scratched at the ground, they flapped their ragged wings, they stretched their necks forwards, opened their savage beaks and cawed menacingly. The smell of rotting meat filled the air.

'The ravens!' Twig muttered, drawing his sword. 'The white ravens!'

Cowlquape grasped his knife, and he and Twig stood back to back, weapons raised, in grim anticipation. Two against so many were impossible odds. Had they come so far only to fail here, almost within sight of Sanctaphrax?

'Listen to me,' he called out to them. 'You must listen to me.'

But the white ravens were in no mood to listen. They stabbed the air with their beaks and cawed all the louder. It could only be a matter of time before the bravest – or hungriest – of them broke ranks and attacked.

·CHAPTER TWENTY·

THE MOTHER STORM

The bright moon shone down impassively on the bleak scene in the Stone Gardens. Two individuals, the blades of their weapons glinting in the moonlight, stood together. In a circle around them, the flock of voracious white ravens scratched at the ground with their scythe-like talons.

'What do we do, Twig?' said Cowlquape.

'I . . . We . . .' Twig fell still. For the first time since he had set out on his quest to find his missing crew, he was at a loss to know what to do. Each one of the crew had been accounted for now, yet the quest was not over – or rather, it had changed. And if Sanctaphrax was not to be destroyed by the approaching Mother Storm, then Twig had to act – and act now.

All at once, the largest of the white ravens stepped forwards. It cocked its head to one side.

'Shooting star?' it croaked.

Twig's jaw dropped. Not only could the great bird speak, but it seemed to recognize him. 'Y . . . yes,' he said, nodding uncertainly.

'Friend of Professor of Darkness?'

'You know the Professor of Darkness?' Twig gasped.

'Kraan know,' the white raven acknowledged.

'Then you must help us . . .' Twig began, only to be drowned out by the raucous cawing of the restless flock.

Kraan turned and screeched at them to be silent, then looked back at Twig. 'Help you?' it said.

'I want you to deliver a message to the professor,' said Twig. 'An important message.'

'Important,' Kraan repeated.

'The Mother Storm will strike Sanctaphrax at midnight,' Twig said very slowly and clearly. 'The floating city must be evacuated at once. Tell him Twig is on his way.' He looked into Kraan's glassy yellow eyes, trying to guess what the bird might be thinking. 'Can you do that?'

Before the white raven could answer, the Stone Gardens were abruptly plunged into darkness. Everyone looked up. Curious dark clouds had swarmed in across the moon, where they squirmed and writhed; it was like looking into a barrel of woodmaggots.

The ravens croaked in unison – a raucous chorus of dismay.

At that moment, a bolt of jagged blue lightning hissed down through the sky and struck the ground nearby. Where it landed, the earth cracked and, as the smoke and dust cleared, the glinting surface of a newly emerging rock appeared from beneath the surface.

'This weather heralds the arrival of the Mother Storm,' said Twig grimly.

The white raven looked at him askance. 'You know what Professor of Darkness does not know,' he said suspiciously. 'How?'

'Because the secret was revealed to me,' said Twig, and pointed beyond the Edge. 'Out there, in open sky – where no professor has ever dared venture. Kraan, you must believe me. If you do not leave now, it will be *too late*. Too late for you, for me, for Sanctaphrax – *life on the Edge will end*.'

'Waaark!' cried the great bird. It beat its wings and rose up into the air. 'Waaark!' it shrieked again, and the circle of white ravens opened to let Twig and Cowlquape pass: they were not to be harmed. *'WAAARK!'*

'Find the Professor of Darkness,' Twig called. 'Give him my message.' Kraan wheeled round and flapped noisily off in the direction of Sanctaphrax. 'And Sky speed be with you,' Twig whispered.

The Stone Gardens receded behind them as Twig and Cowlquape hurried along the path that would take them to Undertown. All around them, the sky hissed and fizzed threateningly. Tendrils of flashing electric-blue light fanned out across the darkness. The Mother Storm was coming closer and the air was charged with her imminent arrival. Half an hour or more had already passed.

'Faster,' said Twig urgently, as he broke into a jog. 'Midnight is approaching. We must hurry.'

'I . . . I'm coming,' Cowlquape panted wearily.

Ahead of them, the spires and towers of Sanctaphrax glinted in the sparking air. And, as the wind grew stronger still, the entire floating city bobbed at the end of

the taut Anchor Chain like a bladder-balloon on a string.

Finally – and much later than Twig would have wished – the outskirts of Undertown came into view. Low wood-framed workshops with corrugated iron-wood roofs, a small tannery, a hull-rigging manufacturer's.

'Nearly there,' said Twig breathlessly.

Behind him, the sky had turned purple, while the electric-blue flashes grew more intense. They fizzed all round the magnificent buildings of Sanctaphrax and down the mighty chain which anchored it to the ground.

'This way,' said Twig, veering abruptly down a narrow alley lined with stalls of basketware and clay pots, still open for business despite the lateness of the hour. Cowlquape struggled after him, his legs rubbery and weak.

They turned left again. Then right. The whole of Undertown was buzzing, thronging. Goblins and trolls stood in anxious clusters looking up at the sky, pointing,

murmuring with disquiet. Something sinister was happening. Something that seemed worse than all the other recent storms put together.

Barging their way through the crowds, Twig and Cowlquape kept on. Right. Right again. Then left. And there it was – in the centre of an open paved area ahead of them – the mooring-platform for the great floating rock itself.

The place was already full of academics. They looked bewildered, frightened and, in their robes of office, out of place amidst the grime and chaos of Undertown. Twig glanced up at the floating rock, where overladen baskets were bringing still more of the citizens of Sanctaphrax down to earth. Kraan, the white raven, had obviously delivered his message and the professor had acted.

The air glistened and sparked, and a deafening clatter of thunder set the ground trembling. The gale-force wind howled down the narrow streets and round the square.

Head down, Twig strode directly towards the platform unimpeded; the gnokgoblins of the Anchor Chain guard had clearly abandoned their posts. He looked at the chain and sighed. No sword could ever sever its mighty links. He climbed up onto the plinth and crouched down to see how the end of the chain had been secured.

The mooring-block was an intricate contraption. An iron plate, with two raised arches in the middle, had been bolted through the platform and into the rock beneath. The end of the Anchor Chain was wound round a cogged-axle, with the final link fixed into place between the two arches by a massive levered cotter-pin. If Sanctaphrax was to be released, the cotter-pin would have to be removed. But how?

'A hammer, Cowlquape!' Twig shouted. 'I need a heavy hammer. For Sky's sake, find me one now.'

Cowlquape darted off into the crowd.

A cheer went up, and Twig looked round to see a stooped figure in black robes climbing from a basket which had just touched down near the dry fountain at the far side of the square.

It was the Professor of Darkness. Twig sighed with relief. If the Most High Academe of Sanctaphrax had left the floating city, then the evacuation must be almost complete.

And not before time, thought Twig, as a low, stomach-churning sound rumbled in the distance. It was the Mother Storm, and she was drawing near.

Where was Cowlquape with that hammer? Twig looked around for something – anything – that he might use to knock the cotter-pin free.

All at once, a brutal volley of hailstones – the size of ratbird eggs – hammered down on Undertown, smashing through windows, and turning fear to pande-monium as everyone ran screaming for cover. With his arm raised protectively, Twig looked up.

Boiling and bubbling, flashing and flickering, an immense ball of pitch-black cloud was tumbling in across the night sky towards them.

The Mother Storm was all but upon them!

Twig leapt down off the platform and levered one of

the slabs of paving from the ground with his sword. He dashed back to the chain-moorings again and slammed the rock into the end of the cotter-pin.

It moved!

Twig tried again. This time the cotter-pin jammed tight. He tried again. But it was no use. The pin wouldn't budge.

'Move, Sky curse you!' Twig roared in his fury and frustration. 'Move!'

'Twig!' shouted a familiar voice. 'What do you think you're doing?'

Twig looked up. The Professor of Darkness was hurrying across the square towards him.

'Please, Professor,' Twig grunted as he slammed the heavy rock into the mooring-block again and again. 'There's no time to explain.'

'Twig! No!' the professor cried. Pulling up his robes, he climbed onto the plinth and seized Twig's arm. 'Have you taken leave of your senses? What has happened to you – you of all people – that you should attack the Anchor Chain?'

Twig shook him off. 'All will be lost if I do not,' he said. 'The Mother Storm is almost upon us! She will strike at midnight.'

'But Twig, how can you say that?' said the professor.

'I have remem- bered what I

learned in open sky,' said Twig. 'What I had forgotten when you found me in the Stone Gardens. If life on the Edge is to survive, then Sanctaphrax must be unchained! The Mother Storm must be allowed to pass on to Riverrise unimpeded.'

'No!' the professor murmured, stunned. 'No.' His breathing quickened. 'I agreed to the evacuation . . . I feared structural damage might lead to injuries, or even fatalities. But to unchain Sanctaphrax! No, it cannot be. I should have remained up there with the rest.'

'The rest?' said Twig, and glanced up at the floating city to see a row of tiny figures peering down from the balustrade. 'Tarp? Bogwitt . . . ?'

'Oh, your crew are down, but several of the older academics refused to leave,' the professor said. 'The Professor of Fogprobing, the Professors of Windtouchers and Cloudwatchers – even that upstart, the Professor of Psycho-Climatic Studies . . . Professors evidently more loyal to Sanctaphrax than myself,' he added as, without any warning, he leapt forwards and shoved Twig with all his weight.

Distracted by the sight of the stubborn academics, Twig didn't see him coming. The heavy blow knocked him off balance and sent him keeling backwards off the platform, striking his head sharply on the edge as he fell. He looked up groggily, to see the Professor of Darkness standing above him.

At that moment, a bell rang out. It was the heavy, brass bell of the Great Hall, chiming the hour.

Bong! it tolled.

The professor looked up. 'You see,' he cried. 'Midnight, and all is well.'

The crowds milled about nervously, eyes to the sky, as colossal banks of clouds tumbled over and over one another. Despite the professor's hopeful words, all seemed very far from well.

Bong!

Far above their heads the massive ball of cloud pulsed in and out, like a great, beating black heart. The air crackled. The wind wailed. The Mother Storm was about to release – and squander – her rejuvenating power here at Sanctaphrax, far from Riverrise.

Bong!

Flushed and breathless, Cowlquape was suddenly at Twig's side. A hammer was clenched in his hand.

'Twig!' he cried. 'What's happened?'

Bong!

The sky rumbled and rolled. Purple and blue bolts of lightning plunged down to the earth, cracking paving-stones, razing buildings to the ground and sending the terrified inhabitants of Undertown and citizens of Sanctaphrax scurrying this way and that in search of safe shelter.

Twig clutched his throbbing head. 'Release the Anchor Chain, Cowlquape,' he croaked weakly. 'Before the bell tolls twelve.'

Bong!

Cowlquape leapt up onto the platform where the Professor of Darkness lay wrapped around the workings of the mooring block.

'Move!' he shouted.

'You'll have to kill me first!' the Professor said defiantly.

Bong!

Cowlquape stepped forwards and seized the old professor by the sleeve.

'No, no!' he cried out, tearing his arm free. 'If you think I'll allow centuries of knowledge to be lost, then . . .' The professor's voice was high and querulous. 'Then you're as mad as he is!'

Bong!

'Cowlquape, hurry!' Twig groaned, as he struggled groggily to his feet. 'Hurry!'

The storm roared. The earth shook. The sky shuddered.

'No, Cowlquape,' pleaded the professor. 'I . . . I'll give you anything you want!' he cried. 'Name your price. Your own department. A professorship. Tell me, and it is yours – only don't release the Anchor Chain!'

Bong!

'Here,' the professor babbled as he tore off his heavy chain of office. 'Take the great seal of Sanctaphrax. It's yours – only don't destroy our great city,' he begged as he reached out and slung it around Cowlquape's neck.

As he did so, Cowlquape grasped the professor by his bony wrist and tugged hard. With a cry of despair, the Professor of Darkness was wrenched from the winding-gear and propelled away from the mooring-platform. He landed heavily on the ground.

Bong!

Cowlquape turned, bent over and hammered furiously at the cotter-pin. Groaning and creaking, the toothed axle moved. Flakes of rust crumbled away as cogs and gears that hadn't been touched for hundreds of years juddered and turned.

Bong!

Above him, the approaching Mother Storm was drifting lower, filling up more and more of the sky as she descended. The heavy air was charged with electricity that set the hair on every head on end, and laced with the smell of sulphur and tar and toasted almonds. A great whirlwind spun round and round, causing Sanctaphrax itself to turn. Fearing for their lives, those beneath the great rock sped off in all directions.

Abruptly, the final link in the great chain sliced through the cotter-pin like a hot knife through butter. Sanctaphrax was free.

Bong!

'No!' wailed the Professor of Darkness, scrambling to his feet. He hitched up his gowns and dashed after the great chain trailing behind the floating rock. 'It cannot be!' he screamed. 'No!'

'Professor!' Twig called after him. 'Listen to me!'

But the Professor paid him no heed. Sanctaphrax was at the heart of his very soul. He would not – *could* not – live without it. He took a flying leap at the end of the chain, and clung on tightly.

'Professor!' Twig cried out.

Bong!

The bell tolled twelve. It was midnight over Sanctaphrax.

The Mother Storm bellowed like a mighty beast. Unchained, the Sanctaphrax rock soared ever higher and out of sight as the Mother Storm – pulsing with power and new life – rolled on across the sky to keep her dawn appointment with Riverrise.

Cowlquape jumped down from the plinth and ran over to Twig.

'Sky protect you, Professor,' Twig called, gazing upwards.

Cowlquape rested a hand on his shoulder.

'The Professor of Darkness was a good person, Cowlquape,' said Twig. 'Dedicated, loyal ... like those other misguided academics who refused to leave.' He sighed. 'They couldn't let go of their beloved Sanctaphrax.'

'There they are!' came a loud, angry voice.

'They cut the Anchor Chain!' bellowed another.

Twig and Cowlquape found themselves confronted by a furious mob – academics, guards, basket-pullers – advancing towards them.

Cowlquape turned to Twig. 'What do we do?' he gasped.

Twig raised his arms. 'Friends! Fellow Academics! People of Undertown!' he called out. 'It is true, Cowlquape here released the Anchor Chain . . .'

The growing crowd hissed and booed.

'But had he not done so,' Twig shouted above the noise, 'the terrible storm you all witnessed overhead would have destroyed not only Sanctaphrax but also Undertown – and all life as we know it on the Edge!'

'Says who?' bellowed a tall robed figure.

'Why should we believe you?' demanded another. The cries grew louder, angrier.

'Because I speak for your new Most High Academe,' Twig bellowed back. The crowd hesitated. 'Yes, you heard me correctly; the Most High Academe!' He pointed to the heavy gold seal hanging from the chain round Cowlquape's neck. 'For that was the title conferred upon him by the old Most High Academe, as is his right, according to the ancient customs of our beloved Sanctaphrax.'

Cowlquape shrunk with embarrassment. 'But . . . but . . .' he murmured.

'There *is* no beloved Sanctaphrax!' shouted an angry voice.

'Good thing, too!' shouted an Undertowner. 'Lazy academics!'

'Undertown scum!' came the furious response.

Scuffles broke out, punches were thrown. Then, the next instant, the crowd froze, each and every one, as their cries were drowned out by the frantic shrieking and cawing of the flock of white ravens circling the sky above them.

'*The chorus of the dead*,' the Undertowners groaned, scurrying away to safety.

'The white ravens,' whispered the academics, holding their ground.

In a great swirling blizzard of feathers the white ravens landed and stood in a protective ring around Twig and Cowlquape. The largest of them turned to Twig and thrust its great beak forwards.

'Kraan,' said Twig. 'Thank you for . . .'

'Lightning bolt hit Stone Gardens,' the bird interrupted. 'Blue lightning bolt. You remember?'

'Y . . . yes,' said Twig. 'I do.'

Kraan nodded vigorously. 'There, a rock grows. Biggest ever. Growing fast. Fast and fast. Must secure it. Secure it now. Before fly-away.'

Twig frowned. He recalled the sight of the glinting

new rock he'd glimpsed beneath the surface. 'You don't suppose . . .' he said, turning to Cowlquape.

'You mean,' said Cowlquape, 'you think this rock might grow big enough to be . . .'

'A *new* Sanctaphrax!' said Twig. 'That's exactly what I think!' He motioned to the academics before them. 'Quick! Go to the Stone Gardens, all of you! Take ropes, chains, netting, rigging, weights – anything you can lay your hands on. For the rock which is growing down at the Edge shall be your new floating city. Together you can build a new Sanctaphrax.'

The academics stared back mutely. Cowlquape stepped forward, hand on the chain of office round his neck. 'Do as he says!' he commanded.

For a moment, the academics remained still. Then a lone voice cried out. 'To the Stone Gardens!' and they turned and began to stream from the square.

Twig turned to Cowlquape. 'Ah, Cowlquape,' he said. 'How I envy you.'

'You envy me?' said Cowlquape.

'Surely,' said Twig. 'For you will be able to start afresh – to create the academic city the way it should always have been. Away with the pettiness, the backbiting, the whispered intrigue. For you are the bridge, Cowlquape, that will bring Undertown and the new Sanctaphrax together. No longer will merchants and academics look down on one another, for you have seen both sides, Cowlquape – and you have a good heart. Now you also have a new floating rock upon which to build your dreams.'

'And what about you, Twig?' said Cowlquape.

'Me?' said Twig. 'I must be reunited with my crew – both here and back at Riverrise.' He sighed. 'If only Spooler had not died . . .'

'Stay here!' said Cowlquape, gripping Twig by the arms. 'We'll build the new Sanctaphrax together. You and me . . .'

'My place is not here,' said Twig firmly. 'It never was. My place is at the helm of a sky ship with my loyal crew by my side.'

Cowlquape screwed up his face. 'But me?' he said. 'What about me? I can't do it all on my own.'

'Follow your heart, Cowlquape,' said Twig. 'Do that, and you won't go far wrong, believe me. Remember, just follow your heart.' He smiled. 'And I will follow mine.'

By the time the sky above the Edge began to lighten, the growing rock in the Stone Gardens had been encased in strong netting to which all kinds of heavy weights were being attached by the scurrying academics.

'Right,' said Cowlquape, satisfied that, for the time being at least, the rock was secure. 'I must hurry back to Undertown,' he said, 'to discuss the matter of a new Anchor Chain with Silex Makepiece of the League of Forging and Founding. In the meantime, I want you to supervise the rock. Ensure that enough weights are attached to keep it from soaring off.'

'Certainly, sir,' Vox, the tall apprentice from the College of Cloud, replied, his voice hushed, oily.

Cowlquape dashed off to the waiting barrow. Vox's eyes narrowed and an unpleasant smirk played on his lips. 'You little runt,' he muttered under his breath. 'I'll get you one day . . .'

When he reached the main square of Undertown, Cowlquape noticed a gathering around the dry central fountain. He leant forwards and tapped the barrow-driver on the shoulder.

'Thank you,' he said. 'If you could let me down for a moment.'

The barrow-driver lowered the shafts of the barrow and Cowlquape jumped out. He ran across to the fountain.

'What is it?' he said. 'What's happening?'

'*Sshhh*, your Most Highness!' said a gnokgoblin insistently. 'Listen.'

Cowlquape cocked his head to one side. From the depths of the fountain echoed a loud gurgling sound. 'What . . . ?' he began.

Then, all at once, as the first rays of the dawn sun fell across the square, there was an ear-splitting roar, and a powerful jet of water gushed up into the air – ten, twenty, thirty strides high – and poured down on everyone standing there.

Cowlquape gasped. 'It's happened!' he exclaimed. 'The Mother Storm has reached Riverrise. She has seeded it with new life. The waters of the Edgewater River are flowing once more. We are saved!'

Forgetting all about their former venerable status, the professors and apprentices leapt for joy with the Undertowners and frolicked in the torrent of water until they were all soaked to the skin. Their doubts were

washed away and, as they opened their mouths and drank the cold, clear water, their bodies were suffused with such energy and optimism, that they cried out in triumph.

'Long live the Edgewater River!'

'Long live Undertown!'

'Long live the new Sanctaphrax!'

And the air trembled with the tumultuous roar that followed. 'LONG LIVE THE NEW SANCTAPHRAX!'

Cowlquape smiled and stepped from the pouring water. The warm sun set his clothes steaming. 'Cowlquape!' came a voice. 'It is time!'

He looked round. There was no-one there, and for the briefest of moments, he wondered whether it wasn't Kobold the Wise speaking to him.

'Cowlquape! Up here!'

Cowlquape looked up, and shielded his hand against the sun. 'Twig!' he cried.

The young captain looked down from the helm of the sky ship, hovering in the sky above. Peering down next to him on one side were Bogwitt, Tarp Hammelherd and Wingnut Sleet. Although they were stand-ing in the dark shadow thrown by the towering aftcastle, nei-ther they nor Twig were glowing: the luminous light had been extinguished with the passing of the Mother Storm. On Twig's other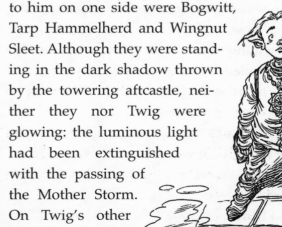

side were Teasel, Stile, Jervis and, bedecked in feathers and jewels, the brogtroll, Grimlock – most of Thunderbolt Vulpoon's crew. Cowlquape noticed the name of the sky ship, its gold letters gleaming. It was the *Skyraider*.

'I found them waiting for me at the boom-docks!' Twig shouted down. 'Now, I will return to Riverrise for the others – Sky willing! For Goom. For Woodfish. For Maugin . . .' He smiled. 'I came to say goodbye.'

Cowlquape's heart sank. Goodbye? 'So soon! You're going so soon, Twig?' he shouted.

'I must. But our paths will cross again,' Twig called back. 'For now though, Cowlquape, your place is here.'

The sails of the *Skyraider* billowed. The sky ship lurched forwards.

'Twig!' called Cowlquape.

'Fare you well, Cowlquape!' Twig cried out, as he turned his attention to the flight-levers.

The sky ship soared off into the sky. Cowlquape watched as it grew smaller and smaller, silhouetted against the lemon yellow of the rising sun. It had been wonderful accompanying Twig on his quest – and part of him yearned to be by his side now, on board the *Skyraider* and heading back for Riverrise. In his heart, however, Cowlquape knew that his place was not on board a sky pirate ship. It was indeed here that his duty lay.

Follow your heart, and I will follow mine, was what Twig had told him. It was all anyone could do. And as Cowlquape took one last, lingering look at the sky ship, he smiled.

Twig was following his heart; now it was time for him, Cowlquape, to follow his.

'Farewell, Twig, my friend,' he cried out. 'And may Sky be with you, wherever you may go!'